D1737061

The Taking
Book Three of the Painted Maidens Trilogy

By Terra Harmony

A Patchwork Press Title
www.patchwork-press.com

Editing team: Jessica Dall and Cathy Wathen

Cover design by Keary Taylor
www.indiecoverdesigns.com

For the characters that refuse to leave my imagination
– thank you sharing your stories with me.

Eternity begins and ends with the ocean's tides.

Chapter One

"Aiden, you are too far out..." The anxious mother's words are drowned out by the next wave. Aiden ignores her anyway. The ocean is rarely warm enough for swimming, and he is going to take full advantage today.

Scanning the water for light-brown tufts of hair, Aiden spots his younger brothers. Both are with a group of human children, throwing a Frisbee back and forth in the shallow surf.

"Aiden!" his mother yells again.

He turns his back to the shore and moves deeper, past the breakers until the swells breach his shoulders. Shuffling through the sand, Aiden stubs his big toe. "Ouch!" He hops a few times on his other foot while he kneads at the stinging pain with his fingers.

Taking a deep breath, he plunges his head underneath the surface. The sensitive senses of smell and hearing dull, allowing Aiden to focus on the sharpened underwater images. Streams of sunlight penetrating the surface send crisscrossed patterns dancing across the sandy ocean floor. A clump of rocks host sea-green coral reaching its spiny limbs toward the light. Yellow-striped fish dart in and out of the plant-like organisms. Gentle tides nuzzle against the boy as he takes a moment to revel in their security.

His fingertips locate the hard object and begin to dig. A quick hiatus to take a breath, and back under he goes, quickly uncovering something round and smooth.

Already short on air again, Aiden wraps his hand around the object. There are convenient finger holds on the other side. He gives it one mighty tug on his way up for air, and it springs free.

He breaks through the surface gasping for breath. Aiden holds the object to the failing light. An off-white sphere, sanded smooth by rough currents rests in his hands. Aiden turns it to see the holes his fingers have breached. They are eye sockets.

Aiden almost drops the skull in shock. There is a large nose cavity; the kind that might hold an elongated snout. But that isn't the most obvious clue that this skull belongs to one of his kind. Two needle-sharp fangs emerge from the upper jaw. Though the waves push and pull at his weight, Aiden stands still, mesmerized by the artifact in his hands. Running the pad of his thumb the length of one fang, he jumps as he feels a hand close over his shoulder in a painful squeeze. The fang slices him.

"Ow!" Blood seeps from his thumb, and he drops the skull as if it came to life and bit him. The discovery splashes back into the water, spraying icy cold water onto Aiden and his mother behind him, who still has her hand on his shoulder.

"Mom—" but Aiden cuts off at the burning sensation that fireballs out from his thumb, up his arm, and straight into his chest. The minor injury paired with his adrenaline rush set off a hormonal reaction; one that Aiden has yet to learn to control.

"Not again…" He throws his head back in pain. "Make it stop mom, please!"

She wraps her body around her son, as if she can forcefully keep the wolf from emerging. But it doesn't help. Spiky, brown hairs spear out from under his skin like needles, and his swimsuit is already ripping at the seams.

Desperate, she looks toward her other sons. They already realize what is happening, and have created a distraction further up the beach by fighting. As they exchange meaningless blows, the only kind a five and seven-year-old can deal out, beachgoers point and whisper at the spectacle.

The mother does the only thing she can do. She moves both further down the shore and deeper into the water, away from the humans. They try to stay hidden behind ocean swells. It isn't difficult; Aiden is buckling at the knees.

Cooler water licks at their feet, and before the mother realizes what is happening, they are moving further and further out to sea, caught in a current. Aiden bends violently at the waist, his head going underwater. Neither of their feet touch the ocean floor, and she kicks, trying bring his head back up.

Once he does, the mother's heart sinks. Her son has fully transformed, and werewolves can't swim.

"Paddle, Aiden!" she encourages.

But he can't even manage to keep his ears above the surface, and his body is now far too large for her to hold up while treading water.

Small ripples nudge at the mother's shoulders. She turns in a full circle, eyes growing wide as she realizes the disturbance is coming at them from every direction.

At first it isn't obvious, but the creatures soon reveal themselves. There is a flick of a light-brown fin, a scaled hand slicing through the air, and then curious eyes emerge.

The mother does the only thing she can. She pleads to the very reason the skull lies buried in the ocean in the first place.

"Help us… please!"

Chapter Two

"Why are you being so difficult?" Serena stands underneath swaths of sunlight streaming down through open holes in the ceiling, bathing the archives in brightness. Her spine is as rigid as Dagon, the trident she holds. She is a stark contrast to her twin brother, who is hunched over an open book.

His lanky arms lope over the table while his feet splay open underneath. "I'm not bein' difficult. I'm bein' reasonable." He lifts an eyebrow, but doesn't glance up from the pages crinkled yellow with age.

"As you say," Serena huffs. It is on the verge of a snort. She watches as he scratches underneath the metal collar hugging his neck. "At least let me remove that thing for you," she says, stepping forward and lowering the tips of her trident.

"No." Now he looks at her, eyes hard and jaw clenching.

"It could kill you, Liam!" She raises her voice.

Liam stands suddenly, sending his chair tipping behind him. Three steps and he is towering over her. "It stays because it protects you!"

Out of the corner of her eye, Serena can see two large figures emerge from corner shadows. The Queen's Guard.

"Stand down, werewolf," says Morven, the largest of all the Queen's Guard.

Serena glances at the guard, then back to Liam. "I have plenty of protection." She lowers her trident, the shadow of the tips floating across her face.

Liam doesn't turn to face Morven. Instead, he closes his eyes. Underneath the stubble on his chin and cheeks, red creeps up from his neck. Serena waits while he takes three deep breaths, and the usual dark creamy beige replaces the red.

"You have more colors than The Painted Maidens, brother," Serena says.

He lifts one corner of his mouth in a half-smile. "Well it's about time someone adds some flavor to this rigid place."

Serena relaxes her shoulders in response, trying not to admit to herself it is mostly forced.

"Listen, Serena," Liam says, his eyes boring into her. "I know you want me to return home—but the pack needs to learn to trust you as their queen, and be ready to follow you. That won't happen if they are constantly lookin' to me. Give them more time."

"They think I hold you against your will; despite the letters you've written. They need more proof."

Liam shrugs. "You gave them Arista as collateral, didn't you?"

"I don't think they see her as collateral," says Serena. "Undine know her as a traitor and the werewolves know her as one of Alaric's lackeys. She's just…trouble."

Sighing, Liam returns to the table, pushes his chair upright, and sits. He toys with the hard corners of the book while the guards retreat back into the shadows. "Let them visit me, then."

Serena can almost feel the tension in the room stretching as tight as the chain that runs from a dropped anchor to its ship. Allow more werewolves to enter Undine territory? If there were another betrayal the Undine would have nowhere to run.

Serena remains silent.

"Okay..." Liam glances at the guards. "Maybe only a few?"

Considering, Serena glanced at the enlarged skylight hanging over the catalogues; the very same one used to throw Liam into the archives a month ago. He has been here ever since, catching up on his Undine reading.

At the time, it was the only place Kai could think of to hold Liam. The archives don't connect with any other Undine caves, and though Serena knows Liam wouldn't harm an Undine, she doesn't think anyone else truly believes that.

"I will confer with my council," Serena finally nods.

"Conferrin', conferrin'," Liam mumbles. "You all are always conferrin'. Why not just make a decision and freakin' get something done?"

Serena patiently folds her hands in front of her. "Are you telling me how to run my kingdom, Liam?"

He runs his palm over tired eyes. "No."

"Then are you telling me how to run *your* kingdom?"

Glancing at her, he doesn't answer.

"Because you are free to leave here at any time and take the clan as yours."

Now he bends all the way forward, dropping his forehead against the table. "This is getting' old, Serena..."

"Tell me about it," she answers, turning her back on her twin brother.

"Your majesty!" Kai runs in from the archive entrance pool, scales that cover his body dripping wet. He isn't wearing the robe required in the archives.

Mariam, the Records Keeper, is not there but Serena stands ready to fill in the appropriate berating. Serena's relationship with Kai makes no difference when book preservation is at stake.

Before she can speak, words spill from Kai's mouth. "There was an incident with one of the boys. Darcy and her boys were attempting an integration mission on the beach, and Aiden shifted."

"When?" Serena and Liam ask simultaneously.

Liam jumps back up from his seat, sending the chair tipping once again.

Kai looks from Serena to Liam, then back again, as if he is unsure whom he should address. "A few minutes ago—"

"In broad daylight?" Serena asks, her fingertips going to her temples.

"Please tell me no humans saw." Liam steps around his sister.

Kai shrugs helplessly. "The beach was fairly crowded. They think something spooked him."

"Probably one of you," Liam's voice rises.

"Okay, everybody just stand down," Serena steps in between the two holding up the palms of her hands as if she might have to physically push them apart. She looks from one to the other until she is sure neither will become uncivil. "Where is the boy now?"

"He is no longer really a boy," says Kai. "And he has been taken out to sea."

"Are you mad?" Eyes bulging, Liam looks as though he is about to strangle Kai. "We can't swim— he'll drown, especially in werewolf form."

Unperturbed, Kai shrugs again. "His mother asked for our help, and we have managed to keep him alive. We tied the bulletproof shields together. With a little help from underneath, it is floating. We'll keep him there until he changes back and it is safe to bring him in, but… "

"What?" asks Serena.

"He is having a little trouble doing that. Not even his mother can convince him."

Liam shakes his head. "It's not a matter of convincin' him. He needs another one of us; his mother is a human. Every other time, it was his father that brought him back."

"Well, there's another problem – finding his father might not be the best choice." Kai glances up at the skylight just as it darkens. "A storm is moving in— and fast."

Chapter Three

Thunder rumbles in the distance, shaking the archives to the core.

Serena snaps her head around to Liam. "There is only one werewolf we can get to in time."

The guards are already stepping forward, their tridents by their sides. "We cannot release him— Murphy's orders."

Liam turns to face the guards. "Are you tellin' the queen how to run her kingdom?"

Serena has to hide her smile.

Morven frowns. "Murphy is the Head of the Queen's Guard—we would be reprimanded, or worse, if we let you go."

"I will be sure Murphy knows you have my pardon," Serena says.

Before the guard can answer, Liam snatches the trident out of Morven's hand. Serena moves quickly, stepping in front of the other guard to keep him from retaliating. Leaning his head to the side, Liam stretches out his neck and slides one prong of the trident underneath his collar. He twists the trident until another prong rests against his cheek. Serena exchanges glances with Kai while keeping one hand in the air, signaling to the guards to remain still.

Using his own face as leverage, Liam squeezes his eyes shut and grunts as he twists the trident. Just as Serena thinks his cheekbone is about to cave, the collar pops off. It sails through the air and bounces on the ground twice before coming to rest at Morven's feet. Without taking his eyes from Liam, the guard slowly bends and picks up the collar.

"Get that fixed while I'm gone," Liam says.

Morven looks to Serena for confirmation.

She nods. "Take it to Ronan."

"As you say, your majesty." Both guards bends at the waist, performing a short bow, then proceed to the archives entrance pool.

Serena looks to Kai. "The quickest way to the boy?"

"With *him*?" He arches his eyebrow at Liam. "Probably up to the Dry and then out to sea."

"Too risky." Serena shakes her head. "We can't let him be seen by the pack and then whisk him away again; they wouldn't let him go without a fight."

"Not sure he'd fit in the passageway," counters Kai. "Then we'd risk him getting stuck and drowning. Not the best way to win over the hearts of the pack, either."

At an impasse, they both look to Liam for the decision. He stops rubbing the red marks on his cheek and neck to look up at the widened skylight.

"I'm not fallin' through that thing again," he says, turning to the entrance pool where the guards just disappeared. "Let's go for a swim."

"Liam, wait—we have to plan this out." Serena walks quickly to catch up with him.

Already almost to the entrance pool, Liam shakes his head. "No conferrin' on this one, Serena. We're out of time."

Another rumble of thunder shakes the archives.

She looks to Kai, eyebrows raised in a desperate plea.

"Sorry – but he's at least right about one thing," Kai says, stepping up to edge of the water. The icy cold laps at their toes. "Werewolves can't swim."

"And so how does this route make sense?" Serena glowers at Kai and Liam both.

"I don't think—"

Kai's mouth drops open as Liam hurls his massive body forward. His splash into the water is less than graceful; it is a belly flop.

Kai laughs. "I like him!"

"Kai..." Serena grumbles, taking off her robe.

Before the material floats to the ground, Kai has leapt into the air. At the apex of his jump, he bends at the waist in a pike, and dives into the water. Serena pauses to watch. Body tight and his back slightly arched, Kai's biceps squeeze his ears. The splash is barely noticeable amidst the swells that still undulate from Liam's entrance.

"Show off," Serena mumbles before jumping in herself.

Underneath the surface, Kai has already found Liam. Serena pauses above them while she melds her legs into fins. Kai is flapping his own fins in front of Liam's face. Liam swats them away, and a myriad of bubbles escape Serena's lips as she laughs.

Insistent, Kai swims in a circle then places his fins back in front of Liam. Finally catching on, Liam frowns but reaches out to wrap his thick arms around Kai's tail. Testing the grip, Kai zigzags around the entrance pool. Finally, he angles up, performing a loop around Serena flaunting his haul. She spins, watching her brother being towed around at Kai's mercy. Kai flicks his tail toward the surface, allowing Liam to take one big breath before the pair angles for the passageway with Serena following directly behind.

Darkness squeezes in around them. The smiles are gone from each of their faces; it is time to concentrate. Serena and Kai are familiar with the necessary dance to get through the narrow corridor unscathed, but Liam is not. She does her best to help Liam from behind. Grabbing hold of his feet, she pulls one up so he turns on his side – better for angling wide shoulders through a tight spot. Next she pushes straight forward, helping the trio pick up speed for the hairpin curve ahead. If they take it quickly enough momentum will carry them through the rotation. It works; Serena has felt only minor vibrations through Liam's body as he grazes the rocky walls.

Pressure decreases as the path ascends the underwater mountain. If it is low tide, there will be a small air pocket just ahead for Liam to catch a breath. If not, it will be a hurried ride out the rest of the way. Serena crosses her fingers, hoping to feel the chain of bodies slow because Kai has found air.

The area brightens a bit, and Serena looks up to see Kai stretching out his chin. It disappears above the water.

Thank Poseidon, thinks Serena.

Serena surfaces on the other side of Liam, squashing him in between herself and Kai in the small air pocket. It is the same place Kai and Serena usually stop to sneak in an unobserved kiss.

"Remember this?" Kai asks, leaning around Liam to wink at Serena.

Her cheeks grow hot despite the icy water.

Liam groans. "I don't even want to know."

"Oh come on," Kai smiles at Liam. "You've been learning about us by reading those books for a month now. The only real way to learn is to live it... by—swimming it."

Liam rolls his eyes. "Let's just get out of here. I feel like a mermaid sandwich."

"We're halfway by now," says Serena. "But even after we get out of the tunnel there will be a bit of swim to the surface. You good?"

Liam nods. "I can go faster—we need to beat that storm."

"As you say." Serena smiles. *This is going to be fun.*

Kai disappears first, sinking below the water.

Liam turns to face Serena. "Why are you smiling?"

But she doesn't have time to answer. Liam is pulled underneath, managing to grab one last breath before he vanishes.

Serena stills her fins and allows herself to sink. In the dark, she finds Liam's feet just as he moves forward. They traverse the tunnels again. Liam doesn't kick; it is much faster to allow Kai and Serena to do the swimming for him. Gradually picking up speed, the three of them make almost effortless progress, twisting and turning, manipulating their bodies to fit the thin molds of the passageway. They make good time until Liam stops short. Serena runs straight into the back of him.

Frantic, she feels around. His midsection is lodged in a tight spot. She tries pushing at him and can feel his body jerk from Kai tugging at the other side of the jam. Serena sends out a signal. Short, short, long. It only takes one repeat for Kai to understand. They coordinate pushing and pulling at the same time on each of Serena's long signals.

They are making progress, but not quick enough. Every moment underwater Liam loses more air.

Suddenly, Liam kicks back hard, slamming Serena against the wall. The underwater clunk is echoed by several more. Liam is pounding at the walls with his fists.

That is never going to work, thinks Serena. Panic rises in her throat. She lunges forward, trying to grab at Liam's ankles, hoping to pull him back the way they came.

But she is kicked away again.

More clunks and finally the hard walls give way. Pieces of rock tumble down the side in a kaleidoscope of pings. Liam is free.

With a rigid tail, Serena pushes against the wall behind her straight into Liam. They move quicker than before, desperation fueling their fins. Breaking through the last part of the tunnel, they barrel into the open ocean. Serena moves up and Kai falls back slightly, each taking Liam under an arm.

Shepherding him to the brightest sunlight, Serena refuses to look at her brother. She doesn't want to know if he isn't breathing—not yet.

When they break the surface, she hears one large gasp right next to her ear, and she sighs in relief.

"You!" Serena lashes out at Kai. "Pulling him under before he was ready. Quit playing games. He could've died!"

"Me!" Kai's mouth drops open. "I saw the look on your face. You were having just as much fun – until things went wrong."

"He is my brother. If anything happens to him—"

"Serena," Kai interrupts. He glances at the water next to her.

Liam is no longer there. Gasping, Serena plunges one hand underneath, latching onto soggy material and pulling up again.

Taking another deep breath, Liam attempts to doggy paddle. It only results in him going back under. Kai moves in, helping Serena hold Liam up.

"Stop moving," she coaxes. "Take a deep breath, and hold it in. The air in your lungs is enough to keep you afloat."

He nods, the panic evident in his eyes. Water splashes against their faces, making it hard to inhale pure oxygen. Liam sputters and coughs, then tries again. Once his limbs go still, Serena and Kai slowly back away. Liam floats. His face turns red from holding in his breath. When he releases his air, his body almost automatically begins to sink. Quickly, he takes another breath in and bobs up until his shoulders breach the surface.

Satisfied he won't drown if she looks away again, Serena scans the ocean. For the first time, she realizes it is rolling and pitching with the oncoming storm. The birds have already left the skies as dark clouds move in.

"This is no ordinary storm," Serena says.

"For this time of the year," says Kai. "I think it is."

"Graveyard of the Pacific," says Liam, breathing out hard before he sucks in another deep breath.

Serena looks at him in question.

"It's what the humans call this area," he explains. "Because of the shipwrecks."

"Well, come on," says Kai. "Before we add to that graveyard."

Chapter Four

"Almost there," Kai coaxes Liam. All three are breathing hard, trying to guide Liam through the rough seas. It seems as though they are under water more often than they are above. The wind grows more fierce.

"I'm cramping up." Liam reverts to doggy paddling again as one leg goes stiff.

"Work through it, work through it!" Kai shouts. "Keep that air in your lungs!"

But the more Kai coaches Liam, the more Liam resists the help. His other leg begins to cramp.

Suddenly burdened with more weight, Kai and Serena find themselves under the surface in order to keep Liam's chin above.

Kai shoots Serena a glare.

Like this is all my fault?! She glares right back.

She can imagine all the arguments he can't speak out loud. *He's your brother. You are the queen. Think of something. Do something.*

Still holding Dagon in one hand, she pokes the stem out toward Kai's tail and draws circles until his tail and the trident are intertwined. Using her hip as leverage she yanks the bottom of the trident back. Following his own fins, Kai disappears into The Deep.

A smile of satisfaction lights Serena's face until her brother sinks to her depth, struggling to keep afloat. Wrapping her arm around his waist, she swims, determined to take care of her own.

Once they both breach the surface, she delivers the same scowl she gave Kai. "Sometimes I wonder how we could possibly have the same parents."

Continuing their labored swim, Kai appears a few moments later. Without a word, and without risking a single glance at Serena, he takes his place on Liam's other side.

Glad to have the help, neither Serena nor Liam protest. Besides, Kai is silent now, which seems to work better.

"There they are!" Serena spots the wolf cub on the platform as they crest a wave. He is surrounded by mermaids holding up the flat panes from underneath.

New energy surges through the trio and they ride the back of the wave down.

"Hold your breath, Liam," Serena says.

After he sucks in air, she and Kai dip below, dragging Liam with them. The swim under will be faster. They lunge forward, aiming for shimmering colors of scales.

Before she has to worry about Liam's lungs, they surface on one side of the panes.

"Darcy... " Serena spots the pup's mother. She makes sure Liam has a good hold on the panes, then swims to the other side to meet the only human out there. "Are you okay?"

Darcy's lower lip quivers. She tries to speak but presses her lips shut again, a high-pitch sob barely escaping. When she makes a second attempt, a wayward wave washes over her head. She loses her grip on the pane and only comes back up with the assistance of several Undine.

"It's okay," Serena puts a hand on Darcy's shoulder. "We'll make sure he gets home safely. You both will." Turning away from Darcy, Serena shoots Kai a worried look across the panes.

He doesn't return it. Instead, he nudges Liam. "You're up, prince."

Nodding, Liam takes another breath, trying to rein in his lungs. He dips down slightly then shoots himself out of the water, trying to get on top of the pane. Kai moves to help him until Serena shakes her head.

As you say, Kai mouths, backing away.

Liam is able to get one knee on top, then the other. He drags himself all the way up just in time to take a wave to the face. The wolf pup on top yelps, sliding to the edge of the pane.

"Whoa there," Liam catches the pup before he goes over. "Easy now."

The pup straightens on all four wobbly legs, attempting to shake excess water from his fur. Panting, the pup looks at Liam expectantly.

Serena and Kai back off a bit, lending their help to holding the glass panes as steady as possible. The sheer size of the glass helps to keep them floating, but in this storm even a boat would easily capsize.

Lightning strikes the ocean further north, and the boom in the sky is heard only a few seconds after.

"Cordelia's baby?" Serena asks Darcy, partly as a way to distract both of them.

"Ervin is at home with Colin," says Darcy, but she doesn't take her eyes off her son.

Liam steadies himself on two knees, squaring off with the small wolf. "Aiden." He looks the wolf in the eye. "I need you to concentrate. If we go over, you won't be able to swim like this, and it will be difficult for the mermaids to save you."

Even though he is young, in his wolf form Aiden is a little bigger than Liam. The pup whines, pacing.

"Something forced this—what happened on the beach?" asks Liam.

Darcy speaks up from the water. "He found a werewolf skull buried in the sand."

"Fear, then," says Liam. "But he should have more control than this—he always has in the past."

Darcy shrugs, her eyes growing more and more desperate.

"Calm yourself, Aiden." Liam's voice is more forceful this time.

The wolf is still hesitant to obey. He edges in closer to Liam, sniffing the air. A jolt in the waves causes him to slide forward, directly into Liam.

The wolf does not show aggression or fear at the sudden contact. He sniffs with curiosity. Serena can almost see a change in his eyes. They sharpen, and he noses Liam eagerly.

Liam laughs, scratching the pup behind the ears. "He thought the skull was my own."

The wolf pounces on Liam now, causing Liam to laugh even harder.

"He didn't recognize me right away; sometimes a wolf's scent is stronger than his sight." Liam pushes himself up, trying to control the excited muzzle that continues to push into him. "Okay, you've had your fun. Come back to us now, Aiden."

There is a moment of calm. The wind ceases to blow, and although the waves still roll, the pane rides on top of a crest. Fins billowing out, the mermaids work to keep it there.

Short, feathery-light hair drops onto the panes of glass. His transformation is quick, and soon a naked boy is curled up in Liam's arms.

"There you go," Liam murmurs, taking off his own shirt to place over the boy.

"Aiden!" Darcy shouts from the water. With a small push from Serena, Darcy slides up onto the panes as well. Wrapping her arms around her oldest child, she inspects. "Are you okay?"

"I'm okay, Mom. I'm... sorry," Aiden says, shivering.

"Don't worry; we'll figure it out," she says, wiping wet strands of hair from his forehead.

Liam puts a hand on the boy's shoulder. "He still shouldn't have been able to shift so easily, not without the full moon."

Mother and son pause, watching while Liam slides his palm down to the boy's wrist, then turns it over to expose soft skin on the other side of the elbow. There are track marks.

"Someone has been giving him my blood."

Chapter Five

"You're sure about this?" Serena asks Liam. Standing in Ungainly form, the ocean is up to her shoulders and his chest, their feet sinking into squishy, water-logged sand. A wave moves in, gently lifting them up, then down again.

Darcy and Aiden were sent home earlier with news Liam would return to the pack that night. Serena squints but can't make out anything in the dark shadows amidst the forest that lies past the beach.

Liam raises his nose to the air and sniffs. "They're waitin'. Besides… " He turns toward Serena, pausing until her eyes met his own. "I've been gone long enough."

"As you say," Serena says, trepidation tingeing her voice.

"You're the one that wanted me to go back." The last word rises in pitch as Liam is pushed forward by another wave.

The pair settle back into the sand.

"Yes, but it was kind of nice having you to myself." Serena smiles. "My own werewolf, tucked away in the archives like a book waiting to be checked out."

"You can still speak to me any time, Serena. Just call." Liam steps forward. "You comin'?"

Serena looks at the shadows again. "You first. Have your reunion. I'll join in a bit."

"As you say," Liam mocks her formal tone, his voice floating away as the waves carry him to shore on their crest.

Serena watches from the breakers. As soon as his feet hit the sand, shadows from in between the trees lengthen, stretching like a myriad of bubbles until they separate and become distinct forms. Hands reach out, sucking Liam into warm embraces. They slap his back and shoulders and prod his midsection while Serena hears snippets of comments.

".....feeding you…"

"….gone so long…"

As each wave moves past, the conversation is temporarily lost to Serena. Soon, Liam's expression slides from exhilaration to caution. Several members of the pack keep glancing over Liam's shoulder, eyeing the waves just as Serena eyed the tree line. The questions grow adamant, the tone of the greeting no longer welcoming. Serena allows the next wave to carry her in a bit further so she can hear.

"Why did they keep you so long?"

"She wouldn't even let us talk to you—let us see you."

Liam takes a defensive step back from the pack, holding up his hands. The ocean dips to Serena's waist, then her knees, and finally her ankles, until its hold on her disappears.

A pack member she recognizes from her time in the fight ring as Alaric's prisoner is leaning forward, his pointer finger raised in the air. "And she expects to lead—"

He cuts off as Serena takes her place on the beach, with Liam on one side and Dagon, her trident, on the other.

Standing tall, Serena waits beside her brother for the ripples of murmurs to die down.

"The decision to stay was my own," Liam's voice booms out.

Serena gives him a sideways glance. His tone is too formal; the Undine may have rubbed off on him.

Everyone that has gathered under the moonlight looks at him, perhaps expecting something more— some better explanation. Finally, there is movement from the back as someone pushes his way forward.

"Conner!" Relief slackens Liam's face and shoulders, and he looks like his old self again. The two shake hands, pulling together and wrapping their free arms around each other's shoulders.

"It's good to finally see you again, brother," Conner says, then raises an eyebrow at Serena.

She has to admit, she is just as relieved to see Conner. Every time she visited the clan while Liam remained in her keep, it was Conner that helped guide her through pack politics.

Conner steps to the other side of Liam, slapping him on the back. "Serena told us it was your decision to stay, and she's done a good job of learning our ways and even helping out with some issues. But I'm glad you're back, because things are about to get a whole lot harder."

"What?" Serena asks the same time as Liam says, "Why?"

Conner reaches into his back pocket and produces a pink, folded paper. He smooths it out and hands it to Liam. "Because we are being evicted from our trailer park."

"How come you didn't tell me?" Serena snatches the official looking paper from Liam's hands. She squints at the writing. "I don't understand any of these words."

"May I?" asks Liam.

Serena hands the paper back to him, clearing her throat.

As Liam reads the paper, Conner explains, "I didn't tell you because it was just served today. Our trailers sit on a national park. I don't know much of what Cecil, the old man, did to keep the authorities away, but our luck has run out since he died."

Liam stops reading at the mention of Cecil's name, his eyes fixated beyond the paper. Serena was there next to him as they watched Cecil being murdered by Alaric, the old pack leader. It seems Alaric is still doing his best to damage their lives, the consequences of his actions taking effect long after his dead body has been returned to the ocean. Serena puts her hand on Liam's shoulder.

Eyes snapping to her, he takes a deep breath and looks back down at the paper. "We have only ten days to move the entire clan."

"Can you fight it?" asks Serena. "I find it hard to believe this flimsy piece of paper, the color of a salmon's soft underbelly" —she flicks at the citation in Liam's hand— "has the power to make you abandon your home."

"It does," Conner and Liam say together.

"Alaric mentioned a lawyer he had that was able to keep anyone from asking too many questions," says Liam. "Somethin' about claiming the ground as native land. But that lawyer died a year before Cecil did. He was talking to someone new but…"

"But he obviously didn't have the chance to solidify anything before he was killed," Conner finishes for Liam.

Liam drops his hands to his sides and turns to Serena. "We can't move, Serena. Our documents are all forged—I'm not sure they would pass if we tried to integrate into some new community. They'd force the boys to go to school, someone would shift—it would be a disaster." He lowers his voice. "And let's not forget that we could never go very far from your society without feeling like we are being ripped in half."

"We would feel it too." Serena nods. She looks out at the few members of the pack that gathered to welcome Liam home. They shift from foot to foot, some of them wringing their hands.

A few ideas are thrown out, each one quickly tossed aside given the complications of the situation. Finally, Serena offers a solution. "If you are forced to leave, you might just have to come stay with us."

The group goes silent as they contemplate Serena's suggestion.

"That won't go over well, with anyone," says Liam. "But we may not have a choice."

"Let's approach it carefully—but the sooner we can get Society and the clan used to the idea, the better." Serena faces the ocean. "I'll meet you here tomorrow night, Liam. So we can confer further." She gives him a playful wink over her shoulder, knowing he hates the word.

"Oh, Queen Serena, speaking of staying with you… here." Conner points to the tree line where two wolves emerge, escorting a maiden in between them.

Serena turns around, squinting into the dark. "Arista?"

"We almost forgot to make the exchange," says Conner.

Arista looks at Serena, head cocked in confusion.

"Oh... did we?" Serena coughs into her hand. "Very well, then. Come on, Arista." Serena turns her back without waiting and walks into the waves.

"I'm glad you came for me yourself, your majesty." Arista rushes to catch up, hopping over the waves. "I have a request."

"A request?" Serena stops, eyes wide. Arista certainly is not in the position to be issuing requests.

"More hydrocoral," says Arista. "I've run out since I've been with the wolves."

"Oh, I see." Serena nods, walking further into the waves.

Arista smiles. "I knew you would."

"But there is a problem," says Serena, wrapping her hand just above Arista's elbow.

"A problem?" asks Arista. Her smile falters.

"Yes. You see..." Serena stops to face Arista, her hand squeezing tight. "You'll have no cause for using hydrocoral."

"But I do," says Arista. "I need it to—"

Serena shakes her head, cutting the maiden off. "Not in prison you won't."

Chapter Six

"You brought her back here? To the Great Hall?" Kai asks, stepping forward from the group of council members, already reaching for the chains in his dry bag.

Arista crosses her arms, mumbling. "That's not all she's bringing."

"What?" Now Kai crosses his arms, asking Serena, "What else?"

Glaring at Arista, Serena takes the chains from Kai and shackles Arista herself. "You know the way?"

Shoulders sagging, Arista nods.

"Kai?" Serena dismisses him from the council to escort the prisoner. The queen could do without his questions right now.

After the pair leaves, Serena takes a deep breath and faces the council. Members present are the Head Gardener, the Head Scientist, Head of the Guard, and the Queen's Second. "We might have to make room in our caves," she says. "The wolves are coming."

"Here? You want to bring them here, to the heart of the Kingdom?" gawks Sarafina.

Serena's eyes snap to the Head Gardener.

"Your majesty?" Nerin, the Queen's Second, leans forward into Serena's peripheral view. "Just to clarify—you want to try to bring the entire clan here?"

Clearing her throat, Serena nods. "If they are forced to leave their home, we have two choices. We go with them, or we allow them to live here."

Sarafina steps forward, perhaps emboldened by Nerin's question. "Surely there is some other—"

"Have you ever tried to leave, Sarafina?" Serena interrupts.

"No, your majesty." Sarafina's spine goes rigid, and she stops short of the first step leading up to the throne.

"I was told several maidens attempted to migrate, once they discovered they were with calfling, to find safer beaches to give birth." Serena pins Sarafina with a glare.

"Yes, that much is true, your majesty. But I wasn't one of them."

"Then go find one, Sarafina, and speak to them. Let them tell you the horrors they experienced when they strayed too far. And if you still do not believe, swim out well past the borders of our kingdom. Experience the pain yourself. But don't turn around too soon. Don't turn when you become sluggish, when your whole body grows heavy. Don't turn when you feel as though you are too tired to continue. The weight that overcomes you will settle deep in your bones until you feel they may snap in half. Then, and only then, Sarafina, is when you may turn back. Because if you go farther, I fear you will never be able to inform the rest of the maidens how it felt." Serena realizes she is on the edge of her throne, leaning forward.

Sarafina herself has retreated several steps.

"Well." Serena forces herself to lean back. "You are excused, Sarafina. Find out what you must."

There is a momentary look of confusion as Sarafina knits her eyebrows together, then she gives a quick curtsey and turns, avoiding meeting the eyes of the rest of the council.

Serena's shoulders sag as she brings her fingertips to her temples.

"Your majesty?" Nerin's soft voice slides through the ringing in Serena's ears. "Do you really think it safe, bringing them here?"

"No," Serena says, dropping her hands into her lap. "It probably isn't safe for anyone. But what choice do we have?"

"We would have to have collars made—for them all. To keep them from shifting," says Murphy, Head of the Guard. He stands as if he is about to go give Ronan the task right away.

"I won't have them wearing collars," says Serena. "The risk is too great; they could hurt themselves."

"They could hurt themselves?" Murphy looks at Serena, eyes wide and voice almost an octave higher. "Since when are you concerned with the welfare of the werewolves?"

"Tell me, Murphy, if someone were to collar you, would you expect me to protest?"

His eyes dart from the queen to Nerin, as if he's suddenly found himself in a trap.

"Well?" asks Serena.

"Yes, your majesty." Murphy bows. "I would certainly appreciate your intervention."

"I am their queen—same as yours," says Serena. "And I will treat them as such."

"May I just point out," Evandre interrupts, stepping forward.

Serena lifts an eyebrow, pinning the Head Scientist with a glare that says she certainly may not.

Evandre continues anyway. "That the Undine were here first, serving—"

"How old are you, Evandre?" Nerin speaks up beside Serena.

"I don't see what—"

"Answer the Queen's Second," Serena interrupts.

"Thirty-eight years, next month."

Nerin turns to Serena. "This werewolf, the one who remains by your side when you are in The Dry, Conner. How old is he, your majesty?"

Serena smiles. "Forty-eight."

"Forty-eight years ago, an Undine calfling was born to Society. By unfortunate circumstance, he was born a weak male and had to endure a life-altering transformation and abandonment. Conner is ten years your senior, Evandre. And, at the very least, we can make an effort not to kill him by strangulation."

Evandre concedes, stepping back.

"Still, your majesty." Nerin dips her head toward Serena. "There are other things to consider. Do we have enough space for them? How can we safely transport them all to the caves? And, most importantly—" Nerin lowers her voice "—will our dying habitat provide enough food to support them all?"

Judging by her tone, the Queen's Second already knows the answer to her last question. Serena sighs. "Have you been to the dining hall, recently?"

"I have, just this pass night," says Nerin. "And may I suggest you do the same."

"There is something you aren't telling me, Nerin." Serena narrows her eyes.

"For sure," Nerin says, attempting a smile. "But I gather Rayne never had any problems in that area."

"No, she hasn't." Standing from her throne, Serena grabs her trident. "I will call Assembly tonight and announce our plans."

A flurry of questions rise up from the council. Only the guards that escort Serena out of the Great Hall remain silent. It is the one saving grace of having to be constantly followed.

After telling the guards to wait at the entrance to the orphanage turned dining hall, Serena calls out. "Mother Rayne?"

The room is as silent as the day Serena moved into a cave of her own. For several years after, the facility was filled only with the ghostly echo of calflings long since grown along with the occasional sweep of Mother Rayne's broom. Recently, the space has found a second life serving as a dining hall for Society.

The unnerving silence causes a pang of worry to bloom at the back of Serena's skull. "Anyone here?"

The sharp clang of pots banging together rings out from the back.

"Hello?" Serena skirts around the weathered table and walks into the kitchen.

"Your majesty, I didn't see you there." Rayne bustles around the floor, scooping up several flopping fish trying to make their escape.

Bending to her knees, Serena grasps a salmon with one hand, placing it back in the red-and-blue cooler—a gift from Liam. "You don't have to call me that, especially when it's just us."

"Wasn't sure, you usually have an entourage behind you." Rayne picks up the last of the fish, then stands, brushing her hands down the side of her legs.

She finally looks at Serena. "I'm sorry, dear. I'm in quite the mood."

"Is that why no one is here?"

"No one is here because I sent them away."

"Why?" Serena uses a jar to fill the cooler with fresh sea water coming up through a hole in the kitchen floor, then shuts the lid.

Walking to her large pantry, Rayne flings open the door. Jars that normally hold drying seaweed and herbs are bare.

"Where is all the food?" asks Serena.

"The past few months, the gardeners have started bringing back less and less. The problem is whatever plants they do manage to harvest are that much less for fish to feed on or find shelter around. The fewer the plants, the fewer the fish. The whole food chain is affected, which poses quite the problem when we are on the top of it." Rayne walks over to a counter carved directly into the cave wall and leans against it. "I've been in denial myself about the situation, which is why I haven't reported it. But yesterday, I went out to see for myself."

"And?" asks Serena.

"And…" starts Rayne. "Well, to put it bluntly, Serena, we don't have much time left."

"We aren't the only ones." Serena looks at the bare pantry again, then back to Rayne's haggard face, etched with lines of worry. The smell of fish rises up from the kitchen floor, taunting Serena and making her stomach turn. She staggers to the dining room table to sit.

Mother Rayne follows, thumping down beside Serena with a sigh. Serena watches out of the corner of her eye as Rayne's shoulders slump deeper, her spine curved in an uncommon Undine trait of resignation.

Each sigh from Rayne helps pump more and more resolve into Serena, until her back is as straight as Nerin's. "Okay. How much time do we have left?"

"Not enough." Rayne shakes her head.

"Rayne!" Serena snaps.

Rayne sits up, looking at Serena. "A month at our current rate, though I could probably stretch it to two or three. The problem would be keeping every Undine from scrounging what grounds are left. Even those considered sufficiently stocked won't last long with every maiden making a grab for what they can. And they will horde, especially once they find out my stocks are low."

"Okay, I'll issue a decree. All personal food stocks are to be brought here. Starting tonight, all meals are to be served from your kitchen. No unauthorized dining, either in the open ocean or in personal caves."

"You want to... regularize eating?" Rayne openly gapes at Serena, but Serena imagines that is one of the milder reactions she will receive when she announces it to the rest of Society.

"We will have to, if we are to make it last. You'll need to put together a schedule, and you'll need help. I'll send some your way."

Finally able to close her mouth, Rayne just nods.

"I'm going to call Assembly tonight—you'll want to be there."

"I can't imagine this is going to go over very well, but I'll be there front and center for you, Serena." Rayne takes a step closer, resting her hand on Serena's shoulder. "May I suggest you keep Dagon close and those guards of yours even closer."

"That, I can do," says Serena, thinking more of Kai than she is of her trident.

Chapter Seven

"This isn't going to go over well," Nerin whispers to Serena as they both watch Undine maidens file into The Great Hall for Assembly.

"So I've been told," mumbles Serena.

Nerin doesn't even bother with the expected *'a queen does not mumble'* reprimand. "You need to announce the new decrees and shoot down anyone that questions them. End Assembly quickly without taking any questions. You know—the way your father used to do it," says Nerin.

"I never liked the way he did it."

"A queen does not mumble, Serena," says Nerin. "Sit up properly. Confidence now."

The last of the maidens are coming in, and Serena knows Nerin is right.

It's time to look like the queen you hope they see.

Reluctantly, Serena straightens her back. Without Nerin having to officially start Assembly, everyone quiets and looks at Serena—it appears half of them know what to expect. Judging from pressed lips and defiant glares, they aren't happy about allowing werewolves into their home.

No problem – I can dispel the notion right now, thinks Serena.

"The werewolves are being forced to leave their home." Serena's voice rings throughout the cavern, clear and loud.

Throughout The Great Hall, Painted Maidens tighten their fists, as if they are already preparing to defend themselves from the beasts.

"And we will go with them." There is no echo from Serena' words. They die without preamble against cold, hard rock.

Nerin's advice was unnecessary—no one argues with Serena. They all stare back at her with blank faces. Serena licks her lips and exchanges a nervous glance with Nerin.

"We will migrate with Clan Werich away from here," Serena says, just in case she didn't say it loudly enough already.

Again with the blank faces.

Serena doesn't think she has ever heard The Great Hall so silent. Even the stalactites have ceased to drip.

"We are given no choice but to go. We cannot be separated from the clan, and as many of our gardeners already know, our food supply runs short." Despite clearing her throat twice, Serena's voice wavers with uncertainty. "Therefore, until we are ready to depart, all personal food stocks are to be given to Raync's kitchen. And starting tonight, all meals are to be served from her dining hall."

Against Nerin's instructions, Serena opens the floor because the silence is unnerving. "Any questions?"

Slowly, the maidens begin to spark to life. One dainty hand rises in the air.

"Yes?" Serena asks.

"Last week was my naming day, and my mother gave me dried nori. It is my favorite." Maidens shift to see who is speaking, and Serena catches a glimpse of orange. Sophia Sunbeam. Her sister Sasha was a casualty the last time the maidens attempted to take the beach.

Serena swallows hard at the memory.

"May I keep those, your majesty?" Sophia asks.

"I'm sorry, but every scrap of food must be turned in so we may ration meals. Society thanks you for your sacrifice." Serena's voice sounds hollow even to her own ears. Everyone knows the Sunbeam family has sacrificed much more than a couple sheets of dried nori. Nevertheless, Sophia nods in acquiesce.

Another hand rises to the air. "Will the kitchen be open at any time? I enjoy… snacking."

"A schedule will be announced," Serena says before turning to the next hand. "Yes?"

"We gardeners work in the coral fields all night. Our midnight meal comes from the open ocean. Are we no longer allowed to dine there?"

"No," says Serena. "Food will be brought to you." The tension eases out of Serena's shoulders. The questions are easy to answer. When one of the elderly crones hobbles toward the front of Assembly, Serena turns her attention to her. "Yes?"

"My large chest contains several family heirlooms," says the crone.

"Okay…" Serena gestures for her to continue. *What does this have to do with food rations?*

"I respectfully request assistance transporting the chest on The Migration, your majesty."

Serena's eyes go wide—the demand catches her off guard. "I apologize. There won't be any room for personal items on The Migration. Society thanks you for—"

"Then I won't be going," the crone interrupts.

"What?" Formality leaves Serena.

"If I cannot bring my inheritance, I cannot accompany the maidens. I won't leave it behind."

Serena glances at Nerin for help, but even the Queen's Second looks to be at a loss for words.

"Why does our food supply run low, anyway?" someone shouts from the back of the room. "What are the gardeners doing all day?"

Stepping out of the council line, Sarafina raises her voice. "My gardeners work harder than any other chosen responsibility."

Out of the corner of her eye, Serena can see Murphy and Kai exchange dubious glances.

"And how do we know Rayne will distribute rations fairly—those who work more will require more sustenance!"

"How do we know the queen isn't leading us into a trap?"

Serena slouches, burying her head in her hands. This is finally the response she was expecting. Ignoring Nerin's disapproving murmurs, Serena continues to slouch, only straightening when she sees Rayne elbow her way out of the crowd. Rayne moves up to the mid-platform then turns to face Society.

Without a word, Rayne fixes the loudest talkers with her stare, tapping her foot. Serena recognizes the stance. It is the same one Mother Rayne used when eliciting the truth from a guilty calfling. In front of her, Society abstains from commenting further about their queen's intentions.

"I will ensure that every Undine receive their fair share of food and, furthermore, that individual rations are stored in preparation for The Migration. If maidens are caught hiding, hording, or sneaking unauthorized food the equivalent will be deducted from your personal allotment." Rayne pauses, looking at Serena for consent.

Serena nods, silently thanking Poseidon for Rayne's interference.

Rayne softens her voice. "I understand these measures seem harsh, but so is the situation. Without the queen's guidance to ration food, we would most certainly starve before we even had a chance to migrate to more sustaining waters."

Serena finally releases the grip she has on the armrests of her oversized throne.

"I, for one," continues Rayne, "am thankful to have such an insightful, clever, and courageous leader as Serena guiding the Undine through these difficult times."

The Painted Maidens remain silent—no one would dispute the character of the queen directly to the woman who raised her.

"Thank you, Mother Rayne," Serena leans forward.

Rayne turns, curtseying to Serena. With her back to the rest of Society, she gives Serena a wink and a smile.

After Rayne disappears into the crowd, dragging the old crone that started the whole thing with her, Serena stands from her throne. "Assembly is dismissed. Those who have questions, concerns, or specific requests, please remain so we may confer on an individual basis."

Now I'm beginning to hate that word as much as Liam.

Serena descends to the mid-platform while maidens either leave The Great Hall or form a line that leads to Serena. Finishing the exchange of hushed whispers with Sarafina and Evandre, Serena turns to the line.

Her shoulders sag. At least half of the maidens remain. Steeling herself, and wishing she had some of Sophia's dried nori to sustain her through the night, Serena receives the first maiden.

By the time she has made her way through most of the line, Serena's back aches, and she has a pounding headache. "You may only bring items that will fit in your personal dry bag," says Serena for what must be the thirtieth time. It is quickly followed by the thirtieth crestfallen face.

The maiden steps away with downturned lips, and the last requestor steps forward. Serena has to lift her chin to look the colossal Undine in the eye.

"You too, Murphy?" she asks. "Are you here to request Society move your valuables?"

"No, your majesty." Murphy bows. "I am here to ask when you might be visiting the werewolf clan again so I may organize some of my men to escort you."

Serena yawns, glancing at the small arched doorway leading to her quarters and the promise of peace. "Liam just returned to them. I thought I might give them some time before infringing again."

"Understood, my queen. But if the werewolves were to catch wind that the Undine are preparing to leave quickly, they could misinterpret it as another abandonment."

"Right," Serena sighs. "We can't have that."

Chapter Eight

"Serena!" Robbie, the youngest of the three boys run at her, full speed, barely slowing before he can wrap his arms around her.

Serena stumbles back, catching her footing only to be knocked to the side by the second boy.

It is a welcome change from the stiff formalities of the court, with all the 'my queen' this and 'your majesty' that.

"Serena!" Darcy follows the noise caused by her boys from around their doublewide trailer. Her oldest, Aiden, follows but hangs back as soon as he sees Serena.

"Boys," Darcy directs, "give her some space."

Despite her own command, as soon as the children clear out, Darcy wraps her arms around Serena. "Liam said you weren't coming back until tomorrow."

A small squeak erupts in protest between the two women.

They pull apart, and Serena bends to look more closely at the baby in Darcy's arms. "Something came up. How is our little Ervin fairing?" Serena asks, wiggling her pinky in front of the baby.

He eyes Serena's finger but doesn't reach for it.

"He sleeps a lot," says Darcy. "And is much weaker than I remember my boys at this stage. But he has a strong will—he'll be all right."

Serena's eyes fall to Aiden, still hanging back by the trailer. She gives a small wave, and he at least lifts a hand in response before looking away. Serena looks back to Darcy. "Is he okay?"

"Oh, he's fine. Mostly just embarrassed about the whole thing." Darcy keeps one arm around Serena's shoulders. "He is grateful for your assistance, along with that of your maidens. We all are."

"It was gladly given," says Serena, trying hard to remain as casual as Darcy is. "But I might ask a favor that you spread the word of Undine assistance to the rest of the pack. We're about to endure some trials, and we all need to be on the same team."

"Done," says Darcy. "Hard to keep something like that a secret for long—especially with these two regaling the story to anyone who'll listen." She ruffles the hair on top of each of her youngest boys.

"Auntie Serena—did you really hold Liam's wolf out of the water for hours during a cyclone?" asks Robbie.

"Not quite," Serena laughs. "I had help." Then she looks at Darcy. "Auntie?"

Darcy shrugs, shifting Ervin to her other arm. "They call Liam 'Uncle'—seems fitting. Unless you prefer 'your majesty'?"

The boys actually giggle at this.

"Can I get *your majesty* some tea?" Robbie mocks while bowing more stiffly than Nerin might.

"They don't even drink tea." The other boy nudges Robbie. "They drink…" he trails off, then looks at Serena for clarification.

She bends, motioning them closer with the crook of her finger. They lean in, turning their heads to hear the secret.

"Fish blood," she whispers.

"Eww!" Robbie staggers back, grabbing his throats while making exaggerated gagging noises.

"Cool!" says his older brother.

"Hush, boys," Darcy admonishes with a smile on her face. "Get back in the house. You can watch TV until the men leave. Aiden—find cartoons for them, please."

"Yeah!" the younger boys cheer in unison, then disappear around the corner, followed by a brooding older brother.

"What men?" asks Serena, starting to follow the boys.

Placing gentle fingers on Serena's elbows, Darcy stops her. "The humans that dropped off the citation earlier still haven't left. Probably best if you aren't seen right now."

The women peek out from behind the trailer.

"They've been inspecting the camp all day. Preparations for kicking us out, I think," Darcy says, her voice low.

Next to a cluster of vehicles—a mix of local police and government cars—a group of men stand in a semi-circle. Liam and Conner are in front of them giving explanations with subtle hand motions. Serena tries to read how the message is being received. There are many crossed arms.

"Some think they're searching for weapons and trying to determine if there will be any resistance," says Darcy.

"Did they find anything?"

Darcy shakes her head. "The back of those cop cars would be occupied if they had. This is national park land—laws on firearms tend to be strict. Besides, Liam got rid of them all after Alaric died. The bigger problem we had was my boys. The authorities wanted to know why they weren't in school."

Serena's head snaps to Darcy. "They wouldn't take your children away, would they?"

"Told them I homeschool. It stood for now but if they look into it any further we'll have trouble. I'm supposed to register my lesson plan with the state, but the boys don't even have social insurance numbers. They didn't exactly have a... documented birth."

Serena shakes her head. "There is no way Undine will be able to integrate with the humans, as difficult a time as the wolves have."

It is Darcy's turn to look at Serena. "You planning on leaving?"

"We have to." Serena shrugs. "If you do. But not only that—our food is running out."

"That's not good. I've got some granola bars if you..." Darcy trails off at the look Serena gives her.

The sound of motors whirring to life attract the women's attention. The officials are shaking hands with Liam and Conner and returning to their cars and leaving. As the dirt kicked up by the convoy settles, Conner sees Serena peeking out from the trailer. He nudges Liam, and the pair begins to walk over.

"Werewolves and mermaids," mutters Darcy under her breath. "How many are there – more than a hundred altogether?"

Serena nods, the corner of her lips pulled back in a grim smirk.

"Where the hell can we go?"

Serena gestures to the satellite on top of the trailer. "Can you research it? Can you find a place?"

"I will," says Darcy. "I'll let you know." Nodding to the guys approaching, Darcy hugs Serena again. "I've got to get little Erving fed and all the kids to bed. Thank you again for your help yesterday."

"Dear god, Serena – if those guys had seen you." Liam is checking over his shoulder as if they might come charging back any moment.

"Good to see you, too, brother. Enjoying your time above the land, instead of below it?"

Having the wherewithal to look sheepish, Liam scratches the back of his neck. "Not gonna lie, as good as it feels to have the sun on my face, it's ten times better to feel the moon on it."

Serena smiles, fully sharing her brother's affection for the moon. She nods at the dust cloud left behind by the group of cars as they pulled away. "Darcy told me about them."

"Liam was able to talk them into a thirty day extension." Conner pats Liam on the back. "But that still isn't a whole lot of time."

"For you or for us," says Serena.

"Why?" Liam asked. "What's going on?"

"Our food sources are running out. We need to move on, too."

"Seriously?" asks Liam. "That is out of the blue." He puts his hands on his hips and taps his foot. "You aren't just saying that for an excuse to force them to move, are you?

"Liam—I just spent the good part of the moon's light sitting in a rigid throne, listening to crones threaten to tie themselves to their grandmother's chest of jewels to prevent me from forcing them to leave." Serena throws her hands in the air in a desperate gesture. "Maidens complained there is no way to bring their wall paintings with them. One actually asked if the guards could use their tridents to break chunks of the cave off so her precious artwork could accompany us. Can you imagine? The tridents would break in two!"

Liam looks as if he is actually stifling a smile. "No, I literally cannot imagine forcin' that whole society to move."

"No need to imagine," says Conner. "We'll be right there alongside them."

Snorting, Liam looks from Conner to Serena. "I'm havin' blatant visions of wolves hikin' the beaches with the Undine out at sea, throwin' over a fish every now and then."

"Well, no—that wouldn't work," says Serena. "The pH levels of the water will change. We can't swim in variable water for long, though we would need the occasional dip. Remember how sick I got last time I was out of the water for only a few days?"

"So, what then? Pack both our clans into boats? They'd be clawin' at each other's throats before long." Liam rubs his own neck at the thought.

"We'll have to work out logistics," says Serena. "We have thirty days?"

Liam and Conner both nod.

"You'll let your pack know to start preparations."

"Oh, no, your majesty." Liam places his hand on the back of Serena's shoulder, pushing her forward. "They don't get their orders from me. Come on. I'll call a meetin'."

Serena sighs, emerging from the shade of the trees. "Just… don't give me an uncomfortable chair."

"We address the pack from the warehouse." Liam looks at her sideways.

"I remember it," says Serena, shuddering at the thought of returning to the makeshift fight ring.

"Don't worry, your majesty," Liam pats her hand. "I've had all the thrones tossed out into the ocean for you."

"Not funny, Liam." She smiles anyway. "Besides, your trash ends up at my doorstep anyway."

"Exactly," he winks.

Chapter Nine

By the time Serena enters the warehouse, the clan has packed it full wall to wall. Gazes fall on her, and she can feel the hostility rolling off of them in waves. They are in their Ungainly forms, but the wolves don't lurk very far underneath.

And this time there will be no Rayne, Serena thinks as she makes her way to an opening around the rink. The crowd here doesn't part for Serena as they did for Alaric. *Not yet anyway.*

"Quiet down, everybody," Liam raises his voice above the chatter and grumbling.

Serena can at least sympathize. After strangers snooping around all day putting everyone on edge, the wolves are called to a meeting by a leader they haven't yet come to love, much less respect.

She skirts around the metal poles and subconsciously rubs at her wrists, cringing at the feeling of chains that are no longer there that held her to those poles. Alaric detained Serena and Liam as hostages, forcing Serena to call her own people. The only one that came was Alaric's mother, Isadora—the Undine psychic. Serena stares at the pillars, wondering if Isadora saw her own death coming.

"Serena..." Liam's voice cuts through her memories.

"Sorry," she says, clearing her throat, but she can't take her eyes off the poles. "You know what? I'm not sorry."

"What?" Liam asks, casting confused glances at the metal poles.

"I want these removed. This clan will no longer take prisoners—Undine, Ungainly, or werewolf."

A stunned silence falls over those gathered inside the warehouse. Serena watches the looks of disgust fade into glimmers of curiosity.

Encouraged, Serena raises her voice. "Does anyone have a problem with this?"

No one answers. Liam sends Conner and another away to find shovels and spades.

"How did you explain these to the authorities anyway?" Serena asks, flicking the ominous-looking chains hanging from the top.

"Tetherball," says Liam.

"Is that like bowling?" she asks, remembering their conversation from the night they met.

Liam smiles. "Not quite."

There is an awkward silence as they wait for equipment to dig. Serena clears her throat, whispering to Liam, "Were you able to find out who is giving Aiden the injections?"

Liam shakes his head. "No, and Aiden isn't talking—about anything these days, really."

"Well, keep me updated..." she trails off as several men return with their tools.

They pause as they make a lopsided circle around the poles.

"Both of them?" Conner turns to look at Serena.

"Yes, both." Serena rubs her wrists. "Quickly."

The first shovel slices into hard-packed dirt. It sounds like the knife slashing through Isadora's throat. Serena turns her back to the arena and swallows hard. She scans the crowd before her for a distraction. The noticeable hostility has left the warehouse, but Serena isn't sure she likes the open mouths and wide eyes any better. "Did I do something wrong?" she asks Liam.

Liam steps closer. "Those poles weren't only used for prisoners. Alaric often kept clan members tied to them for punishments. Sometimes for a whippin', sometimes he just kept them there for a couple days without food and water."

Serena's face grows hot with anger. "I had no idea."

"This is a good thing. It's like the last of Alaric's rule is comin' down."

Serena glances at the crowd again. As one pole falls, she can almost see tension lift right out of the pack. The other pole drops with a loud thump in the sand, sending a plume of dust into the air.

Conner sticks his shovel into the ground. "What do you want us to do with these?"

Serena turns to the crowd. "Any suggestions?"

Everyone is quiet for a long time. No one can tear their eyes from the now harmless, fallen poles. Finally, someone steps forward. He is shorter and skinnier than most of the others. Stumbling a bit when he walks, he opens a flask, and the pungent smell of liquor floats out. He weaves his way in between Serena, Liam, and those who dug up the poles. He stops in front one of them and pours out the entire flask of liquid.

When the last drops fall, he gives the flask a violent shake, then throws it against the back of the warehouse. Turning to Serena, he growls much more fiercely than she would expect from that small a man. "Give them to me. I'm goin' to melt them down."

"Danny has more hours tied to those poles than any of us," Liam whispers to Serena.

Without another word, Danny turns his back to Serena and Liam and removes his shirt. Pink and white scar tissue crisscrosses his skin. Serena couldn't lay her palm anywhere on his back without touching the raised welts.

When he turns around once again, Serena looks him in the eye. "They are yours for the taking."

Danny bends to pick up the poles and throws them both over his shoulders. Exiting the warehouse, he leaves his flask and his shirt behind.

"Danny was the second wolf transformed after Alaric," says Liam, his voice low. "They were friends for a while, but when it came time for one of them step up as Alpha... well, things didn't go well. Hopefully Danny won't need his liquor anymore just to get through the day."

"He won't try to step up as Alpha now that Alaric is gone?" Serena asks.

"No," says Liam. "There already is an Alpha." He extends an arm, motioning for her to step forward and take the stage.

"Right," says Serena, taking a deep breath. No point in delaying the inevitable. She raises her voice so everyone can hear. "We are leaving."

"Who's leavin'?" shouts someone.

"All of us. Werewolves and Undine. We will be traveling together to seek new land to share together. Somewhere we can be safe."

"Where, exactly?" another voice calls out.

"I'm leaving that to Darcy. If you have any suggestions, please see her. It will be next to water, obviously, but a lot of research is required." The more Serena talks, the more she believes Darcy is the best to make the decision. The clan already trusts her, and she'll want to find a place to raise her boys. As far as the Undine go, they already have taken a liking to her. She is the only woman in the clan, after all.

"How soon?" Someone else asks.

"One month," says Serena.

"It will still be difficult to be ready that soon," says Liam. "I might be able to get another extension from the authorities to stay longer."

"It isn't just the clan we have to consider," says Serena. "The Undine are running out of food. We leave in a month." She turns to Liam. "Start your preparations. I'll be on the shore one hour after dusk every night if it is clear of Ungainlies. You can report your progress, and I'll inform you of ours."

As soon as Liam nods, Serena walks forward, straight toward the crowd. She keeps her steps long and quick and her chin held high. Those in the front step to the side, and an even line parts as the queen exits the warehouse.

Chapter Ten

During the next few weeks, preparations to move two entire societies get underway. Except for nightly updates on the wolf clan progress from Liam, Serena's focus is on the Undine kingdom, and they are proving to be a resistant bunch.

"Seven of the elderly maidens have barricaded themselves inside a cave. They say they are refusing to leave with the rest of Society," Murphy tells Serena as each council member reports progress for The Migration.

"Have the crones stolen any of Rayne's food?" asks Serena.

"No." Murphy clears his throat. "My guards made sure of that. As a matter of fact, the crones insist no food is left for them. They want to send it all on with us for The Migration."

"So they will be traveling to the afterlife while the rest of us travel to bluer waters?"

"If it will be as they say, your majesty." Murphy bows.

Serena sighs. "And the strength of their barricade?"

"I could have it brought down in a matter of minutes."

Serena nods. "Leave them there, for now. They will cause less trouble than they have been. And make sure to pass food through."

"If they refuse it?" Murphy asks as though he has already attempted it.

"If they refuse the food, let them know they will be bound and gagged until we reach our destination. Is that all, Murphy?"

"One more thing, your majesty. Arista has once again requested hydrocoral."

"Denied." Serena waves her hand in dismissal. *At least that one was easy.*

Murphy bows and steps aside.

"Health?" Serena asks Hailey.

Hailey flits in front of Serena on light toes. Loose skin hangs under tired eyes, but she acts as though she has energy to spare. "Weight loss is prevalent, though not dangerous."

"Good," says Serena. "Hopefully it means sneaking extra food in the coral fields has stopped."

"Right," says Hailey. "But with less sustenance, the polluted waters seem to have more of an effect. Almost half the population has been to my quarters as a result of torn webbing. And thanks to your Ungainly apparatus—"

"The microscope?" Serena interrupts. For some reason, Hailey refuses to use the Ungainly word.

"Yes, apologies," she chirps. "Scale samples are showing more fissures and weaker structures."

"I'm not sure there is anything we can do about that until after The Migration," says Serena.

"Most likely not, your majesty," agrees Hailey. "But it means we will be very vulnerable during The Migration, and we will need our werewolf protectors more than ever before."

Hailey's words caste a somber silence over the council. Though Serena has had plenty of experience with the wolves, not many other Undine have. All that remains in their memory is the recent battle on

Cliff Beach and perhaps even the Maiden's Massacre. There are bonds of trust that need to be established before the two groups can embark on their journey as one.

"Understood, Hailey. I will see to it."

Hailey curtsies and hops aside for Evandre, who barely waits for the Healer to vacate the area.

"Your majesty," the Head Scientist bobs her head without lowering her eyes. "I must insist we delay departure until I can travel to the selected destination myself. I have to check salinity, acidity, temperature, and food sources before we can even think about sending forth our Painted Maidens."

"We've been over this, Evandre," says Serena. "If we delay any further we risk starvation. And the wolves will have to move on anyway—neither species will survive if we separate."

"I can investigate and find a way to survive the separation—"

"And how long do you think that will take? One month? Two? A year? Odds are we will run out of food before you can find a cure for separation. And that cure still won't solve our own problems. Please focus, Evandre," Serena looks at the council member before her.

They all stand as stiff as planks. It is obvious Evandre is dead against rekindling an alliance with the werewolves—and there are plenty of maidens that follow her lead.

If I could convince Evandre, maybe I could convince the rest Society.

Serena speaks carefully. "I understand your need to see that the Undine are traveling to a safe place, and Society thanks you for your protection. The one

Ungainly who lives with the wolves left a week ago to seek a new home. She is tasked with bringing back water samples. I will arrange it with Liam so that you may confer on our new home with her. Will that suffice?" asks Serena.

"As you say." The Head Scientist doesn't even curtsey before she walks away.

Serena sighs. "If that is all from the council?"

Several heads bob up and down.

"Kai, I'll take leave to visit Liam. Do you wish to accompany me?" Serena stands from her throne.

Kai jaunts up the few steps, holding out his elbow for Serena to take. The council members have conveniently turned their backs in whispered conversation, and Murphy is giving the guard their orders. While no one is paying attention, Serena takes her time descending the few stairs to the mid-platform. Running the pads of her fingers along the inside of Kai's arm, she allows herself to break decorum and look up at him. He is already smiling back at her, both of them anticipating time alone, even if it is just for a short trip to The Dry.

* * *

When Kai and Serena reach the surface of the Pacific Northwest waters, the beaches are empty of Ungainlies, but it isn't quite dusk.

"The sun is taking its sweet time to retire," observes Serena after dipping her hair back under to keep cool from the harsh rays.

"Let it," says Kai. He wraps one arm around Serena, bringing her closer. "More time for us."

"And if someone sees?" asks Serena. She raises the pitch of her voice and over-annunciates, imitating Nerin. "It wouldn't do for the queen to be caught flirting with a guard member. What would Society think?" Despite the fact their relationship has been publically known for at least a month, Nerin insists Serena and Kai cannot show affection for one another in front of anyone else.

Kai laughs. "Like Murphy has never been caught—by Nerin herself, her own mother."

"Kai Forest, don't lie!"

"I swear to Poseidon, I'm not."

"Which maiden was he caught with?" Serena's jaw drops.

"Hailey."

A rolling wave comes through, bumping the pair together. They laugh again.

"She talks about him sometimes, but I never thought the feelings were mutual." Serena remembers the look on Nerin's face when she caught Hailey merely discussing Murphy with Serena. If his feelings were mutual, they were kept well under wraps, on account of his mother.

The waves grow rough as the wind picks up.

"Come on," says Kai. "I have an idea." He takes Serena by the hand and swims them both into rougher surf.

"Kai, what are you—" The next wave crashes over their heads, cutting Serena off.

Tossed and turned, colliding into each other and pulled apart just as quickly, they flounder like guppies in the water. Serena straightens herself out, finding the surface and popping above just to be pushed below again by the next wave. Kai rolls by in front of her, sticking out his tongue while his tail is tangled in kelp.

Serena laughs as she breaks the kelp apart for him. As soon as he is free, he pulls her up. Picking up speed, Kai and Serena glide along the surface, angling in to join another wave. This time, they slide in front of it just as the crest folds forward, wrapping them in a tunnel of brackish blue. Kai continues to jut forward, but turns on his back and dips below the surface. He pulls Serena on top of him so her chest rests on his stomach. She rides the wave just as she has seen the Ungainly surfers do, lying down on their boards.

Holding her arms like wings, Serena's fingertips skim the watery tunnel on each side. Here in the ocean's breakers, between The Deep and The Dry, Serena is finally afforded a little privacy from both worlds and her title as queen.

A wide grin spreads across her face as she looks down at Kai in gratitude. She pulls him up just as the tunnel condenses, then collapses in on itself. They endure the chaotic aftermath, tickling each other as they roll into calmer surf.

Catching their breath, their heads bob above water. Pure delight dances across Serena's face with the last light of the sun, and she looks at Kai. "I want to pair with you." The words are out of her mouth as soon as the thought enters her head. Her eyes go wide. Kai looks just as stunned.

"Are you sure?" he asks, giving her a chance to retract the statement.

Serena bites her lip, her eyes falling to the frothy water surrounding them. The time between waves lengthens, as if the ocean herself awaits Serena's answer. Finally, she looks up to Kai. "No more waiting, Kai. I'm ready, and I wish to pair with you—if you'll have me."

His eyes light up, and he squeezes her face in between his hands, drawing her lips to his. A breath she doesn't know he was holding escapes as his lips relax open. He tastes of salt. Another wave finally breaks, taking them both by surprise. He wraps his tail around hers as their arms snake around each other.

The wave pushes them under in a tumultuous celebration, and they hold on tight as the world spins around them. Hitting the sandy sea floor, they break apart. Serena's hair has escaped her braid and black tendrils reach out, brushing Kai's cheek.

Right here, right now, there are no worries in the world. There is nothing but Kai and all the fun, the security, and the affection he brings. Serena can't pretend the moment will last forever, but she knows if Kai is by her side then she can face anything.

The sun dips below the horizon, and Serena's blood tingles with the strengthening rays of the moon. One hand interlocked with Kai's, Serena leads the way into The Dry. Scales sink into skin and she barely registers the sting. All she can feel is the smooth ridges between Kai's knuckles with the taste of him still lingering on her lips.

Water gives way to earth and her legs disconnect from each other to form feet. Wiggling webbed toes in grainy sand, Serena and Kai stand together as a wave recedes, taking the last of the salty seawater shed from their bodies with it.

Liam hasn't made an appearance yet, and Serena is thankful for a few more moments alone with Kai—

especially with the prospect of a pairing fresh in her mind.

"Should we wait until The Migration?" asks Serena.

Kai turns to her, taking both of her hands in his. "More than likely, we will never see these beaches again," he says. "Everything is about to change—but before it does I'd like our pairing to be in the same place as each generation of our ancestors." He brushes the pad of his thumb across her knuckles. "And may Poseidon bless us with a strong, healthy calfling of our own."

Serena swallows hard, squeezing Kai's hands. She doesn't even want to think of what it might mean birthing a calfling in new waters. "I'll announce The Selection as soon as we return to the Great Hall."

Kai smiles again, then presses his forehead against hers. "I love you, Serena Moon-Shadow. And I am yours."

"I love you, too." Serena feels as though a cloud lifts her straight into his arms. "And I am yours in this world and the next."

Chapter Eleven

By the time Liam arrives, the moon has trekked halfway across the sky. He emerges from the tree line out of breath and tired, finding Kai and Serena constructing a sprawling castle in the sand.

"Is that your underwater kingdom?" Liam asks, his shadow falling across a series of towers flourishing detailed stonework.

"No," says Kai, looking up at Liam. "It's a sandcastle."

"Stop it, Kai." Serena stands to brush sand from her lap, trying to keep a smile off her face.

Liam does not hide the frown on his. "Preparations for the Undine must be goin' well, seeing as you have time for sand art."

"They are going better." Serena squares her shoulders with her brother. "Now that a group of crones have barricaded themselves in a cave, refusing to participate in The Migration. At least they are staying clear of our bustling corridors."

"Some are refusin' to go?" asks Liam. "What will that do to the… connection?"

Serena knits her eyebrows together. "I hadn't considered. I'm of the opinion everyone will be convinced to go, in one way or another."

Squatting to inspect the main castle structure, Liam runs a palm across the top to even it out. "I don't know, Serena. Maybe forcin' our will upon our people is not the way to handle this."

Serena bends to the side, allowing her untamed hair to brush across the sand as she looks at Liam upside down. "What are you implying?"

He doesn't seem to appreciate her silliness. Instead, his cheeks grow pink as he stands. "These people have lived in this one spot their entire lives. You and I are the youngest of our species. We ain't cemented into the ways of our people, but they are. They don't want to leave their damn home behind, they don't want to say goodbye to their damn stuff, and they are damned scared." Liam kicks at one of the towers, and it explodes into a shower of sand.

Kai steps forward, inserting himself in between Serena and an angry werewolf.

"Liam," Serena says, voice soft. She peers out from behind Kai. "What troubles you?"

Up until now, he has been fully immersed in preparations for The Migration and unfazed by any obstacle put before him.

He takes a deep breath, looking between Serena and Kai. "Sorry," he mumbles, glancing at the maimed castle. "But I'm gettin' pushback from some of the older wolves as well. They haven't so much as flat out refused to go yet, but I think it's comin' to that."

"What do you propose we do about it?" asks Serena, more careful with her words and her actions.

Taking a deep breath, Liam glances down at his boots until the pink drains from his face. He sits in the sand, making a point to shore up the shattered side of the castle. "Pieces of us will always be with our homes, no matter why we leave." He gestures to the rest of the castle, sturdier as a smaller structure. "The places you make for yourself along the way will always be a part of you, they build you up—just like the experiences you have and the people you meet."

Kai grasps Serena's hand and squeezes.

"I think," says Liam slowly. "We should let each Undine and each werewolf make their own decision about stayin' or goin'. Hopefully, whatever magic binds us together will... understand. But I ain't goin' to make people do somethin' they don't want to do. I ain't Alaric," Liam finishes softly, rubbing at the needle scars on the inside of his arm.

"And I'm not my father," says Serena. She catches Liam's eye. "I mean *our* father. He was always demanding."

"And stubborn," offers Kai.

"Exactly," says Serena.

"Well, that settles that," says Liam, standing up with sand caked to his pants. He glances at Kai and Serena's interlocked fingers. "Wait—what's goin' on?" He looks over his shoulder then out into the ocean. "I mean, I knew you two were together but not openly."

"I think that is about to change," says Serena, drawing strength from the heat of Kai's hand to break the news for the first time. "We wish to hold a pairing, and we want it to be on these beaches before we leave."

"Oh." Liam reverts his eyes back to the castle. His cheeks are turning pink again.

"And if we are leaving some behind, particularly the older generations who wish to stay," says Kai, "then what better way to honor them than to have a completely traditional pairing, with the blessing and protection of the werewolves."

"You're goin' old school with this?" he asks.

Kai and Serena exchange confused glances at the phrase.

"It could work." Liam runs a hand through the stubble on his chin. "And it would be a good way to build trust between the two groups before our journey together."

"It's about all we have time for," says Serena. "Unless we want to dangle maidens from the cliffs for each werewolf to rescue." She looks up at the cliffs towering above the beach and shudders in memory.

Liam surprises her with a laugh. "That doesn't end well for anyone but us, Serena."

Kai still has his eyebrows knit together.

"The ceremonial procedures are in the archives," says Serena.

Liam rolls his eyes. "The Undine and their ceremonies and books. Takes the fun out of it if you ask me. Besides, I already know the general gist of it."

"How?" asks Kai.

"I read the book. I had a lot of time sittin' in those archives. So besides your new love affair that's actually old news, do you have anything else to pass on?"

"Our Head Scientist wishes to speak to Darcy on her findings when she returns," says Serena.

"She flies back tomorrow night—should get home by midnight. Should we make a ceremony out of her return?" Liam teases.

Serena smiles, mostly in relief he is back to his old self. "No, but I want to be there, too. I need to keep Evandre on a short leash, as you might say."

"I most definitely would not say," says Liam. "Dog metaphors don't go over too well with the pack."

"Noted," says Serena. She looks at Kai. "Remind me to announce as much at the next Assembly."

"You have your portions of food for The Migration under control?" asks Liam.

"We think so, but of course that all depends now on how many stay and how many go."

Liam nods. "Let us know if you need us to supplement. We are more than covered in that department. And with Doug's business, we have enough boats to transport all of us plus supplies. If we have to go over land, though, that will become a problem."

"We'll see what Darcy comes back with," says Serena. "We'll meet again tomorrow at nightfall, and I'll have Evandre with me. In the meantime announce those that want to stay have my permission and get a count." Serena sighs. "By Poseidon's good graces, this will all work out."

"Poseidon's graces and a bit of luck," mumbles Liam. "Until tomorrow, your majesty." He imitates the bow of the king's guard and turns on his heels, stalking into the trees.

"We may make an Undine out of him yet," says Kai.

"Let's not even broach that subject," says Serena, turning toward the waves. "I'm going to send out a call now. I can't wait a second longer for the announcement about the pairing." She skips along wet sand, prospects of a Selection and Pairing she actually wants to participate in overshadowing the possibility that she will leave some of her Painted Maidens behind.

Webbed toes touch cold saltwater, and Serena breaks into a run, picking her knees up higher and higher until the next swell is deep enough for a dive. She jumps, bends at the waist, and streamlines her body. Plunging in, the transformation back into fins is quick enough that by the time the swell subsides, her fins are already working. Kai splashes in behind her, and Serena follows the coral-covered slope down to The Deep.

Passing a large bloom of jellyfish, Serena scoops one up and pushes it back toward Kai. Unable to dodge it because he is looking away, Kai is punished with a sharp sting. He wags his finger at Serena, silently chastising her for playing games common amongst caste mates. She smiles back, but her mood has dampened. There are no more caste mates—the last of the school-age Undine graduated, Serena was one of them. There were none to take her place until her own caste mate, Cordelia, gave her life to birth a son.

And how will the newborn fair during The Migration? Serena wonders. Hopefully Darcy's theory that they might do better together will help them cope with the stress of travel.

Undine working the coral fields come into view, with the guards watching their backs not far away. The Queen's Guard, highly proficient in marksmanship with their arrows and trained to use their tridents to defend their people against any threat, is now relegated to cafeteria duty.

Serena's somber mood deepens. Playtime with Kai is over, and as much as she has to look forward to with him, she needs to focus on the problems of her people. She opens her mouth and calls to them. Elongated whistles studded throughout with clicks— it is Serena's echolocation signal, but she knows her call is well recognized by all of Society now, whether emitted above or below the water.

The sound comes back to her, and with it Serena can see the detailed patterns and vibrant colors each maidens' scales boast. Heads turn and tails angle their fins to follow Serena—her call is irresistible to her subjects. By the time she emerges from the entrance pool to the caves, more than half the Undine population is behind her.

Walking down the corridor, Serena continues to sing. Up ahead, Murphy stands guard at a fork in the hallway, his trident rigid by his side. He gestures to the right—this is where the elderly maidens have barricaded themselves. Serena doesn't follow the hallway to the closed-off cave, but stands her ground at the fork.

Changing her harmony to appeal to a different generation, her melody follows the tune of an ancient song. Gradually, Serena adds words only the long-standing members of Society can remember. Deep bass-like notes thrum out from the end of the hallway. The crones send their answer.

We are coming, my queen.

Serena turns away but does not cease her song. It follows her into the Great Hall, where she opens up her throat and pushes more air out from her lungs. Keeping her pitch high, Serena makes it obvious her song is missing something. It is only balanced once the group of crones, delayed by their own barricade, enter the Great Hall. Aged vocal chords add a weathered flavor to the melody. It is a balance of young and old—fresh notes supported by a confident beat.

The song ends after one last reverberating note. Serena stands at her throne with the crones in front of her on the mid-platform. She runs her eyes over them and they give a slow curtsey in response.

"I understand you wish to stay behind, instead of embarking on The Migration with the rest of Society," says Serena.

"Yes, your majesty," one gravelly voice rings out as the eldest of the group takes a shaky step forward. "We don't—"

Serena holds up one hand, cutting off the crone. "You don't owe an explanation. But you are aware of the invisible thread that binds us together? Separating from the group will not be pleasant."

"We are aware, your majesty, and will swear as much to Poseidon if needed." The crone removes a sharp instrument from her hair and presses it into her pockmarked skin. In the old ways, swearing to Poseidon always requires a blood oath.

"That will not be necessary," Serena's voice rings out. "I give permission, for those who wish it, to stay behind."

A collective gasp runs through the crowd. From the corner of her eye, Serena can even see the Queen's Guard look at one another in an unprecedented break in decorum. Council members who weren't given the time to take their place on the mid-platform now push their way through the crowd.

Nerin is one of them. "Your majesty, council has not been given the opportunity to advise you on this matter."

"And I thank council for their concern," says Serena. "But the decree is made."

Nerin nods her head, then moves slowly and stiffly to stand by Serena's side.

"Each maiden should know that The Migration will be dangerous. However, as our food supply runs short and falls under peril, which only increases with every passing day, it is far more detrimental to stay here in the sea of our ancestors." Serena watches the faces before her. Many look to each other and several hands join as they are faced with the sudden prospect that Society may split apart. Standing up from her throne, Serena picks up her trident, clacking Dagon against the ground. Everyone's attention snaps back to her. "I expect any Undine wishing to stay behind announce their decision within the week."

Maybe my father was on to something with his no nonsense attitude during Assembly, Serena thinks.

"Before we leave for The Migration, there is one other ceremony we must carry out." Serena softens her voice causing maidens to lean in. "We will hold a traditional pairing on our beaches."

"Traditional, your majesty?" asks Evandre. The exasperation in her voice is pronounced. "As in werewolves?"

"As in protectors," Serena says. "We will hold The Selection before the next full moon, and it will be open for any maiden to participate."

"My queen, I must protest—"

"In order to assuage any fears the wolves' presence may create," Serena interrupts. "I, myself, will be participating." Her eyes bore through Evandre. "I know you will not work to contradict my desire to take part in this ancient ceremony, Evandre, and I thank you for that."

Chapter Twelve

The swim to the archives goes quickly, with high tide pushing Serena through the narrow tunnel. Once she hits the wide entrance pool, she forces her transformation into legs, rolling her body in a dolphin-like kip. Having lost some speed with the transformation, her body crests the surface just enough so she can land on the platform. But instead of hitting jagged cave rock, there is a splash. Water covers the platform up to her knees.

She looks up. Robes hanging from the hooks move with the push of the tide, the hemmed material at the bottom soaked through.

"Mariam?" Serena calls as she enters the archives. She lifts a foot over the lipped doorway that should be plenty high enough to stop encroaching water. The ocean is gushing over as though there is no obstacle at all. "Mariam?" Serena calls again.

"Serena – thank Poseidon. Come help me over here!"

Following Mariam's voice through shelves of books, Serena wades through ankle-deep water.

"Careful!" Mariam says. "Don't splash them."

"Oh, sorry." Serena drops to her knees, causing even more of a splash, and tries to wipe at the water spots on the books with her wrist.

"Oh never mind that. Help me get these books out of the way." Frantically collecting hardbacks off of the lowest shelf, Mariam throws them in lopsided stacks on higher shelves.

Mariam pauses to rub at her lower back. Looking behind her, Serena realizes the older woman has already done two long rows. "I could go back to the open ocean and call for help," Serena offers as she scoops up an armful of seaweed encyclopedias.

"I don't want to risk water damage to any more books," says Mariam, getting back to work. "The tide should start receding within the hour. Let's finish this section."

Soon, water ceases to rush into the archives. What is left lies in stagnant pools on the floor.

Mariam and Serena finish moving the last of the wet books, then sink to the ground with sore backs.

"Are you okay, Mariam?" Serena asks.

The archives master looks to be on the verge of crying.

Instead of tears, laughter comes. "I am a mermaid librarian. What did I expect?" She shakes her head, allowing her hands to go limp by her side. "I was so worried about the wolves above me, maybe clawing their way through the sun shafts... " she glances up at the ceiling, "that I didn't even notice the ocean creeping up behind me."

"You talked about taking measurements, and keeping track. I remember."

Mariam shrugs. "Didn't get around to it. But I've never seen the water above the platform—never."

"The combination of high tide, the stormy season, and rising seas probably helped," offers Serena.

"Thank you for your assistance," Mariam stands, offering a hand to Serena. "I could never imagine asking your father to do such a thing."

Serena laughs. "Bound to his tail as he was, my father couldn't even make it this far in the archives." Her laughter fades as they walk in silence. "I came because I called Assembly and made an announcement. Well, several, in fact."

"Murphy was already here, delivering the news," Mariam says. "And inspecting. I don't think he likes the look of those sun shafts, either." She turns her back to Serena, busying herself with the catalogued tracking system.

"He told you about each maiden having a choice in The Migration?" Serena asks.

Mariam makes a noncommittal noise in the back of her throat, but she doesn't turn to look at Serena. "I'm going to have to find entire sections a new permanent home," she mumbles, continuing to rearrange cards in the catalogue.

"I told those who want to stay to let me know at the next Assembly. Not that you need to be there, though it may be—" Serena cuts herself off when she sees Mariam's hunched shoulders. "Mariam?"

Finally, the archives master turns to look at Serena. "Right. I won't be there. I'll just tell you now." Mariam takes a deep breath. "I choose to stay."

Serena feels as though her breath has been stolen. She rounds her lips to ask the question *what*, but only a squeak comes out.

"Look around you, Serena. This is my life. How could I leave my books in the clutches of high tide?"

Hands going to her midsection, Serena forces herself to speak. "I… can't leave you. Food is sparse, and your health will deteriorate. You'll die!"

Mariam sets down the cards in her hand and steps toward Serena. "We all die, Serena. And in the end, the only thing that matters is what we leave behind. This" —she holds out her arms wide— "is my life's work. And I will see it through to the end."

Tears sting the corners of Serena's eyes. She shakes her head. "I take it back—all of it. I'll say everyone has to go. And we'll find a way to transport your books. Every last one of them."

Mariam closes the distance between them and wraps Serena in a tight hug. Burying her face in Mariam's shoulder and hair, sobs rack Serena's body. When she can finally speak, she looks at Mariam with a tear-streaked face. "You've been my friend and my mentor for as long as I can remember. *I'm* your life's work. Will you not go with me?"

It sounds selfish, even to Serena, but right now she will say anything to keep Mariam with her.

Mariam smiles at Serena, pushing stray strands of jet black hair away from her face. "Serena—I couldn't be more proud of the maiden you've become. You are queen now. And you face harder choices than any leader before you. But you are making the right decision."

Serena sucks in a shaky breath but nods.

"Let me make this decision for myself," says Mariam. "I'm sure there will be others, and we will take care of each other. Now, let's talk about The Pairing. Is Kai pressuring you into this? Because I will have words—"

"No, Mariam." Serena releases her mentor to wipe her cheeks dry, trying to calm herself. "It was my idea."

Mariam stares at Serena with her dark-brown eyes. Serena knows the look well—it exudes innocence, trust, but demands honesty at the same time.

"So you are ready?" Mariam asks.

"I am ready to take Kai as my mate for life," says Serena. Her voice is no longer shaky.

Mariam persists in her questions anyway. "Are you yielding to pressure from your status as queen? You are young yet… and have time. Don't feel like you have to grow up all at once."

Serena pauses to think about her friend's question. "I am the youngest Undine. But I am also the queen. The thought has crossed my mind—how could I truly know what it means to be Undine, and how could I make the right decisions for Society if I haven't undergone one of our most sacred rituals myself?" Serena bites her lip, looking at Mariam.

Mariam remains silent, her eyes prod Serena to answer the question herself. Serena is thankful for the safe reprieve in which to talk.

"But it isn't about what everyone else has done or is doing," says Serena. "And it isn't about growing up or proving myself. Even if The Selection and The Pairing were completely private matters, I'd still want it." Serena looks down, wiggling her toes in a puddle of water. "It is about the way Kai makes me feel. With him by my side I feel stronger—more independent. He lifts me up." Serena smiles, remembering their surfing tunnel. "He makes me a better me. He is my anchor and my best friend. And I am ready to share myself with him."

When Serena looks at Mariam, the archives master exhibits the same smile Serena holds. "I've seen that much myself," says Mariam. "I just wanted to make sure you've seen it, too. I'm so happy for you, dear."

"Thank you, Mariam." Serena steps closer for another quick hug, then clears her throat. "So, um, do you have any knowledge or advice for me during The Pairing—or anything that comes after?" Serena remembers Mariam's words. *I am staying.* Her throat closes up at the thought.

"Knowledge? Yes, of course. I have an entire library of knowledge. But who is to say that any of that can translate into good advice for the youngest Undine, who has stunned Society by all she has accomplished as Werewolf Liaison and then as queen? You forge your own path, Serena—you always have."

"Right," says Serena. "And I'm about to forge it straight away from you."

"No more of that. I will not have you doubting yourself because of my choice to stay," Mariam's voice turns hard. "But there is one thing I want to tell you about The Pairing."

Serena lifts her eyebrows in interest.

"The first time can be many things. It can be thrilling, awkward, or downright painful. It is different for everyone, and I want you to be prepared. Just know that a pairing is meant to improve with time, trust, and communication."

"Thank you, Mariam."

Though Mariam is more than twice Serena's age, the mentor has always spoken to Serena with candid respect. It is time to return the favor.

"And I will honor your wish to stay, and give you anything you need to survive," says Serena.

"As long as it doesn't put those on The Migration at risk, of course," interjects Mariam.

"Of course," says Serena after pausing only slightly. "Now, point me to the books on The Pairing.

The werewolves will be there, and I need to know their role."

"Old school, huh?" Mariam smiles.

The phrase catches Serena off guard, but then again, Mariam did spend a lot of time with Liam when he was held in the archives.

Mariam turns to the catalogues, opens a drawer toward the bottom, and pulls a card. "I always did appreciate the presence of the werewolves at The Pairing. Makes it more exciting—heightens the experience." Mariam winks at Serena, waving the card in the air. "Follow me, dear."

Chapter Thirteen

"Why must we stand here? You are their queen. Their… habitat is yours." Evandre taps her fingers impatiently at her hip as both she and Serena stand on the beach looking out into the dark forest.

Liam is late meeting them tonight, but especially with another Undine, Serena insists they be escorted into the camp. "We will wait to be invited to their home. It is a sign of respect. How can they come to respect me if I do not respect them?"

Evandre turns up her nose. "Your father would not be left waiting. He would be bold—march straight into that camp and bellow his demands."

"My father could not walk as a result of some of the very bold choices he made." Despite her insistence on patience, Serena gives Evandre an irritated look. "Besides, I am not my father."

"That you are not," mumbles Evandre.

Shrubbery rustles in front of them, putting an end to the argument. Liam emerges from the trees, dressed in his bowling alley shirt and ripped jeans. His eyes hop from Serena to Evandre and back again.

"May I present Liam of Clan Werich, brother to the queen." Serena smiles. It is a playful jab at Liam. "And this—"

"Evandre," says Liam. "I could hear her whine from a distance." Liam shoots back with his own jab.

Evandre frowns.

"Evandre Sea-Bird," Serena says, pushing propriety back into the conversation. Serena needs this meeting to go well. "She serves as the Head Scientist for the Undine."

Evandre lifts her chin, her ego slightly recovered. "I apologize for my tone, earlier," she tells Liam. "I am not used to waiting, especially in a place that has had such petrifying connotations for us for so long."

"Understood, Head Scientist of the Undine," Liam adopts a formal tone, and Serena can't tell if he still mocking Evandre. "But we are here to change all that, aren't we?" He holds out his elbow for her to take.

"Yes, I suppose we are." Slowly, Evandre raises her fingertips to rest her hand inside Liam's arm. Serena watches the pair of them walk into the woods before she follows, wishing she could paint the scene in the caves below just to remember it. Serena keeps her distance, trailing Liam and Evandre to camp, hoping the pair can find some common ground.

"Here we are," says Liam, holding back a leafy branch for the Undine maidens.

The first trailer comes into view, and it is one of the worst Serena has seen. Siding hangs off in sheets, duct tape—perhaps a temporary fix—blowing in the breeze.

"You… live here?" Evandre asks, the corners of her mouth turned down in distaste.

"Well, not that one. I'm on the other side. Wanted to get as far away from Alaric as I could. That there is Danny's trailer," says Liam.

As they pass the dilapidated structure, the sound of hammer on metal rings out.

"Sounds like Ronan's armory," says Evandre.

"He is doing somethin' with those poles." Liam looks at Serena.

"Something" —Evandre puts the emphasis on the ending of the word— "good I hope."

Serena pauses. "Maybe we should check."

"Let's not bother him," says Liam, urging the maidens along. "He announced his intentions to stay and others have been givin' him a hard time about it. Come on. Darcy's trailer is right over here."

Liam ascends three steps and knocks.

"More waiting," Evandre mumbles, fingernails tapping her hip again—the clicking noise grates on Serena's nerves.

The rapid reverberation of several pairs of running feet get louder and louder until the door bursts open. Evandre gasps, stumbling back in surprise as two young boys launch themselves at Liam.

Letting out a deep-throated guffaw, Liam lurches backward. He lands on his behind—the boys squeal in delight as they pounce on Liam's chest. Evandre stands behind them, eyes wide with her hands clutched tightly together over her chest.

"Ruffians!" shouts Evandre. "Stand back, my queen."

"Evandre, calm yourself. They are only wrestling," Serena explains.

One boy has both arms wrapped around Liam's neck while the other is attempting to wrangle his legs.

"Ow—no biting!" says Liam.

"Ruffians, indeed," Darcy's voice rings out from the top of the stairs. She leans against the rickety railing wiping her hands on a dishtowel. Small wrinkles form around the corners of her eyes as she smiles down at Liam. "Okay, enough torturing your uncle. Inside, boys."

"Go on now. Listen to your mom. Isn't it past your bedtime?" Liam nudges one boy to the door while picking the other up off the ground by his shirt.

"Hi, Aunt Serena!" they escape Liam's grasp to wrap their arms around Serena's waist.

She laughs, holding her hands up to ensure Evandre they mean no harm.

"I said now!" Darcy shouts.

The boys yelp at their mother's command, but she whips them playfully with a towel as they run past. "Come on in," she gestures to Liam, Serena, and Evandre. "Make yourself at home. I'll just put them to bed, and I'll be with you. Colin's at the alley." She sets a baby monitor on the round kitchen table. "Ervin is asleep."

Darcy's guests shuffle in and sit around the monitor—it plays a repeating lullaby. Evandre sits with her back stiff and her hands folded on the table in front of her. She turns down Liam's offer of drinks and food while they listen to Darcy running through the nighttime routine with her boys.

"I'm sorry about that," Darcy says, coming back into the kitchen after most of the rambunctious sounds from the back of the trailer die out. Her shirt now dons a toothpaste stain down the front. "I'm Darcy." She nods at Evandre across the table. "And you've met two of my four little heathens."

"They are quite… wonderful," says Evandre, clearly at a loss for how else to explain them.

"Thank you. They aren't always this crazy, but I think the move has them on edge." Darcy's hands flit around the room at the boxes, some half-filled, some stuffed and taped.

"Are you taking all of it with you?" asks Serena, casting a nervous glance at Liam. They've talked several times about how difficult it will be to bring personal effects.

Darcy sighs. "Almost all of it is going to storage. Until we figure out what to do with it."

"What did you find out on your trip?" Serena asks.

"Okay." Darcy retrieves a folder from the counter. She spreads it open in the middle of the table and notes, maps, and pictures scatter. "I narrowed it down to three places before I left, all accessible by water. I picked secluded but protected lands, with water that best matches salinity, acidity, and temperature to here—or as best match as I could find with my limited research methods."

"Which are?" asks Evandre.

"That," says Darcy, pointing to the corner of the room.

Serena and Evandre both squint. It is a square box with a screen on one side.

"Here are the samples I brought back for you." Darcy produces a small box from under the table and opens it. Corked vials fill the box. "A dozen water samples from each location. Yours for the taking." Darcy winks at Evandre.

"Thank you. I will begin tests right away." Evandre fills the waterproof satchel tied around her waist. "We should know if any of these places are habitable by the next moon, your majesty."

Serena almost flushes at the formal title in such an informal setting.

"Which places did you find?" asks Liam.

"All up north in Alaska," says Darcy, unfolding a larger map. "Here, here, and here."

"The U.S.?" ask Liam. "We don't know much about their government."

Darcy shrugs. "I'm hoping that doesn't matter, if we stay secluded enough."

The door to the trailer home slams open, and everyone hops back from the table, heads swinging toward the entrance. Colin stomps in. "Darcy!"

Serena is beginning to think Cordelia's baby can sleep through anything.

"Great Poseidon, woman," says Evandre. "How many heathens do you have?"

"One too many, apparently," says Darcy, stepping toward Colin. "Excuse me a moment."

Darcy and her husband leave the trailer, shutting the door behind them. Hushed whispers buzz in through thin walls.

"Are you sure it's him?" asks Darcy. "How do you know?"

"He answered all the questions right when I quizzed him about the old man," answers Colin.

Serena and Liam exchange glances, their interest peaking.

"Well you can't let him in—not with the mermaids here."

Serena automatically looks at Liam. "We can leave out the back."

"Hold on," he says, standing up from the table. "Let me see what this is all about."

Poking his head out the door, Liam exchanges more hushed whispers. Finally, he looks back at Serena, excitement lighting his eyes. "It's Cecil's lawyer. He has a will."

Chapter Fourteen

"Put them on." Liam hands Serena and Evandre both a long-sleeved jacket, then turns off most of the lights in the room.

Holding the jacket up between two fingers, Serena looks at Liam. "Or I can just retract my scales."

Liam shakes his head. "Doesn't matter. Your skin still has a bluish tint to it. There's nothin' we can do about your face—maybe he'll think you are in some exotic stage show."

"What about me?" asks Evandre. She already has the jacket on and is scratching at the itchy material on her arms.

Studying her elder with renewed interest, Serena has to admit Evandre's cheeks and the sharp lines at her jaw have a strong purple hue.

Staring, Liam finally shrugs. "I don't know. You can pass for a carnie, maybe."

"Everyone ready?" Colin asks, holding the door open.

Mumbles of hesitant agreement sound off around the table.

"Good," he says. "May I present Mr. Donelly."

A thin man in a dark suit with a stiff white shirt buttoned up to his neck appears in the doorway. "Oh." He looks startled as his eyes flit around the room. They come to rest on Serena and Evandre, and he lifts one finger to point. "You are..." he trails off as his finger curls back into his palm, and his thumb extends, pointing to the waves sounding in the distance behind him.

Serena gives a cautious nod. "As you say."

Mr. Donelly swallows hard. "Let's get this over with. Liam, I presume?"

"Yeah." Liam steps forward. "Let me guess, the old man is still ordering me around."

"I'm not sure I would call it that," says Mr. Donnelly. "More like helping you." He takes a seat at the table, glancing up at Serena and Evandre again.

Mr. Donnelly stares at the pair of Undine until Liam sits beside him. "May I present Serena Moon-Shadow and Evandre Sea-Bird."

"Pleasure to make your acquaintance," Mr. Donnelly mumbles, but the words sound strangled, and they come out in a high squeak. He clears his throat. "Cecil left everything in joint custody to Liam and Serena. His house, his business, and this… " Mr. Donnelly takes a small, locked box out of his bag, placing it on the table. "Here is the key. I don't know what's inside. Though I was informed it is necessary for both species survival."

Liam takes the key, turns it over in his hand once, then inserts it into the lock on the box.

"Please don't open it now!" says Mr. Donnelly. "I prefer not to be present. I don't need any more information about this situation than I already have." He takes a deep breath and pulls a stack of papers out next, sliding them toward Liam. "Sign here."

The room falls silent as Liam's pen scratches across paper after paper. Serena keeps catching Mr. Donnelly's eye and self-consciously pulls her sleeves down to her wrists.

Liam signs the last paper and pushes the stack and the pen toward Serena. Her eyes hop from the pen up to Liam and down to the papers.

"A simple X will do, right next to Liam's signatures," says Mr. Donnelly.

Pinching the pen between her forefinger and thumb, Serena fumbles as she draws an X on each page.

Once she finishes the last page, Mr. Donnelly scoops up the documents and stuffs them into his briefcase. "I thank you for your time, and I do apologize for not coming sooner, but trust me, I believe everything Cecil told me, which is probably why my first instinct is to run in the other direction." He zips up his briefcase, stands, and pauses. "The only reason I am here now is because I heard about them closing down the trailer park. I can't imagine your lot loose in the towns. Thought I should do something about that before my big move." He turns and walks toward the door.

Darcy holds it open for him, the dishtowel clutched tightly to her chest.

"Where are you moving?" asks Serena.

He stops at the door, turning his head slightly. "To a landlocked country, Ms. Moon-Shadow. Somewhere very far away from any ocean." Mr. Donnelly reaches into his pocket and produces a small slip of paper. "Here is my card." He hands it to Darcy. "But don't come visit me. Just call if you have any questions."

After Darcy shuts, then locks, the door behind Mr. Donnelly, all heads turn toward the box on the table.

"Do you think it's a bomb?" asks Colin.

"Please—this is Cecil we're talking about," Liam growls at Colin. "He raised us."

"Cecil was the human that kept our sons?" Evandre asks.

Liam nods, all of them circling around the table.

"I left my son with him," she says.

Every pair of eyes in the room is glued to the box. No one dares look at Evandre.

"Do you know which of us he is?" asks Liam, his voice almost a whisper.

Evandre shakes her head, swallowing hard. "We gave him the transformation potion, but he did not survive it. It was in the very early days, even before Alaric. We didn't have the potion right—not in time for my boy, anyway."

Running her hand over the box, Evandre smiles. "The human left his windows open that night."

Liam frowns. "Cecil never left his windows open."

"That night he did." The smile dies from her face. "Because I was singing. I was singing to keep him alive, and the human knew it."

"Your songs are very powerful," Darcy speaks up. She looks at Serena. "Yours helped my boy."

"Well." Evandre breathes in and stands straight. "Are we going to open this thing or shall we break into song right now?"

"Right—here goes," says Liam, inserting the key and unlocking the box. He pulls out a mess of paperwork, flipping through it. "Titles, business documents, official papers makin' sure everything is in our name, Serena."

"Won't do us much good," Serena says. "We're leaving."

"I can at least give the trailer to Danny. Maybe he'll pick up the business and continue to keep tourists away from your maidens that are staying behind."

Serena nods, a lump forming in her throat. If she is going to leave Mariam behind, at least her friend will be as safe as possible.

"And..." Liam pulls out a map, rolled in a cylinder tube with a rubber band around it. "It looks like he left us something much more important."

"What could be more important than...?" Serena trails off as Liam snaps the band and unfolds the map.

A vial of water comes out with it. Rolling across the table, Evandre stops it right before it crashes to the floor. "It looks like one of yours, Darcy," she says.

"What is that old man up to?" Darcy eyes the vial then leans over the map. "Will you look at that? He's already picked a place for us."

"Where?" Serena and Liam ask in unison.

"A place called Ivvavik National Park—on the northern border of Canada, right next to Alaska. I didn't consider it because it would be a long migration. We'd have to skirt all the way around Alaska." Darcy stands, furrowing her eyebrows in thought.

"But he's made arrangements," says Liam, reading a note from Cecil that was tucked into the map. "Ivvavik National Park is only accessible by aircraft. There are no roads leadin' there—it is very secluded. And it appears as though his cousin works there." Liam looks up at the group. "He says it's safe for us."

"I'll test the water," Evandre says, peering at the tube.

Liam nods. "And I can correspond with his cousin. He left contact info."

"Wait a minute guys." Colin is flipping through more of the paperwork. "Cecil left some research notes. It looks like he has some ideas of the pack splitting and cutting whatever is binding us together."

"Oh?" Liam lowers the papers he is looking at. He exchanges glances with Serena.

"He thinks if both sides have an Alpha, the pack can split without any pain." Colin looks at Liam, excitement flashing through his eyes. "I wonder if Danny would still be willing to take the job?"

"I'll talk to him." Liam turns and starts pacing. "This could work. This could all work out thanks to Cecil."

"Wait…" Colin is scanning the page further. "He thinks not just the pack, but also the Undine need an Alphas—one to cover each side. That's the only way the split will work."

"It makes sense," says Evandre. "All along the Undine and the werewolves have both had an Alpha. They counter each other. Well, I suppose until Serena took on both rolls."

"Which can easily be remedied," offers Serena.

Liam's eyes snap to hers, and she feels a tinge of sheepishness for it. She looks down at the map, running her finger around the borders of the protected land. The park is almost four thousand square miles and sits right on the Arctic Ocean. "Ivvavik," mutters Serena. "I wonder what that means."

Colin turns Cecil's research notes in his hand, showing Serena. "In the local aboriginal language, it means 'a place to give birth'."

Chapter Fifteen

When Serena enters the Great Hall, trailed by Evandre, energy and excitement hums through both their bodies. They walk to the front quickly, smiling at each other as they go. Other members of the council stand toward the front of the massive cavern, raising their eyebrows in interest.

Serena leans toward Evandre. "Let's not announce what happened quite yet. Test the water and make sure it is compatible."

Evandre nods, a gratified smile on her face.

"You have news for the council?" Nerin asks as soon as the pair of maidens approaches.

"We might, but I've asked Evandre to confirm some facts first," says Serena.

Evandre lets out the quietest, shortest squeal beside Serena. But Nerin misses nothing, and wide eyes gawk at Evandre.

"Very well," says Nerin. "The Selection is to begin shortly, anyway."

Evandre's shoulders sag a little when her important task is brushed off so easily.

The sounds of chattering, webbed feet brushing over hard rock, and fingers running through hair in a final attempt to prune enter the Great Hall. It grows louder as more maidens, and then the Queen's Guard enter, Murphy marching his formation straight to the front. Standing in a group with the council, Serena watches Kai at the back of the formation. Her stomach tightens into knots. The Selection is about to begin. With the reading of Cecil's will, Serena hasn't had a chance to even think about The Selection or The Pairing—until now.

Kai frowns at Serena, and she realizes she is biting her lip. He shakes his head in disapproval, much like Nerin would, but he looks determined to do something about Serena's mood. Keeping the rhythm of the guards' march, Kai lifts his feet higher and higher, legs straight so he is goose-stepping down the Great Hall. It is the old way of marching, and it looks so awkward it was a wonder they ever did it at all. When Murphy calls the guard to a halt, Kai rears back his leg in an over-dramatic attempt to stop himself. He spins once and does a pony hop as the other guard members are clacking their heels together.

A smile wide on her face, and barely able to hold back laughter, Serena mouths the words *'thank you'* to Kai. He lifts his legs in quick sequence, as if he is jumping over an obstacle, then bows to the queen. His endeavor to lighten the atmosphere in an otherwise stressful ceremony has worked—several maidens giggle in tight groups.

"Will you take the throne, your majesty?" Nerin asks. Even her words have a softer edge to them.

"Yes, of course." Serena turns toward the looming throne but pauses. "Evandre, unless you wish to participate, you are excused from the ceremony."

"Thank you," Evandre says with a more respectful curtsey than Serena has ever seen the maiden give. "I shall report my findings as soon as I have them."

As Evandre leaves the Great Hall, the last of the maidens filter in, and Serena takes her seat. The council arranges itself on one side of the mid-platform opposite the guards. Once everyone quiets, heads begin to turn toward Serena. She clears her throat and sets her trident against her throne. "Will the maidens who wish to be considered for The Selection please step forward?"

There are subtle shifts in the crowd as maidens attempt to squeeze their way to the front of the Great Hall. Simone is one of the first. Serena narrows her eyes as the maiden previously paired with Kai takes the first spot in line. Simone does not glance at Kai or Serena—she keeps her eyes trained directly forward. No one else from the Temporal Caste steps forward, but several other maidens of various ages do.

"Very well." Serena gives her approval of the six maidens in front of her. "I—"

Serena cuts off as movement from the council catches her attention. Hailey steps forward. Serena's eyes go wide, and she can't help but glance at Murphy. There is only one reason Hailey would participate in The Selection. Her face is flushed as she takes her place at the end of the line. Standing beside Serena, Nerin has gone very still as her eyes dart in between her son and Hailey.

Before Nerin can say anything, Serena stands. "Let The Selection begin," she bellows.

The maidens in line jump at her words.

Damn it, Serena thinks as she sits back down. The tension that Kai managed to ease is slowly slipping back into the room. She looks at the Undine Maidens lined up in front of the throne. Many are fidgeting, with their fingers constantly in motion rubbing at the scales on their hips. Even those who have stood through The Selection before are nervous. No one looks happy.

Serena frowns. If The Selection and The Pairing are successful, these women will endure the hardship of a changing body as calflings grow inside them, then the difficulties of birth. They will face possible death, as many have before, or worse—the death of their calfling. There might still be the decision they all face if their calfling is born a weak male. Would they give them the potion?

Heat washes over Serena. This feels all wrong, but it is the way it's been done for generations. She feels powerless to stop it.

At Murphy's nod, the first of the Undine guards step forward. It is Morven, the biggest one. Almost simultaneously each of the maiden's eyes go wide, then shoot to the ground in front of them.

"Stop!" Serena shouts. Her voice snaps throughout the cavern as though the former king himself just clacked his trident against the ground.

Every head in the Great Hall turns toward her. She stands from the throne slowly. "I will not have my maidens cowering in fear as they wait to be inspected and picked up like seashells in the sand." Serena scans the line of maidens as she speaks. They raise their eyes in interest.

"They are worth more than that," Serena continues, her voice softer. "And they must go into The Pairing knowing the value of themselves."

Now she looks at the guards. Morven has paused mid-step, one foot still raised.

"I decree The Painted Maidens shall select their mate themselves. And after tonight, The Selection will no longer be a public ceremony. Parties may confer in private whenever they feel ready. They shall report their intent to pair only so that we can arrange appropriate protection on the beach." Serena finds herself on the mid-platform, having descended the stairs as she speaks. She is eye to eye with the line of maidens in front of her. "Do any maidens participating in tonight's Selection wish to withdraw from the line due to the change in ceremony?"

They each shake their heads no. A new kind of excitement jitters through them as they shift from one foot to another, glancing over at the guards.

Serena turns to the male Undine. "Do any of the Queen's Guard wish to withdraw their eligibility from The Maiden's Selection?"

Most of them shake their head no, but Morven slowly lowers his foot as his opposite hand rises into the air—just as slowly. "Apologies, your majesty, but I'm not—"

"No apologies are necessary," interrupts Serena. "You may stand by my throne, Morven."

Her dismissal is not harsh. In fact, standing next to the throne is a place of honor usually reserved for the Queen's Second and the Head of the Guard himself.

"As you say, your majesty." Morven bows and jogs up the steps toward the throne. Nerin offers her own spot, then goes to stand with the council. Morven does a perfect about face then comes to rest, his chest heaving with pride.

"Anyone else?" Serena asks.

"Your majesty," one more guard, the one standing beside Kai, steps forward and bows. "I will also request to abstain from the ceremony."

"And so it will be. Please take your place by my throne."

The guard bows again. As he dips his head, Serena catches Kai's eyes. All at once, she realizes what her own decree is going to mean for her. She will have to select him.

She turns to Assembly, mouth dry. "We will perform this last rite of passage to honor our ways of old before The Migration. The ceremony has been blessed by our elders."

The aged maidens who stand toward the front of Assembly nod their heads.

"Given the change of ceremony, does the court still have your blessing?" Serena asks them.

There is a moment of tense silence, then one steps forward from the group. "I should've liked to seen it done such a way in my days," she says, her voice deep and scratchy with age. The rest murmur in agreement.

"Thank you," says Serena, breathing a sigh of relief.

Surveying the maidens before her, Serena works a bit of moisture back into her mouth. Her eyes come to rest on Simone, standing at the end of the line. She remembers the snarky smile on Simone's face when Kai chose her at the last Selection, after Serena made it clear she wasn't ready.

There is no way I'm going to take a chance this time, she thinks. *I am the queen, damn it.*

Stepping forward, Serena lifts her chin. "Very well—let The Selection begin."

Before the echo of her words bounces back, Serena performs a right pivot worthy of the Queen's Guard and takes quick strides toward Kai. Her fingers jitter and her vision blurs as nervous tears spring to her eyes.

Don't think about it. Just do it.

Her pace quickens. She doesn't want to give herself the chance to back out of this. But when she meets his eyes, warmth envelops her body, and her beating heart calms. With locked gazes, Serena stops in front of Kai. She curtsies and he returns the gesture with a bow—then they step forward and come together.

"You will have me?" Serena asks.

Kai nods, swallowing hard. His lips form the word 'yes' but barely a sound squeaks out. He appears to have lost his voice.

At least I'm not the only nervous one, she thinks.

"And I will have you," Serena says.

Their lips press together in modest kiss that lingers just long enough for Serena to revel in the taste of smoke and salt. Smiling, the couple breaks apart, Kai taking her hand. Serena falls into the line of guards by his side.

An awkward round of clapping rings out but doesn't spread among the crowd. After all the deviations in decorum, applause is asking too much.

Looking back toward the line of maidens, Serena prays to Poseidon. It is their turn now, and she hopes they will embrace the change.

Surprisingly, Hailey, the oldest of the maidens, steps out of line first. She treads toward Murphy, her footfall light and airy. Like Serena, she will not risk losing the only one she desires. Hailey stops in front of Murphy and extends her hand. Without hesitation, Murphy bends to kiss Hailey's knuckles. The union is agreed to by both parties—but instead of taking her place by Murphy's side the pair steps forward and turns to where Nerin stands with the council.

With her telltale rigid spine, the Queen's Second looks from her son to his new mate and back again. Finally, she gives the slightest nod.

Bending in unison, Murphy and Hailey graciously accept his mother's approval of their pairing, and they return to the line of guards.

The diverse manner in which the unions are being made encourage the rest of the maidens. Two step forward at the same time. After an awkward pause, they actually laugh out loud. Joining hands, they walk to the line of guards together, then separate after a brief hug and well-wishing to choose their mate. The next maiden walks toward the Queen's Guard with a slight skip in her step. That skip morphs into a prance, and the maiden finishes with a spin in front of her chosen mate. The smile on his face is wide and he responds in kind with his own tap dance, finishing with one toe forward as he takes her hand. When she wraps her fingers around his, he spins her into place by his side.

The last maiden to step forward is Simone. She doesn't glance at Kai even once. Instead, she moves to stand in front of one of the quieter guards and extends her hand to him.

He doesn't take it. "I was going to choose you during The Selection of the Temporal Caste," he says. He gives an accusatory glance to his right, not directly at Kai, but everyone knows who Kai selected in the last pairing event.

Simone doesn't break her gaze. "I'm here now," she says. Her face softens into a smile. "And this time, I am allowed to make my own choice."

Understanding blooms over the guard's face. "Thank you, Poseidon… and your majesty, for that."

The guard takes Simone's extended hand, pulling her into the line next to him.

With two guards having abstained from the ceremony, every other guard is matched, and there are no remaining maidens. The Selection is complete.

Nerin steps forward from the council, a pleased smile on her face. "The couples are excused to prepare for The Pairing."

Chapter Sixteen

Kai turns toward Serena and squeezes her hand. "I'm going to go get ready. You'll be okay?"

Serena nods and forces a smile even though her nerves feel stretched too thin.

"Good." He smiles back. "I'll meet you on the beach, beautiful." He kisses her on the lips.

The warmth that floods her body is enough to anchor her. She walks the length of the Great Hall to her room, fingertips scraping the sides of the hallway.

Normally, the maidens and guards who will participate in The Pairing retire to their own caves. Family members and friends visit to give congratulations, advice, and sometimes gifts.

The Pairing has been built up into such a stressful event—no wonder they are hardly ever successful.

Serena stops in the middle of her room, glancing toward the barren entrance hallway. She does a full circle around the cavern, then glances at the hall again. It is still empty. Serena has no family, and it is doubtful anyone will be visiting, since no one is allowed in the queen's quarters. Lying back on her bed of stone, she sighs. Poseidon stares back.

"At least I have you," Serena says to the inanimate carving.

Candles begin to flicker out around the room. Serena remains staring at Poseidon. Without as much interfering light, his eyes twinkle back at her.

His long beard and square face remind her of her father, and she wonders, not for the first time, if they are related. She wonders what kind of advice her father might give right before the pairing, or if he would steer clear of the issue all together. She wonders if her father could ever be convinced to leave the place he grew up.

"Am I doing the right thing?" Serena swallows a hard lump in her throat, thinking past The Pairing to the upcoming Migration. The carvings of Poseidon will of course stay behind, and there will be no more reminders of her father.

Will I forget what he looks like?

She closes her eyes, trying to burn Poseidon's image into her brain, but lids fly open as she hears footsteps coming down her hall.

"Murphy?" she asks, scooting out from the sleeping rock.

"It is only me, your majesty." Evandre halts at the entrance to the room.

"I am sorry." Morven bows to Serena. As one of the only two guards not participating in The Pairing, he must have been posted to her quarters. "But she said she has very important news."

"Yes, your majesty." Evandre has a wide smile, as she waves a test tube in the air and steps into the room. "I have results."

"It's fine, Morven. Thank you," Serena says.

Morven bows and leaves. Serena watches as Evandre walks right over to the rock, sits down, and pats the edge for Serena to join her. Shocked at Evandre's brazen conduct, Serena slowly walks over and sits. "Have you been in here before?" she asks.

"No, I haven't." Evandre purses her lips, looking around. "It's smaller than I thought it would be."

Serena clears her throat. "You said you have news."

"Oh, yes." She looks at the vial in her hand as though it just appeared. "The water tests out okay. The pH balance more or less matches the waters here as they were thirty years ago. The water, on average, will be about ten to twenty degrees cooler, but Undine will adjust to that well enough."

"So we're going," Serena says, her voice quiet. She turns to look at Poseidon as though it will be the last time.

Evandre follows her glance, then puts her hand on Serena's shoulder. "Poseidon will grace our journey," Evandre says. "And, Serena, your father will always be with you. Tonight, for The Migration, and whatever comes after."

"Thank you, Evandre. We will need the blessing of every Undine that has passed to the afterlife. They at least know what it is to migrate."

This elicits a small smile from Evandre. She clears her throat and straightens her back. "Someone has spoken to you about what to expect during The Pairing?" Her lips go tight, as if she is preparing herself for some gruesome task.

"Mariam has," says Serena, feeling formality creep back into the atmosphere.

"Good." Evandre stands, smoothing her scales down her midsection. "If anything, Mariam is forthright and thorough."

"That she is." Serena stares at the last flickering candle.

"If I may, your majesty." Evandre looks to the hallway. "Maybe a visit to Mother Rayne would benefit you? Now is the time to be with family."

"Very well." Serena stands, allowing Evandre to lead the way without looking back. Behind them, the candle sputters out, leaving Poseidon alone in the darkness.

* * *

"Serenita." Rayne hops up from the table to greet Serena. "We weren't sure if you would come."

Across from her, Ronan stands a bit more slowly.

"And we didn't think the guards would let us in your quarters, even given the circumstances and the fact that we raised you," Rayne continues. "I had a half a mind to march in with a frying pan should they give me any grief about it."

Behind Rayne, Ronan grunts. Both he and Serena know Rayne would have done it.

"Please don't beat my guards, Mother Rayne." Serena says with a chiding eyebrow. "That would make for a very awkward trial."

"Awkward trial, indeed." Rayne crosses her arms. "As if we haven't seen enough of those already."

Ronan grunts again, then scratches his rough chin, looking at the kitchen.

"Yes, well—Ronan and I will cook dinner for you. You'll need your energy tonight, after all," says Rayne.

Blushing at the wink Rayne gives, Serena keeps her head down and follows Ronan into the kitchen hoping Rayne also doesn't feel the need to talk about The Pairing, or worse, give advice.

Thankfully, Rayne whips into action as soon as she enters her domain. She opens the storage cupboards and pulls out the coolers while Ronan lights a small fire in the cooking pit.

"Is her majesty still a vegetarian?" asks Rayne, plunging her hand deep into the cooler. Something splashes back at her.

"Yes, I am—and I'll thank you to respect as much tonight." Serena doesn't usually use such a harsh tone with her orphanage mother, but she really, really doesn't want to fight about food.

Rayne makes a quick snatch and pulls out a small, pink salmon. "The fish is for me and Ronan. We've collected enough hijki to make your favorite."

Rayne opens a large pot, and Serena can smell the makings of sea lettuce soup. Her stomach grumbles in anticipation.

"Grab the hijki, Serena. Just in that jar, on the middle shelf."

Relieved to be rid of formal titles, bows and curtsies, however temporary, Serena almost begins to sing as she fumbles through the cupboards. Finally, she finds a clear jar full of the thin, dried algae that looks like twigs. "Did everyone else eat?" asks Serena, feeling guilty that the three of them are indulging.

"Anyone that cared to show up during supper hours," Rayne says, stirring the soup. "I sent a small tray of anything we could spare for those participating in The Pairing."

Serena opens the jar and selects a crunchy stick. She lets the salty flavors roll around in her mouth as she looks about the kitchen. The cupboards designated for Migration food storage lie open too. Rayne has bundled food so each maiden will be capable of carrying her own. Serena counts the individual packages as she swallows the last of the hijki stick. "We are short a few."

She doesn't miss the quick glance that Rayne and Ronan share.

"Nerin stopped by today to inform me of two more maidens that have chosen to stay," says Rayne.

"Still short." Serena recounts just to make sure.

"Put the fish on, Ronan, or he'll barely have time to heat up." Rayne concentrates on her stirring.

"Rayne?" Serena asks, a sliver of worry gnawing at the back of her brain. Instead of waiting for the answer, Serena marches over to another cupboard and flings open the doors. This holds bundles of food for those planning to stay. They aren't nearly as big—the hope being the ecosystem will once again begin to thrive with fewer Undine picking at it. Ten bundles sit on the shelves, like stubborn barnacles that refuse to budge.

"Mariam, the seven elderly Undine who have already announced their intent to stay, plus the two more you mentioned. Who are the other two bundles for?" Serena asks.

Ronan stands up from the fire, and Rayne stops stirring. She closes the pot back up, and her shoulders hunch.

Understanding hits Serena like an iceberg. Tears automatically spring to her eyes. "No," she says, wiping away the tears because she refuses to believe it.

Ronan moves to stand by Rayne, and they both look at Serena, clasping hands.

"We didn't want to tell you until later," Rayne says.

"No," Serena repeats. "I can't leave Mariam and everything that reminds me of my father and say a final goodbye to the two people who raised me."

Rayne wipes away her own tears, then shrugs. "We would just slow everyone down, Serena. And we probably wouldn't make it."

Lifting her chin and closing her eyes, Serena swallows hard. "I cannot imagine life without either of you in it."

Serena hears shuffling, then Ronan's large arms wrap around her. The scales that have been singed and blackened until they curl back scrape at her, but the hug feels good, as though he is forcing her to pull herself together. Only when Serena's tears cease does Ronan let go. He cups her chin in his hand. "You'll be just fine, little calfling. Just fine."

"We'll speak more of it later," Rayne says. "But now, let's eat."

After the devastating news, Serena isn't able to swallow much food, even if it is sea-lettuce soup sprinkled with hijki. But Rayne doesn't nag her, and the meal is finished in relative silence. By the time the dishes are scrubbed and put away, Rayne announces it is time.

What food Serena does manage to swallow has somewhat filled the hole that gets bigger in her chest every time another Undine announces their intent to stay.

"We'll take you to the beach, if you wish," Rayne says.

"Yes." Serena nods. "I would like that. Thank you."

The swim to the beach takes longer than it should—Serena's orphanage parents are slow. At first she thinks they are just trying to prove a point, until she reminds herself she hasn't seen them actually swim in a long time.

Serena stays behind Ronan and Rayne, watching as they nudge each other when the current pushes them together. Ronan reaches out for Rayne's hand, and their fingers intertwine. Calloused palms and raw knuckles find their comfort, wrapped in the warmth of another. All at once, Serena can't wait to start her life with Kai.

Chapter Seventeen

Once Serena reaches the breaking waves, Ronan and Rayne pause. They each give her one last hug. Rayne tucks a stray strand of hair floating out from Serena's braid, and Serena swears she can hear Ronan grunt, even underwater. They nudge her forward, and Serena surfaces.

As each wave pushes against her, the transformation from Undine tail and fins to Ungainly legs takes place. The rest of the maidens participating in The Pairing stand in the water, while the guards are on the beach. They are inspecting the sand and the tree line—venturing into the forest as far as they dare. The Undine are taking their own precautions for safety. It is something the wolves should be doing, but recent fighting is still too fresh in everyone's memories.

As the guards continue to inspect, Serena glances down the line of maidens standing in the frothy water. Moonlight refracting off their colored scales shades the water around them, so they stand in a halo of their own making. Turquoise, yellow, and deep red—the colors of the painted maidens make their impression upon the ocean.

Serena notices each of the maidens in turn are looking at her—and not in a good way. Furrowed eyebrows and nervous twitches in their hands give away their agitation. It isn't until the maiden standing next to Serena begins to call forth more of her own scales that Serena realizes she is still fully scaled, and it is customary to mimic the dress of the superior present.

Sighing, Serena begins to retract her scales. Starting from the bottom, diamond-shaped plates sink into skin on her feet, ankles, and calves. The armor glows softly and Serena keeps it displayed above her knees, going to her upper thighs and above her hips.

Down the line of maidens, Simone leans forward. Her entire midsection is exposed.

Serena crosses her arms, clearly indicating she is not going that far with it.

But Simone has stuck out her bottom lip in a pout, gesturing to her mate who is on his hands and knees sifting through the sand looking for traps. She has come to impress and is determined to do so once the boys stop playing around on the beach.

Oh fine, Serena thinks. She looks down, watching as scales retract to reveal her abdomen. Aware she has put on extra weight from long hours in the throne with only the rare chance to romp around in the forest, Serena is pleasantly surprised to find a flat, toned midsection. The weight has settled in all the right places, her chest and her hips.

Maybe Nerin's constant harassment about posture has some merit.

Finally, Serena hides scales along her arms shoulders and her lower neckline, wiping away sliver-thin stripes of blood and seawater left behind. She looks at the maidens who are happily copying Serena's covering, if they weren't there already.

"You look like an angel," says Kai.

Serena turns, surprised to find him ankle-deep in the waves in front of her.

"An angel?" she asks. She looks at the other maidens standing in their circles of color. Serena is the only one without a halo.

"Your shades match the water almost perfectly tonight," says Kai. "Like an extension of the ocean herself."

He wades closer, and Serena fights to keep her breathing steady.

"The skin that shows…" Kai lays one hand on her bare shoulder while the other one wraps around her waist, "…glows. Like an angel." His fingertips run down the side of her face.

Serena can feel her cheeks heating at his touch. He moves beside her, wrapping his hand around hers. "Are you ready?" he asks.

Nodding, Serena walks forward, trusting her legs more than she does her voice. The rest of the couples follow suit until everyone stands on the beach.

"Where are the werewolves?" Serena asks. She doesn't need to look behind her to check if the moon is full and if they have the right night. Her blood tingles with the knowledge of the perfectly round orb that shines above them. It pulls at her life force as surely as it pulls at the tide.

"No sign of them yet," says Kai.

Raising her nose to the air, Serena inhales. "They are coming."

The Undine wait in nervous silence, their eyes glued to the dark forest. A breeze tousles Serena's hair and moves through the leaves before disappearing amongst thick shrubs. There is rustling in response, and Liam emerges from the shadows of the tree line, dressed in only a cape. He carries a basket of wolfsbane, the poisonous yellow flowers brimming over the top. Once he stands in front of them, he bows, flourishing one arm out to his side.

"Hello, Serena Moon-Shadow, Queen of the Undine Kingdom and Kai Forest, Second to the Head of the Guard," Liam says. "I will be your werewolf protector this night."

Both Kai's and Serena's mouths drop at the formality of Liam's words and actions.

He sets down the basket. The rest of the werewolves on the beach, one per Undine pair, finish their lines addressing each couple by their full name and title.

"Did you learn every Undine's name?" asks Serena.

Liam breaks his rigid stance to step toward Serena. "With help from Evandre," he whispers. "We weren't sure which of you would be here." He steps back, gesturing to the basket again and raises his voice. "I bring you this peace offerin' and swear by my own life that no harm will befall you tonight."

Serena eyes the wolfsbane. "How did you collect the flowers without poisoning yourself?"

"We have gloves. Now, would you please let me finish?" Liam says in a hushed hiss. "We're sort of the example, here."

Serena looks to her left and right. Each of the werewolves, and in turn the Undine couple in front of them, is glancing nervously toward Serena and Liam. "Continue," says Serena.

Liam takes a deep breath and then furrows his eyebrows as if trying to remember his lines. "I will give you complete privacy, but I will be nearby should either of you call for help. We've also made private dens by bendin' trees together and drapin' vines in the tree line, should you seek further privacy from your peers."

Serena and Kai glance into the forest, just now noticing darker inlets along the line of trees.

"Or, if you prefer, we've built a small but sturdy platform on the whale rock." Liam points just past the breaking waves, where a large boulder in the shape of the majestic sea giant sits. "And I have one more gift." Liam produces a small, square package from the inside of his cape and hands it to Kai.

Kai turns over the thin blue piece in his hand. Plastic crinkles between his fingers. "What is it?"

"It's somethin' we… and the humans use, in case you prefer not to be with calflin' right now." He raises his eyebrow at Serena. "You should know, it isn't always one hundred percent effective."

Kai and Serena look at each other. When Serena opens her mouth to speak, Liam cuts her off. "It is for you two to decide once I am gone. I ain't one for details." Liam breaks his formal decorum, turns with his hands on his hips, and takes a deep breath. "This is very, very awkward for me," he mumbles. He takes another deep breath and turns again. "I will leave you now and take to my wolf form. Please do not be alarmed—it is my strongest form and will give me the best chance of protectin' you should anything occur. Which it won't." Liam gives an extra nod as if he is trying to reassure himself. "Thank you for givin' me your trust, and may Poseidon grace your union." With that, Liam turns on his heel and walks toward the trees, untying his cape.

Pulling at the final string that holds the cape together, he catches it by both ends and holds it out wide. Liam bends until his entire body is shielded, and the cape shudders. When it drops to the ground, he is already in his wolf form.

"Liam!" Serena calls.

The wolf pauses and turns.

"We thank you for your protection this night." Serena isn't sure if the words are part of the formalities or not, she didn't get a chance to read the book, though it is obvious Liam did.

The wolf bows his muzzle to the sand, then vanishes among the shadows of the trees.

Chapter Eighteen

After Liam disappears, Serena and Kai glance at the other couples. Their wolves have already left them, and some are making their way into the dens in the tree line.

"A few will stay on the beach, but spread out. And some will go into the breaking waves, where they can be with the earth and the ocean," says Kai, glancing out over the water. Both their gazes fall on the whale rock. "No one has gone to the platform yet..." he glances at Serena.

"I'm not sure I can," says Serena, remembering the gruesome scene of the last battle.

She shivers and Kai wraps his arms around her. "Wherever you want," he says.

Serena glances out at the ocean again. "Come on." She takes his hand and pulls him into the breakers. He still holds the basket of wolfsbane flowers in his other hand.

"Here?" Kai asks, once Serena stops as the crest of a small wave tickles the backs of their knees.

"Remember when you let me glide on top of the water, wrapped in a breaking wave?" she asks.

Kai nods.

"Here, where the ocean meets the earth..." She pauses, bracing for a stronger swell that crashes against her body. Instead of knocking her over, it curls around her, embracing her in its hold. "This is where I feel strong," she finishes.

"Do you want to use this?" Kai holds up the blue package Liam gave them.

The moonlight hits it, emphasizing how small it is. Serena wonders how it can make such a huge difference in their lives. *To have a calfling or not?* "What do you think?" she asks.

"I think…" Kai lets his hand drop to his side. "We have all the time in the world, Serena, now that we've made a promise to be together. Can we enjoy each other now and look forward to a family later?"

Turning toward the full moon, Serena allows its silvery light to hit her face. She feels its pull, just as the waves do. The ebb and flow of Serena's internal tides are stimulated when the lunar orb shines at its brightest. It is why the maidens must be on shore to complete The Pairing.

Will I dishonor the ancients by using the gift from Liam? Serena asks herself. But Kai already put it perfectly – *let us enjoy each other now and look forward to a family later.*

Serena turns back to Kai and gives him a shy nod. Then she takes the basket of wolfsbane flowers and tips them into the water as another wave makes the trek to earth. Yellow petals curve up to a crest then dance, spinning in circles in the frothy turmoil after the wave breaks. They follow the tide toward the sandy beach.

Kai gathers Serena into his arms. She rises onto her tiptoes, and their lips meet. Hand splayed out on his chest in between them, Serena can feel his heart thundering inside. She responds by wrapping her other arm around his neck and pulling him close, anchoring him as he does for her. By the time the last of the flowers wash ashore, Serena and Kai are tangled together, sinking into the vibrant waves.

Chapter Nineteen

Serena is floating in a kelp forest. The long strands of seaweed sway in the current, the canopy above letting in snatches of soft sunlight. Velvety tendrils wrap around her waist, seeping warmth into her body.

"Serena." Her name floats to her through thick plants.

"Hmm?" she says.

"Serena!" It comes across more urgently.

Serena stirs, and the slow realization that she is not floating dawns on her as her shoulder rubs into hard rock. She opens bleary eyes. It is not kelp wrapped around her waist, but a single arm.

She blinks her eyes all the way open. Murphy stands at the entrance to the queen's quarters.

He clears his throat and bows. "Your majesty, Assembly awaits."

"So let them wait," Kai's says, his voice still heavy with sleep and muffled by Serena's hair. His breath tickles the back of her neck. "*Her majesty* hasn't even had breakfast yet." He unlatches Serena's waist and stretches. "And neither have I," he mumbles under his breath.

"Unfortunately, there is no time. The couples from last night are present to report The Pairing a success," says Murphy, shifting from one foot to another.

"I forgot about that part," says Serena. After she and Kai left the beach, they came straight to Serena's quarters. With the changes in ceremony to accommodate for a more all-around private affair, she'd just assumed there was no need to report details of each pairing.

"Council is delaying Assembly by giving reports on progress of preparations for The Migration," says Murphy. "You have a few minutes to make ready." Murphy turns on his heel and leaves, his footsteps fading into Evandre's voice in the background describing the ecosystem and geography of the new destination to the rest of Society.

Kai yawns as he rolls to his back. He puts his hands behind his head, then freezes as he stares up at Poseidon for the first time. "Well, this is awkward," he says.

"Tell me about it." Serena scoots closer to Kai.

"You sleep under Poseidon every night, while he stares at you with those twinkling eyes and that chiseled jaw?"

Serena smiles. "Not to mention that bare chest and... what really lies underneath his tunic anyway?" She sits up halfway, squinting as if to inspect.

"Oh no you don't," says Kai. He covers Serena's eyes with his hand, then pushes himself on top of her.

"Kai, stop." She giggles.

"Look away, Poseidon." Kai shields Serena's body with his. "She isn't decent!"

Serena's lungs open up in a full-bodied laugh that ends in a snort. She clamps her hand over her mouth, and they both go still, glancing at the hallway. Evandre's voice is droning on about polar bears and caribou in the arctic.

"I don't think they heard," whispers Kai.

"I don't really care if they did," she whispers back.

He knits his eyebrows together, feigning confusion. "Then why are you whispering?"

"Shut up and kiss me," Serena says.

Their lips meet, and Serena inhales the briny scent of Kai. Lips breaking apart in a smile, Kai helps her off the sleeping rock. "Ready to face them?" he asks.

"With you by my side—always."

They pause together in the hallway, calling forth scales until they are formally garbed for appearance in the Great Hall. As they walk forward, and the crowd comes into view, maidens shout out questions about human interference at Ivvavik National Park.

"What about Ungainlies?"

"Ivvavik is true wilderness," answers Evandre. "It is ice-covered and rarely visited in winter. There are no facilities, trails, services, or campgrounds for Ungainlies in the park. The most likely time for Ungainly presence is the four months during summer."

"And who will keep the Ungainlies away then?" another insists.

"The werewolves will," answers Serena, stepping into the light of the Great Hall.

Startled, the maidens closest to her turn and start bobbing their heads or bending in a full curtsey. The end result looks like an uncoordinated wave.

Serena decides to ignore it. "Thank you, Evandre." Serena nods to the Head Scientist as she makes her way up to the mid-platform. "We'll establish more question and answer sessions over the next few days," she addresses Society before ascending the stairs to her throne. Kai has already taken his position in the line of the Queen's Guard.

Several of the maidens from The Pairing stand on the mid-platform. Serena looks them over. "I trust everything went well last night?" She sits in the oversized chair.

All of them nod, refusing to announce any details. Serena is grateful for that. Her eyes come to rest on her former caste mate.

"Simone?"

The red-scaled maiden snaps her head up at the Queen's inquiry.

"The wound at your arm?" Serena asks.

Simone looks at it before glancing at her partner. Her cheeks flush to almost the color of her scales. "We... accidently tipped over our basket of wolfsbane flowers."

Serena arches one eyebrow.

"Then we accidentally rolled in them," says Simone in further explanation.

A quick glance at her partner reveals he has the same superficial burns along his arms and legs. There are a few snickers from the crowd.

"The pair of you, please see Hailey directly after this," says Serena. She turns toward the Head Doctor. "Hailey, I trust you managed to pass the event unscathed?"

"Yes, your majesty." She steps out from the line of council members. "But it will be my last stock of charcoal to treat them."

"That's fine," says Serena. "I don't think wolfsbane grows in the arctic."

Sarafina and Evandre both acknowledge the assumption, but Serena isn't watching them. Instead, she catches the unsure glance Hailey sends straight across the mid-platform to Murphy. Even standing at attention, he seems to stiffen at her look.

Serena sighs. "Murphy Air-Spirit and Hailey Sage-Brush..." Serena trails off, wondering if Hailey will take his last name now that they are paired. A sharp pang of realization runs through her – will Serena take Kai's name? *Serena Forest.* It doesn't have quite the same ring as Serena Moon-Shadow.

"Your majesty?" Murphy says.

Serena realizes with a start he is already standing in front of her. She takes a deep breath. "Do you have anything to report?" *Please don't report anything – I don't want any details.*

"As a matter of fact, your majesty," Hailey says. "We do."

Murphy stiffens even more.

Oh, Poseidon go easy on me. Closing her eyes, Serena grips the armrest of the throne, steeling herself. "Proceed." When she opens her eyes, the pair is holding hands.

Looking Serena straight in the eye, the Head of the Guard lifts his chin. "We have decided to stay, your majesty."

By the time his words register with Serena, her ears are already ringing. She shakes her head, as if to clear it of extraneous noise and focuses her increasingly blurry eyes on Murphy, trying to decide if he is joking. But he is not known for his jokes. She turns to Kai, the only guard member notorious for pranks, and it is his wide eyes and dropping jaw that convinces Serena this is real.

The Undine have just lost the Head of the Guard and their Healer as they are about to embark on a treacherous journey.

Stunned into speechlessness, Serena snaps her mouth shut at the movement out of the corner of her eye. Nerin is leaving her position at Serena's side to descend the stairs. She stops on the mid-platform, standing next to Murphy and Hailey.

"And I respectfully request to abstain from The Migration, your majesty," says Nerin. "I will stay by my son's side and, by Poseidon's grace, see my first grand-calfling."

Mariam, Rayne, Ronan, Hailey, Murphy, and now Nerin. Serena's closest friends, family, confidants, and advisors—all choosing to stay, leaving Serena to fend for herself.

Slowly, she rises from her throne. "Is there any other Undine that wish to announce their intent to stay?" Her eyes bore into the crowd, almost daring someone to speak. She bangs the stem of her trident against the ground. The boom echoes throughout the cavern. "Speak now! This will be your last chance," Serena shouts, taking one step down and pointing Dagon at the three before her. "I could not bear any more. I will not leave anyone else behind."

Nerin shrinks away from the tips of Serena's trident, and Hailey edges behind Murphy. Serena's arm shakes, and she knows she is about to break down. She turns and throws Dagon against the throne, chest heaving. "We leave at moonrise tomorrow," her broken voice croaks.

Keeping her eyes locked on the ground, Serena descends the steps toward her own chambers. "Inform the wolves," she hisses to Evandre as she passes the line of council members, every head turning to follow Serena as she leaves Assembly.

"No one is to disturb me until I emerge," she says to the guard standing at the entrance. "No one."

Serena disappears into the hallway, intending to have a long talk with Poseidon.

Chapter Twenty

Under the next moonrise, Serena stands on the beach alone facing the darkened forest looming before her. Her hands at her sides, she does not waver as she waits.

Eyes catching a shifting shadow, Serena turns her attention slightly to her right.

Liam steps out, taking deliberate strides toward Serena.

"Where are your maidens?" Liam asks.

Serena turns her head, glancing over her shoulder at the ocean. "They are here, awaiting your wolves."

Sniffing the air, Liam scans the breaking waves. His eyes settle back on Serena. "I wasn't sure which form we should come in. Werewolves might scare you back into the water..." Liam trails off as small beams of light begin to appear in the ocean.

One by one, the bioluminescent hair of each Undine flickers to life, illuminating their faces. Angled cheekbones underscore colorful skin while sharp chins lift in confidence. Dark clouds roll over the silvery moon, and more maidens appear bathed in their own light. Some are already on the beach, startling Liam back. Arista stands behind Serena, flanked by guards and wrists in chains—yet her thin lips are curved in a smile. More Undine stand where waves crash against their bodies, and there are several still waiting further back, both above and below the surface.

"My maidens can hold their own, Liam of Clan Werich," Serena says, stepping closer and lowering her voice. "Let your wolves come in animal form, brother. It will even the playing field."

Adam's apple bobbing once in his throat, Liam nods. "It shouldn't be a problem for us to transform, since we are still close to a full moon, and energy runs high tonight. Give us a minute to distribute capes, then we'll proceed to the docks as a group."

The entire fleet from Doug's Pier has already been prepped for the journey and stocked with supplies for both sides. Five boats in all, including a fifty-foot wooden trawler, a sailboat, an ocean tug, a center console fishing boat, and the smallest of them a twenty-eight-foot cabin cruiser. The rest of Doug's fleet was deemed unsuitable for the long journey and will be left with Danny to manage.

As Liam disappears back into the trees, Serena turns to the sounds of webbed feet in ankle-deep water. A small group of Undine walks onto the beach, led by Murphy and Nerin. There are fifteen in all—it is everyone that chose to stay.

Serena meets them at the high-tide line, where the ocean leaves its mark up and down the coast. Dotting the sand are scraps of kelp, broken shells, and other bits of debris from the home Serena will never see again.

She bends to pick up a whole shell that has washed ashore and runs the pad of her thumb over reddish-purple ridges. It is a thin specimen, showing small fissures along its length. Serena can't help but think of the same happening to the scales of the Undine she leaves behind. She closes her hand around the shell and looks at Murphy. "Rayne and Ronan, my adoptive mother and father, are staying. My best friend, Mariam, has elected to stay. Nerin, my most relied upon mentor, will also stay behind." Serena swallows hard as her eyes run over the group. "And so does my trusted Head of the Guard." Her voice cracks.

Murphy steps forward, hand going to his chest. He looks as though he himself is about to crack.

Serena puts up a hand, stopping him. "Murphy… I put them in your hands to protect. And I know you will do it."

He smiles, bowing deep. "As you say, your majesty."

"Murphy." Serena frowns.

"I know, I know." He straightens, then steps forward to scoop Serena in a tight hug. It stitches her back together. "I will take care of them, Serena."

When Murphy sets her back down, Serena still rolls the shell in her hand and turns to Nerin. "I am confident that separation will not hurt anyone this time. There is a theory that the Undine may break apart from one another without pain if there are two alphas. One to lead each group. Nerin—you have advised my father and me through many trying obstacles. It is time to take the reins yourself."

In an unprecedented break in decorum, Nerin's eyes go wide. "That is a very great honor, your majesty."

Serena raises an eyebrow.

Nerin clears her throat and curtsies. "One I shall carry out with respect, duty, and morality. Thank you, your majesty."

"I bestow the title of Queen and leader of the Undine… Vancouver Chapter" —Serena smiles— "to Nerin. All hail the Queen."

"All hail the Queen," echoes the group behind Nerin. But there are so few, their voices are lost in the next wave.

"Make the ancients proud," says Serena.

"Thank you, your majesty," Nerin answers. "I'd tell you to do the same, but you already have."

Serena glances out at the whale rock. "Is this how my father would do it?" she asks Nerin, voice almost at a whisper.

Nerin doesn't hesitate to answer. "I don't think it matters. I never liked the way your father did it, either." Nerin curtsies to Serena for the first and the last time, then steps back.

Hailey comes forward, her hands filled with vials. "The last remnants of the transformation potion, should you need it," she says.

Serena places them gently in the dry bag latched around her waist.

"I've trained my three apprentices well. They will be able to address any medical needs as I would myself. They have already packed the bulk of my herbs and medicines. And I've given Darcy my notes on the biology of Undine. She is a good nurse and can help with emergencies. But don't—"

"Hailey," Serena interrupts. "You are babbling."

Hailey's lips press together, then burst out as she sobs. "I'm stalling." She hugs Serena almost as tightly as Murphy did. "Just… be careful. And stay away from the wolfsbane."

"I will," Serena promises. "We'll be fine. You be careful, too."

Serena turns to Mariam, who has inched her way to the front along the outskirts of the group. "I have a gift for you, too," Mariam says before Serena can speak. She holds out a package. "The Ancestral Book. It should go with the youth of our Society, so they don't forget. Besides, I don't think you've ever had a chance to read it."

"Thank you, Mariam," says Serena.

"I've wrapped it carefully. It should be protected even if your dry bag leaks."

This time, Serena doesn't wait for the hug. She steps in and takes one herself. Mariam smells like the archives—solid, strong earth and musty books. "I will never forget you," Serena whispers into the woman's shoulders.

"Nor I you," says Mariam. "Be good to yourself."

"Be good to those books." Serena sniffs as she detaches herself from Mariam.

Mariam smiles. "Always am."

As Mariam retreats to the back of the small group, more maidens with glowing hair come ashore, preparing for The Migration. Serena does a quick count in her head. They are all almost here.

Next, Serena turns to Ronan and Rayne. Serena's adoptive mother is smiling so big little wrinkles appear around her eyes. But the corners of her mouth quiver. "Here," she says, thrusting a jar in Serena's arms. "Hijki—your favorite."

"Thank you." Serena puts the jar in her dry bag, along with the shell she keeps turning over in her hand. Not even that can distract her anymore—she is about to say goodbye to the Undine that raised her. No words come to Serena, and her arms feel as heavy as the whale rock watching quietly from a distance.

Serena glances at the monument standing alone in the sea, where her father once ruled… and died. She thinks of all the decisions that led to her standing here in a defining moment as she is about to split Society, most of them never to return to their ancient lands. She looks at Ronan and Rayne. "I'm so… sorry," she croaks out.

Rayne's eyes snap up to Serena, the lines disappearing from her face. "Don't be, Serena. Do you hear me? We are so very proud of you." She continues to pin Serena with an unwavering gaze.

"I hear you, Mother Rayne," Serena says, the lump in her throat disintegrating. It is replaced with a bit of confidence.

Serena steps in and two pairs of loving arms wrap her in an embrace. The moon comes out from behind the clouds, warming the trio. When they finally release each other, Serena's eyes fall to Ronan. He cups her chin in his rough, leathery hand. "You'll be just fine, Painted Maiden—just fine." It is the first time Ronan hasn't used the term 'little calfling' with that phrase.

Ronan stares directly over Serena's shoulder. "Take care of our daughter."

Serena turns to find Kai, fully scaled and gripping his trident.

"I will her protect her with my own life," Kai says.

Ronan grunts in return.

Serena finally releases her mother's hand and watches in silence as the group bids their farewells to others, then retreat into the water. As the last of the group, Mariam pauses when her shoulders are just above the surface. She turns to give Serena one final wave. And when her chocolate scales disappear into the water, Serena exhales, her body shuddering as it releases the stress hovering over her the last few weeks. She takes in a new breath. Wind blows in from the northwest, fresh and crispy cold. A hint of what is to come.

"All is well?" Kai asks.

"Yes," says Serena. She scans the water, waiting for signs of anyone changing their mind in the last minute and reappearing. No one comes. Serena latches her dry bag closed and folds extra flaps over the opening.

"You almost forgot this." Kai hands Dagon to Serena.

She takes it, turning the stem so the three prongs on top gleam in the moonlight. "I was considering leaving it behind." Serena shudders as she remembers throwing it against the throne in a fit of rage right in front of all of Society. "Apologies for my actions."

"Forgiven before they even occurred." Kai winks at her. He looks out at the maidens on the beach. "And what of your father's old trident?"

"Resting," says Serena, her voice soft. "In his chamber beneath the gaze of Poseidon. Along with mother's jewel from my breastplate." She smiles back. "They can all keep each other company."

"You aren't bringing your armor?"

She lifts her chin, soaking in confidence from the moon. "We aren't traveling to fight. We are traveling to live."

He narrows his eyes. "What did you do last night?"

Running her webbed toes in the sand at their feet, Serena traces the shape of a crescent moon. "I had a long talk with Poseidon."

Kai grunts, reminding Serena of Ronan. "What did he say?"

She brushes the pad of her foot across the sand, smearing the moon away. "He said to let go of the past." She pauses, taking Kai's hand. "To look to the future and believe in myself."

The pair turns toward the moon, high and bright in the sky—ready to lead the way. It is full besides a sliver, waning into the new moon.

Kai squeezes Serena's hand. "I could've told you that."

"I know." She squeezes back, and her smile grows wider.

The wind dies down, and with it the soft noise of webbed feet shuffling ashore goes silent. Serena turns to find all of the maidens in line down the beach. She starts to count but stops when she realizes Kai's lips are already murmuring numbers.

"They are all here," he says a moment later.

The last of the saltwater slides down scales in a shimmery cascade, then sinks into the sand below them. Serena steps forward and turns so all of the Undine can see her. "Calm yourselves, maidens," she says, trusting the still of the night to carry her voice. The rest of the maidens need to get their glow under control.

Council members, spread throughout the line of Society, take the hint first. The bioluminescence of Evandre and Sarafina flickers away and the maidens surrounding them follow suit. When the last of them go dark, Serena turns back to the forest, watching the shadows.

It isn't long before Liam reemerges, this time as his wolf. Yellowed talons sink into the sand underneath matted fur...and Serena can't be sure, but he looks much larger than she remembers. The rest of his clan isn't far behind. Dark shapes slink out from in between trees, and when the shadows release their hold, the hulking forms of more wolves take shape. Up and down the tree line, the wolves stand across from the Painted Maidens, their numbers almost equivalent, one clawed set of feet for every pair of webbed feet.

When all the wolves are present, there is nothing left to do but to stare at each other. Liam and Serena exchange nervous glances. The last time all of the species were present, they were killing each other. Bonds of trust have been reestablished at the upper levels, but not down in the ranks.

Adrenaline, almost as thick as the smell of salt itself, spikes down the line. Serena can see hairs bristle on the back of wolves' necks, and in response her own maidens call forth more scales.

Liam turns his head, growling. The warning is directed at his own. The energy of the area is escalating, and one wrong move could set the The Migration off in disaster.

Quick feet bouncing across the sand draw all eyes to one end of the line. Darcy is marching straight through the beach in the middle of werewolves and Undine, her kids in tow and Cordelia's infant son in her arms. The only human among a sea of creatures almost ready to square off against each other has shocked the atmosphere into submission. The tension decreases as Undine stare at the tiny, mewling baby in Darcy's arms who has recently undergone the transformation potion out of pure necessity for survival. It is a good reminder why The Migration is so important and why the wolves and the Undine must work together.

Darcy's two youngest boys skip behind her, delighting in the unabashed attention and mesmerized by the Undine. When they bound too close to the line of werewolves, they get a playful nudge back toward their mother. Their mere presence calms the wolves.

But it isn't the youngest boys or Darcy or even Cordelia's baby that stills Serena's heart. It is the oldest boy, Aiden. Coming out from behind his younger siblings, Aiden is in werewolf form. He lengthens his stride and puffs out his chest. Embracing the beast that is a part of him, Aiden is not fearful or ashamed of his transformation.

Serena turns as she watches Aiden lope by. The werewolf bows his head slightly to Serena as he passes, then to Liam across from her—and they each return the favor.

Once Darcy and the kids have crossed the beach, Serena, Kai, and Liam turn to face north, and everyone else follows suit.

"Ready to go?" Serena asks Kai.

"With you by my side," he says. "Always."

The werewolves and Undine take the first steps of their journey.

Chapter Twenty-One

One long column of Undine and one long column of werewolves, side by side, take little more than an hour to hike to Doug's Pier. Beforehand, strict instructions were given to Undine that they must stay out of the water. The entire journey is to be taken alongside the wolves, and Serena and Liam agreed the first few steps would be important in setting the tone.

Nonetheless, Serena keeps catching her Undine glancing out at the ocean, especially when the wind catches the top crest of a wave, spritzing the maidens with crisp saltwater. Needing a distraction from her maidens and the teasing ocean herself, Serena concentrates on the werewolves. They are an impressive sight with stalking strides, shifting the weight of their muscle-wrapped frames from shoulder to shoulder. Trying to look past their yellowed talons slicing into soft sand and red eyes that constantly scan their surroundings, Serena focuses in on the slight twitches of their ears and tails. Every time they glance at Undine, ears perk forward and hackles stand tall. But when laughter from one of Darcy's boys floats down the pack, their tails give a friendly swish. Occasionally, with barely perceptible whimpers, the wolves look into the tree line, pining to enter their protected domain of the forest.

The rolling columns enter hills and traverse one tall cliff at the edge of the sea. Finally, Doug's Pier comes into view. Their transports, a fleet of five boats and ships of varying sizes stand ready at the docks. Serena, Liam, and Kai pick up their pace so they move to the front of the lines. Standing with Doug, all in Ungainly form, are the pack members who have chosen to stay. And like the Undine who will remain behind, they are all older members of the clan. They busy themselves passing out clothes and collecting capes from those who transform back into their Ungainly forms.

Liam briefly disappears to change. Once he returns, he directs the incoming columns onto boats. Every vessel will hold equal amounts of each species. Continuing to force them to mix until they are comfortable with each other is the only option.

"You are all set up in Cecil's cabin?" Liam asks Danny.

"Me and five others," says Danny. "It'll feel cramped for a few days until we can have some trailers pulled over to the property. But we've got new scenery—so it sort of feels like Christmas. Oh," Danny looks at Serena. "Speakin' of Christmas, I have some presents for you."

She can't help but put a hand to her already bulging dry bag. But the device he hands her is small.

"I've seen these before," Serena says, turning it over and pushing at the buttons on the front.

"It's a phone—a satellite phone," explains Danny. "I'll keep one with me in Cecil's cabin, and I'll let them mermaids that are stayin' come to use it anytime they want."

She turns it over in her hand, then lifts a questioning eyebrow at him.

"You can talk through it," Liam explains. "You won't see them, but you can hear them."

Danny nods. "This ain't the dark ages. We can and will stay connected."

Serena's eyes light up. "I may confer with the remaining Undine?"

"Sure. Just don't get it wet," says Danny. "And try not to crush it."

"Thank you," says Serena, trying to keep tears from her eyes. "Truly the best gift you could have given me.

"I've got somethin' else," Danny mumbles.

Serena places the phone in her dry bag at her hip. When Danny extends his hand and opens his palm, a silver-chained necklace with a small charm rests on it. Leaning in for a closer look, Serena and Liam both emit an awed sigh. The charm is a tiny mermaid, her tail curved up so the entire shape makes a small 'U'. Her upper body is bare but only her back shows. Serena runs the pad of her thumb down the long locks of hair cascading down the mermaid's shoulders almost to her scales at her waistline.

"You made this?" whispers Serena.

"Out of them poles you let me have." Danny nods. "Except the hair. That comes from a special stone."

"What is special about it?" asks Liam.

"It has luminescence."

"Like our hair?" asks Serena.

"Of sorts," says Danny. "But this one lights up only when another type of stone is close. The energy of the both of them together creates the light. Look…" Danny motions down the dock and another man with two large boxes comes forward. As he walks closer, the hair of the mermaid in Serena's hand begins to glow. At first, only subtle glimmers are perceptible, but by the time the man with the boxes is next to them the charm is at full radiance.

Danny reaches into one of the boxes pulling out several more mermaid charms. "These are for your maidens. They won't glow—that quality is unique to yours, meant to help you find a maiden if she gets lost along the way."

"Danny," says Serena. "Thank you. I don't... I mean..."

"The least I could do," says Danny. "You are the best thing that has ever happened to the clan, well, since Liam here anyway."

"Hey!" Liam protests.

"I've got somethin' for Mr. Second Best too," Danny reaches into the next box.

Liam crosses his arms. "I ain't wearin' no necklaces."

"What about a bracelet?" Danny smiles. He pulls out several silver bracelets. The twisted band ends with a wolf head on either side. "Don't worry, yours is just as special." Danny pulls out an envelope, emptying the contents—one of the wolf bracelets— into Liam's palm. "In yours, the eyes light up when one of your wolves is close."

Turning his arm, moonlight flashes along the ridges of the bracelet until Liam's wrist is pointed toward the heavens, and the eyes of each wolf glow red.

"Brilliant," Serena says the same time as Liam says, "awesome."

"I've got three smaller ones for them wolf cubs, and they're all flexible so they won't just break off during transformation."

"Thank you, Danny." Liam looks at the older werewolf with a steady gaze. Eyes flitting past Danny's shoulder, Liam motions to the rest of the pack members who have chosen to stay. They line up behind Danny. "You got this?" asks Liam.

"I do," says Danny.

Serena realizes that short exchange is their way of designating the alpha of Clan Werich.

With Poseidon's luck, the magic that binds us together will realize that, too.

"Liam." Danny motions to the side.

The two men bow their heads together deliberating, but Serena can hear their words anyway.

"Just so you know, those phones won't turn on until you put the batteries in." Danny slips Liam a separate package. "I don't recommend you do it until you are plenty past the breakin' point, if you get my drift."

Serena looks toward her kingdom, understanding that Danny doesn't want to give the migrating group any reason to come back. If those left behind feel the pain of separation for some reason, Liam and Serena aren't to know about it.

She tries telling herself she wouldn't have known anyway but now the temptation will be there, within reach.

"Serena?" Liam asks. "Ready to board?"

"Yes," Serena says. "After one last thing." She walks to the end of the pier where a thin but long trunk sits, its lid pushed open. It is the perfect size for tridents. She stops, staring into the dark shadows of the box, refusing to look at Dagon.

I am hiding away my status symbol; the one thing that sets me apart from the rest of the maidens, besides my blood.

Serena almost reels at her own admission. *There is more that sets me apart from them than my trident.*

Maybe I've relied on it too much. She runs her palm up and down the two interlacing poles that create its stem.

But the trident is more than a status symbol. Murphy, Kai, and Serena's deceased friend, Ervin, had all sacrificed their own beloved tridents in order to make hers. Dagon has gotten Serena through some sticky situations, in the forests and in her own Assembly hall.

I think it's time to walk on my own now. Sorry, Dagon. We will meet again at Ivvavik.

She lay the trident down in the chest and turns away quickly. All of the Undine guards have come up behind her with their own tridents. She nods once, then pushes her way through them, unable to look back at the chest. Behind her she can hear the soft clink, clink as each of the guards submit their own tridents to the box.

The box will be sealed under lock and key for the duration of The Migration. If the Undine are spotted by Ungainlies, the least they look like mermaids, the better.

Serena looks to the fleet. Almost everyone is already seated. Rather, the Undine are seated with stiff backs, knees together, and hands in their lap. On each craft, they line one side of the boat. Across from them, the werewolf groups are chaotic, at best. They jostle for seats, settling differences with wrestling matches that tilt even the largest of the ships as if it were in the midst of a storm.

When one wolf gets launched into the knees of Sophia Sunbeam, she draws them up into her chest. Serena shoots an accusatory glance at Liam.

"They're nervous." He shrugs.

The rest of the maidens surrounding Sophia stand, fully scaling themselves. Serena and Liam rush forward together, boarding the fifty-foot wooden trawler. Putting two fingers to his mouth, Liam whistles loud and shrill. The wolves stop wrestling and turn toward Liam, ears perked. He stares them down until the ship's rocking settles. Slowly, those in human form ease back on the benches and those in wolf form stretch out on the floor.

Serena walks to Sophia, placing a hand on her shoulder. "Take ease, maiden. It was not done on purpose."

Slowly reestablishing a poised position on the bench, Sophia gives Serena a tight smile. "I apologize, your majesty. It's just—"

Sophia cuts off as one of the beasts rolls over on his side, letting out a loud yawn. Serena shoots him a hard glare then squeezes Sophia's shoulder in reassurance.

"I've never been this close to them before," Sophia finishes.

"You sure about that, sunshine?" The gruff voice blares out from across Sophia. A pack member leans forward, elbows on his knees, looking at the maidens. Serena remembers Zeke from the truck ride to the motel. On all accounts, he was friendly enough toward Serena.

"What do you mean?" asks Sophia, drawing courage from her own kind surrounding her. Her own mother sits next to her, leaning close.

"You must be... what? Twenty-three?" Zeke asks.

"Twenty-four next full moon." She narrows her eyes. "How do you know that?"

"I was there patrollin' the moon of your birth. I will never forget them orange scales."

Serena takes a small intake of breath that results in a squeak. That would have been before the Maiden's Massacre, when the wolves served as protectors.

Exchanging a nervous glance at her mother, Sophia presses her lips together before turning back to Zeke. "And my little sister, Sasha?" she asks. "Did you witness her birth? Her scales were orange like mine, though some say they were even brighter."

"I did," he says quietly. "And they were." Zeke stares at the floor in front of him—he knows what is coming next.

Sophia squeezes her mother's hand. "Did you witness her death?"

All Undine heads turn toward Zeke, who by now looks like he wishes he had never said anything. He looks up, glancing over his shoulder at the dock. One man is untying a rope that moors the sailboat to the pier, looping the line in a coil around his arm.

Sophia follows his gaze, watching as the man throws the rope into the ship and jumps in, giving one of the maidens an unnecessary nudge with his shoulder. Serena remembers watching the wolf tear into Sasha's soft middle—there is no way the maidens could distinguish who that was… but the wolves can.

"His name is Xavier," says Zeke.

Giving the slightest nod, Sophia acknowledges the exchange of information.

"Liam…" Serena mumbles in warning.

"I know," he says. "We should've just let them keep wrestlin'."

Jittering with nervous energy, one of the pack members paces the length of the boat then stops to peer into the lifejacket bin. He pulls out canned soup—one in each hand. "Where are all the lifejackets?" he asks.

Liam smiles and crosses his arms. "They are sittin' across from you."

The pack member looks at Sophia and her mother, sitting side by side on the bench with rigid spines. "Well ain't that some karma," he mumbles. He tosses the cans of soup back in the bin and slumps down onto the deck, swallowing hard as the boat's engine rumbles to life.

Chapter Twenty-Two

Liam, Serena, and Kai decide to part ways, each choosing a boat. They can only cover three of the five, but hopefully at least those three will be peaceful. Leaving Kai with Sophia and her mother on the trawler, Serena crosses the pier to board the sailboat with Xavier. Liam gives her a grateful nod. An attack against a wolf—retribution style—would be an unfortunate start to their journey.

"All ahead full!" A wolf calls beside Serena, making her jump. Sails unfurl, and Serena presses herself against the ship's railing to keep clear of the bustle. A crew of at least five scurries around the deck until the sailboat pulls away from the pier.

The same call echoes out from each of the other ships as they are forced away from their moorings. Colin, Darcy, and their boys are on the sturdy tugboat which takes the lead. The other four ships pair side by side in an inverted 'V' formation, like migrating geese. The boats that hold Liam and Serena end up together, in the middle of the fleet. As the ships pick up speed, Serena glances at her twin. Liam stands near the bow of the smaller fishing boat, the longer strands of his hair wave in a wild whirlwind around his face. Smoothing back her own, tame braid, Serena can't help but feel a bit of pride in her unruly brother. Liam scratches at his face before his hand falls to the small, cylindrical lumps in his pocket—the satellite phone's batteries.

Those batteries are the key to making the phone work—the only lifeline Serena now has to her orphan parents, Mariam, and the rest—she turns to look in the direction of Society. Dark grey clouds behind Serena part, allowing a swath of moonlight through. A pale band of silver marks a clear path over choppy waves into calmer waters. It is the way back home.

"You are facing the wrong direction, your majesty."

The clear voice turns Serena's palms cold. She presses them to her outer thighs as she turns toward Arista. The maiden sits cross-legged on the wooden-planked floor, her hands chained to the side railing of the boat.

"There, that is much better," says Arista.

The moon illuminates a path in this direction, too. But the waves are so high the light only touches the frothy white crests. Every trough in between falls into exaggerated darkness.

"It means you have a tumultuous journey ahead of you," says Arista, following Serena's gaze over the agitated waters. "I've foreseen as much, anyway."

"Foreseen?" asks Serena. She doesn't want to get dragged into a conversation with Arista, especially now that those around them turn their heads in interest. But Serena needs something to distract her from her jittery nerves. "What do you mean?"

"Apologies, your majesty. I forget you may be too young to recall."

Serena grits her teeth. Every time someone mentions her age, she detects doubt of her leadership capabilities. "Recall what?"

"Before I was tried and sentenced, I served as assistant to the Undine Psychic." Arista moves her cuffed wrists to face Serena, the chains rattling as she readjusts.

"You...?" Serena trails off. "No, I don't recall. I didn't have much occasion to visit Isadora."

Arista throws her head back and laughs. The high pitch cackle causes several wolves on the boat to shudder. "You think it might have been helpful, given all that has happened?" Arista says in between more giggling.

"Perhaps," Serena says, pressing her palms even harder into her sides just to keep them from going for Arista's throat. "And yourself? Did you foresee prison and chains in your future?"

Laughter dying on her lips, Arista looks at the ground, sullen. Clouds slowly move to cover the moon once again, and the lighted path over the ocean disappears.

"The first thing Isadora..." Arista's voice cracks as she mentions her former mentor. She swallows and tries again. "The first thing Isadora taught me was never to look too closely at my own future." Raising her chin, Arista looks at Serena with a hardened stare. "Sometimes it is better not to know when death is coming."

Serena's body goes rigid. She can't decide if Arista is threatening her, or just speaking the truth. Choosing to let it pass, for now, Serena nods. "As you say."

Arista blinks once, then leans back. "If you ever want a reading, your majesty, just let me know." She holds up her chains. "I'll be here."

"Noted," mumbles Serena. She scans the line of maidens and wolves, this time for a distraction from conversation with Arista. Entrenched in the middle of the ship is the cockpit. One pack member has his hands on the oversized wheel, shouting out orders to the crew. Doug sits beside him, a map sprawled open on his lap. He wears his work shirt with 'Doug's Rentals' scrawled across the back and a red handkerchief hanging out of his front pocket.

Leaving Arista to toy with her chains, Serena descends two steps into the small cockpit area.

"Doug." She bobs her head at the navigator.

"Hey, there's my favorite singer." Doug smiles at Serena before shouldering the man with his hands on the wheel. "This one can belt a tune.".

The man only grunts in response, not bothering to glance at Serena.

"Seth ain't so appreciative of music," says Doug turning away from his map. "Maybe because he hasn't heard you. Go on and let him hear it, Serena."

"Apologies," says Serena. "But I don't wish to cause a disaster on the first day of our travels."

Seth bursts into laughter, finally looking at Serena with an appreciative twinkle in his eye.

Trying not to take the outburst as a slight, Serena glances at the map. "Planning our route?"

"The route is planned," says Doug. "I'm just checkin' and double checkin'. Wanna look?"

"Please." Serena bends over slightly to see.

"We travel through the night," says Doug, "then stop for a short break."

"What then?"

"Then…" Doug sits up straight in his small, swiveling chair as if ready to make a big announcement. "We join up with a race."

"A race?" asks Serena, her eyes snapping to both of the men with renewed interest.

"A race," both Doug and Seth confirm with wide smiles on their faces.

"Well, more like a derby," says Seth. "It is the Capital to Capital Yacht Derby. Goes from Olympia, Washington to Juneau, Alaska."

"It will be one week of navigatin' a labyrinth of channels, sounds, whirlpools, bays, fjords, rivers, and the open Pacific Ocean through one of the vilest stretches of water in the world." Doug leans forward, almost standing.

"And this is a good thing?" asks Serena, her stomach doing flip-flops.

"It's perfect!" says Doug. "We enter the race and join the other boaters. Any other time our fleet would have to face customs at some point. Besides, during the race fuel and supply stations are set up along the way just for the boaters."

"What about the sheer number of bodies we have on these boats?" asks Serena. "Won't it look odd for a race? Won't the other racers surely notice?"

"Yeah, well..." Doug runs the back of his hand across his nose. "We'll have to stash all the wolves and as many mermaids as we can below deck in the tug boat and the trawler."

Serena looks across the water at Liam, still standing at the bow of the fishing boat. They lock eyes for a brief moment, then he looks down, busying himself with unraveling then coiling a length of rope. He knows what information is being relayed to her.

Serena narrows her eyes at her brother, then turns her attention back to Doug. "And what about the rest of the Undine? What about those we cannot *stash* below deck?"

Swinging around in his chair to look at the row of Undine sitting on benches, Doug rubs his chin.

Finally, he looks up at Serena. "They can swim, can't they?"

"Doug!" Serena looks down her nose at him. "Not *that* far—why do you think we are all on the boats now?"

"Honestly, I thought it was because this would be a fun experience for them. Sort of like a carnival ride. I mean—how often do they get to ride on boats?"

Serena buries her forehead in the palm of her hand.

"Tumultuous journey…" taunts Arista from just outside the cockpit.

"Doug?" Serena asks, staring at the rough waves ahead. "May I borrow that handkerchief?"

He glances down at the red plaid material sticking out of his shirt pocket. "Sure—why?"

"I am going to gag the psychic."

Chapter Twenty-Three

The remainder of the night is uneventful. The ocean calms as day begins to dawn. Most of the passengers of the fleet doze off just as the stars in the sky fade under the brightening sun. Serena herself has found a cozy spot next to the ship's railing. Lulled to sleep by gentle rocking, Serena's eyes flutter closed. It feels like no more than five minutes when the ship stops suddenly and she is forced awake with a rude jolt.

"Land ho!" Doug laughs, jumping out of the cockpit and nudging wolves aside as he and the crew pick up coils of rope to tie off to the dock.

Reluctantly, Serena forces life back in each of her limbs, stretching and yawning. The land beyond the pier is more of the same thin strip of beach followed by looming forest. "Where are we?" asks Scrcna.

"Hope Island." Doug begins nudging some of the slower-to-rouse wolves. "Wake up! Gonna camp on land today."

Serena frowns. "Hope Island? That is no more than a stone's throw from Vancouver Island." Twisting to stare past the stern, Serena squints. "In fact… isn't that our island right there?"

"Quite the navigator—want the job?" Doug tosses his rolled map to Serena, leaving both hands free to wrangle the rope.

"Hardly," mumbles Serena. But she unfurls the map anyway as maidens edge around her to disembark the boat.

"See here." Doug points to the map – it has been enlarged and shows their path. "We wait until late afternoon when the racers will be sailing right past this point. We'll trickle in between them; it is toward the end of the day, so they should be spread pretty far apart. With luck, no one will even notice."

"So this is the race route?" Serena traces a purple line up the northern coast of Canada.

"Yep," says Doug.

She follows the line from Olympia harbor through Puget Sound and into the Strait of Georgia. The Undine left behind could even witness the racers passage, if they poked their heads above water at just the right time. It will be as the racers enter Queen Charlotte Sound that The Migration will sneak around from the back of Hope Island, where they are now, to merge with the race. The rest of the way is wrought with twists and turns through tight passages, straights and sometimes even rivers. It reminds Serena of the narrow tunnel leading to the archives, and she feels a pain of loss for her home, and for Mariam.

Blinking back tears before they can take hold, Serena focuses back on the purple line outlining her fate. "The race stops here" Serena holds out the map for Doug, pointing at the final leg through Clarence Strait near the finishing point at Juneau. "Yet we still have to skirt the entirety of Alaska before we get to the northern coasts and Ivvavik. Five thousand miles, at least."

"Seven thousand, give or take," says Doug.

Serena looks at him with wide eyes. "The race is just the beginning."

He nods. "We'll have to make a choice in Juneau. Easy way or hard way."

"What do you mean?"

"To go over land" —he traces a potential path with his finger— "would be under three thousand miles. Cut the trip by more than half."

"Yes, but my maidens may not be able to be away from the water that long. Besides, Darcy said Ivvavik isn't accessible by roads. How would we get there if not from around the coast?"

"We are just figurin' out as we go along, sweetheart."

Serena gives Doug a hard look. She isn't sure if it is for the nickname or the unacceptable lack of planning, on both their parts. She blinks, then turns her attention back to the map, folding it in frustration.

"Gentle, gentle!" says Doug. "I take it back, you'd make a terrible navigator. You've got to *roll* the maps."

As Serena relinquishes the map to Doug, she spots a small commotion just off the pier on the sandy dunes of the small island. One of the pack members is bent over, heaving. Several friends come to his aid, but there is nothing they can do to help. Serena leaves the boat, walks down the aging pier, and crosses the sandy beach.

"Sea sickness." Liam stops her. "Best just to let him ride it out."

"As you say," says Serena. She turns away, trying to block out the gagging noises. "So glad we don't have to worry about that with the Undine—"

Serena is nudged out of the way by a maiden running for the water. An incoming wave reaches the maiden's feet just as she expels the contents of her stomach.

Liam bites on the back of a knuckle to keep from laughing.

"Not funny, Liam!" Serena elbows him in the side before she follows the maiden into the ocean.

"Kiera," Serena says, recognizing the Undine gardener. "Just try to breath."

Kiera looks at Serena. Recognition dawns on her face and she straightens. "Your majesty!" Attempting to curtsey, Kiera pauses just as she bends, grasping her stomach again. "Oh, no." She looks up at Serena, mortified.

They both know what is going to happen next.

"I'll just go get a healer," says Serena, backing away.

Kiera nods, looking a little green in the face, though her natural color is a light pinkish-purple. Her cheeks puff out, and Serena turns away from the maiden at the sound of thick chunks hitting the water.

"We have a long way to go," Liam tells Serena once she is back on the beach. "This could turn serious if they keep it up."

"I know." Serena turns around to look for Hailey's medical assistants. "We can't have them wasting all our food." Spotting Simone's bright red scales, Serena waves her down.

Simone makes her way over to Serena, taking longer than necessary.

"Your majesty?"

"I'm hoping you have something for seasickness." Serena gestures to Kiera, still bent over in the waves. Serena's eyes widen slightly when she peers closer at Simone. "Are you okay, Simone? You look a little pale."

"Fine, fine," says Simone. But her nod is sluggish and her hands uncoordinated as she fumbles with the knotted dry bag at her waist. "Hailey insisted I take the rest of her ginger stock..." Simone mumbles to herself as she stumbles toward the sick maiden. The first wave nearly knocks her over.

"Your healer doesn't look so good herself," Liam tells Serena.

By now, Simone is rubbing Kiera's back and giving her instructions.

"I don't know," says Serena. "Hailey has taught her well. She at least knows what to do."

As if on cue, Simone herself turns away from her patient to vomit in the waves.

Serena sighs, shoulders sagging. "I'd better go find the other healers."

In her search for the other two healers—who, by the grace of Poseidon, are in good health—Serena finds five more maidens with seasickness. She herds the entire group, plus Kiera and Simone, to a discreet spot shielded by thick trees and shrubbery, lest the smell and noise inspire more sickness.

"There are a few members of the wolf clan who have seasickness, too," Serena tells one of the healers.

The maiden goes still, glancing at her dwindling supply of ginger. The vials have been collected and stacked in neat rows on a fold-out table. They sit beside a mortar and pestle for grinding.

Serena frowns at the hesitating maiden.

When the healer notices, she looks down at her feet. "I apologize, your majesty. But as you know, Undine are extremely sensitive to herbs grown in The Dry. And we aren't aware if there are any other remedies for upset stomachs that we can take. Surely the wolves have their own remedies – or at least are better suited to trying others."

"Perhaps," says Serena, tapping her fingers against her hip, glancing from the maiden to the ginger and back again. "Okay," she says. "We will leave the ginger to the maidens for now. But if the ailment gets any worse, we will have to share. And remember – you are healer to Undine and werewolf alike now. Understood?"

"Of course, your majesty," the maiden mumbles, avoiding Serena's eyes altogether.

Sighing, Serena leaves the healer to her patients, vowing to send any wolves should they look even worse for the wear. Returning to the main group, Serena finds Liam has organized the camp. There are cooking fires and a few tents set up to rest while shaded from the searing sun. The seasick wolves have been relegated to their own tent.

"You did well," Serena remarks to Liam's back. He squats over a fire, roasting a skewered salmon.

"Your maidens are good fisherman." He glances out to the waves where two pack members in Ungainly form stand. Past the breakers, there is a flicker of a scaled tail breaking the surface of the water, then a fish goes sailing through the air. One of the pack members reaches up to catch it. He can't get a grasp on the slippery, flopping fish, and after juggling it from hand to hand, the creature splashes back into the ocean and swims away. Liam smiles. "The fish are more easily caught when they are in wolf form, but no one likes teeth marks in their food. Besides, it was freakin' out some of your maidens."

Serena smiles back. "We will have to work on that."

"Fish?" Liam holds the charred salmon in front of Serena's nose. Its eyes are wide with shock, the makeshift skewer protruding out from its open mouth.

"Ew, no." Serena grimaces, stepping back.

Liam shrugs, blows on the dead creature then tears a chunk out of the soft middle. With a full mouth, Liam gestures further up the beach. "Well if you ain't goin' to eat, you might as well get some rest. I set up a tent for you."

"I couldn't sleep now. We should keep an eye on everything. Besides." Serena glances at those spreading blankets in the open air or retreating under the shade of trees. "It seems unfair I should get a tent when there aren't enough to go around."

Liam puts an arm around Serena and walks, steering her toward the tents anyway. "I insist."

Serena leans as far away as she can from the smell of burnt fish on Liam's breath.

"I don't want to see anythin' between the two of you anyway," Liam continues to talk in between bites.

"What do you mean?" Serena narrows her eyes but doesn't wait for an answer. "Liam, seriously. I have things to do."

She wiggles out of his grasp just as they reach the tent and bumps straight into Kai. "Apologies." Serena turns her attention to Kai. He is wet all over. "Have you been swimming?" Serena asks. The water that drips off him is all wrong. "You look… shiny."

Liam leans in close to Serena's ear, still chewing. "It's sweat."

"Ohhhh." Serena looks at Kai again. He smells saltier, if that is even possible. Sun glints off his chiseled midsection and chest as he swings an axe up to rest in the dip of his shoulder.

"I was chopping wood for the fires but took a break to set up the tent Liam provided for us." Kai runs the back of his hand across his forehead. "Just enough room in there for the two of us." Leaning over to unzip the opening, Kai gestures to a plate chiseled out of dried driftwood, holding a pile of food on top of it. There are sea vegetables only—no fish.

Beaming, Serena looks up at Kai. "Camping… suits you."

Beside her, Liam snorts. "Hand over the axe, I'll finish choppin' wood."

Without his eyes ever leaving Serena, Kai surrenders the axe.

"You just make sure she gets enough rest." Liam points the axe at Kai.

Scowling, Serena turns to her brother, nudging him away. Liam holds his hands up in innocence. "Alright, I'm goin', I'm goin'."

She watches him stride away, axe in one hand, the last of the poor fish on a stick in the other hand. Satisfied he will leave them in peace, Serena turns back to Kai. He is holding the tent flap open for Serena. "Hungry?" he asks.

Chapter Twenty-Four

After eating, Kai and Serena lie down together on smooth mats, listening to the camp settle down around them. She can hear Liam's voice in the distance assigning shifts for patrols as well as lookouts for the race. He recruits help in creating nets that can drag in the water alongside the boats to keep freshly caught fish preserved for consumption later. He checks in on sick members and makes sure everyone will get at least a few hours sleep before the fleet has to be ready to join the race.

Grateful for the short reprieve with Kai, Serena knows it won't occur too often during The Migration. Making a mental note to thank Liam and ensure he gets enough rest along the way as well, Serena scoots closer to Kai. Her head rests in the depression between his neck and bicep, and she wraps one arm around his waist.

She listens to Kai's deep breathes slowing until a slight whistle with each exhale lets Serena know he is asleep. She begins to drift off herself when Kai jerks in his sleep. Alert, Serena tunes into him. His breath comes faster now, and he jerks again. A combination of mumbling and moans bubble out from his lips.

Pushing herself up on one elbow, Serena looks at Kai. His eyelids flutter in deep sleep. The jerking grows more consistent until he has Serena in a painful squeeze. Riding the nightmare out with him, Serena leans into Kai. She murmurs back, just loudly enough to overtake his own whimpers. It lasts for several minutes until finally Kai settles back into a slow, rhythmic breathing pattern. He relaxes his hold on Serena but doesn't let go altogether.

Serena releases a breath she didn't know she had been holding. Squeezing her eyes shut, she bites her bottom lip. This was no ordinary nightmare. The Migration is going to be all that much more difficult because Serena knows the rock that supports her is cracking.

* * *

When Serena awakes, Kai is already up and rolling his mat. Shifting on her other side to face him, she searches for any sign of the stress that plagued his sleep. If it's there, it is pushed behind the Queen's Guard façade.

"Good evening, moonshine." Kai winks at her.

Serena smiles, tucking unruly hair behind her ear. "Moonshine?"

"You know..." Kai pauses with mat only half rolled. "Instead of sunshine... because you are a maiden of the moon."

Serena continues to stare at him.

He shrugs. "Or I can just keep calling you 'Your Majesty'."

"You'll call me that." Serena rolls onto her back, folding her hands behind her head. "If you never want to sleep with me again."

"Oh, really?" Kai flops down next to Serena, his forgotten, half-rolled mat unrolling itself. Gathering Serena in his arms, they each lie on their sides, nose to nose. "Sleep with you? Or pair with you?"

Serena lowers her voice. "Do you want to pair again... already? I mean how often can maidens...?"

Her sentence trails off, sounding stupid to her own ears.

Kai's lips graze Serena's, putting an end to the awkward moment. "As often as they want," he whispers back.

Responding more forcefully to his light touch, Serena presses her hips into his and she takes him by the mouth, rolling them both over so she is on top. Her tongue grazes his teeth as her loose, black hair falls around them like the night's veil. His scent fills their small cocoon, and for a moment, Serena can pretend they are safe in a cave of the Undine Kingdom, with nothing but each other to fill their time.

Sounds of the camp coming to life infiltrate the illusion. Kai and Serena break apart once they hear cooking fires being stamped out. She rolls off him, pushing her hair behind her shoulders. The ceiling of the tent comes into focus as they listen to Liam bark out orders for moving what supplies came off the ship back onboard.

"I suppose I should go help him," Serena says, but she doesn't move.

"Yes," Kai agrees. "I need to check in with the guard. I'm going to divide them up evenly amongst ships today." He doesn't move either.

"If possible, can you put at least two near the werewolf who killed Sasha?" Serena snuggles closer to Kai. If they discuss plans, at least they will feel productive.

"Why?" he asks. "Do you think he might try something?"

"No," Serena says, tilting her head back to look at Kai. "I think the maidens might."

Kai gives her a gentle squeeze. "Okay."

Moments of silence pass and more guilt settles in as they delay with helping the rest of the camp.

"Kai?" Serena asks.

"Hmm?" Sleepiness tinges his voice.

"When you fell asleep... did you have a nightmare?"

Kai's shoulders tighten and he hesitates just a moment too long before he answers. "A small one." He gives her a quick kiss on the forehead and pushes himself off the ground. "Nothing to worry about. Come on. Let's pack."

Serena watches as his hands fly into motion, rolling both their mats and gathering their small collection of things around the tent. He is avoiding more questions, and Serena lets the conversation pass for now. Tucking herself into a small corner of the tent to steer clear of Kai's whirlwind, Serena folds her unruly hair into a tight braid. By the time Kai unzips the tent and holds a flap open for her to step out, Serena at least looks ready to face the day.

She leaves Kai to finish breaking down the tent and glances around the camp, acknowledging maidens who curtsey as she passes. For the most part, the pack members ignore her. They seem busier, having more personal possessions like tents, blankets, and pillows to store on the boats. They have more food and personal grooming paraphernalia. Then there are the cooking pots, cigarettes, and extra changes of clothes.

"High maintenance," Serena mumbles to herself.

"Who is?"

Serena jumps at Liam's voice. She gives a nervous laugh as she recovers. "Your wolves are."

"More than you know." He smiles at her. There are dark circles under his eyes. "The racers haven't been spotted yet. But we expect to see the first of them in about an hour. We'll need to be packed and ready in time." He looks at the maidens. Most are standing or sitting in the surf just off the beach. "Soakin' it in?" Liam asks.

Serena nods. "This water is very similar to home. They know they won't see it again. Let them be—it will invigorate them for the long journey."

Serena and Liam watch as Kiera enters the water. She looks to have recovered a bit from her bout of seasickness, though she gives the boats bobbing up and down at the pier a weary glance. The green tinge is gone from her pink-purple cheeks. Wavy blonde curls hang loose at her shoulders. Treading tentatively into the chilled water, Kiera's azure eyes sparkle to life with each step. Once she is deep enough, she bends her knees until the ocean rushes over her shoulders. Translucent water turns into frothy white as a wave builds in front of Kiera. She dips below just as it breaks over her. Emerging on the other side, Kiera stands, thoroughly revitalized, with a wide smile on her face.

Maidens further out to sea turn and look, but their gazes drift past the wet strands of Kiera's hair to something behind her. She turns, and her smile dies on her lips. A pack member has entered the water. He stands at least a foot taller than Kiera, watching her from only a leap away. With locked eyes, the pair slowly circles each other. One of the closer maidens reach out for Kiera's hand, pulling her away from the man.

"It's Conner," Serena whispers to Liam. "He wouldn't hurt her, right?"

Liam shakes his head. "He's not there for her…"

Conner's eyes drift from Kiera to the ocean that surrounds him. Wind pulls water from the crest of a wave and spritzes him across the face. He runs his palm across his chin in wonder, and when he takes it away, Serena can see it is not only the ocean dripping from his cheeks but also tears.

"He never goes in the water," Liam explains, his voice cracking. "Most of us just… don't."

Conner's knees buckle. Lifting his chin high, he howls. Just before a wave washes over his head, Serena can see hair, pointy ears, and needle-like fangs emerging.

She isn't the only one to have seen it. Maidens run from the ocean, giving wide berth to the transforming wolf. Several nearby guards rush forward with their tridents, placing themselves between the wolf in the water and the retreating maidens.

Glancing down the beach, Serena sees that the chest that holds the tridents has been brought ashore and unlocked.

"He ain't gonna hurt no one," Liam shouts.

The water settles in between waves, and Conner breaks the surface, in full animal form. Panting, he turns to face the ring of guards around him. He emits a short whine at the shock of half a dozen tridents pointed at him.

Groups of wolves have gathered on the beach, but other than that, no one moves for fear of igniting a bloodbath. Serena feels a hand on her shoulder, and she turns to find Kai standing beside her.

"Kai—help."

Eyes trained on the wolf and his whole body tense, Kai moves forward. The setting sun flashes off Kai's trident, and Serena can't help but remember his night terrors—maybe he is the exact wrong person to diffuse the situation.

Joining the semi-circle of guards, Kai raises his trident, then points it at the wolf.

Liam steps forward.

Serena stops him with a quick grab at his arm. "Just wait."

Turning his head slightly to each guard beside him, Kai issues an order. Slowly, they lower their tridents and step back. Kai says the same to the guards on each end of the semi-circle. As they move away, the wolf licks his snout and wags his tail. When it is only Kai left, he and the wolf regard each other for several moments. Finally, Kai lowers his trident and his shoulders relax.

He gestures to the open ocean around them. "Enjoy her."

The wolf gives a short yip, then turns to jump into the next wave, kicking his hind legs up and out behind him. Kai rejoins Serena and Liam, who are now watching Conner's wolf roll along in the next wave.

"Thanks, man," says Liam. "I wasn't sure which way that was gonna go."

"Me either," says Kai. He turns to look at Liam. "And I am no man. I am Undine." With another glance back at the frolicking wolf, Kai stalks away.

"It's just an expression," Liam mumbles to Serena.

"He knows that," she says. She tears her eyes away from the ocean to look around.

Pack members are cheering Conner on—several have already decided to join him. Maidens continue to stay in tight groups, turning their backs to the wolves.

"Tensions are still too high," says Serena. "How is he able to transform anyway? Did he take your blood?"

"Conner would never," says Liam. "But if we are close enough to the full moon, and his system floods with emotion—any emotion—it can happen."

"I don't know." Serena doubts their former decision. "Maybe we should separate them."

Liam shakes his head. "If we can't get them to make amends during The Migration, they never will once we reach Ivvavik and are able to establish separate domains." He rests his hand on Serena's shoulder, squeezing. "It's now or never, sister."

Chapter Twenty-Five

Serena leaves Liam to wrangle his wolves out of the water—she needs to make things right with her maidens. But when she approaches the pier, they are all already boarding the ships. They follow the same protocol as earlier, splitting themselves up among each vessel, and sticking to only one side once they are aboard.

Standing at the end of the pier, Serena watches as more maidens pass her. They give a slight curtsey in her direction but never make eye contact. It can't be outright labeled as disrespectful, but Serena can feel their cold shoulders as much as if she were laying her cheek on them.

The last of them board, and Serena is left staring at their backs, just as she did in her caste days as the youngest at the back of the formation. A lump of frustration filling her throat, Serena turns to look at the wolves. Their matted fur is sopping wet, but they look invigorated by the short romp in the sea. Dragging themselves toward the beach at Liam's insistence, they keep glancing back as if they are debating which call takes precedence.

Colin, Darcy, and their boys emerge from the tent set up for the family. As their parents are occupied with breaking down camp, the boys take the opportunity to rush into the water themselves. The newcomers give the wolves an excuse to reignite the mad scuffle for last minute ocean fun. From across the beach Liam gives Serena his best 'what-can-I-do' shrug, then takes off his shirt and joins his pack mates.

Watching her brother tackle another wolf directly into a large, breaking wave Serena boards the tugboat, the vessel that contains the most maidens. She continues to watch the wolves, smiling and laughing every now and then. She waits until she can see most of the other maidens watching as well, then she turns to face them.

Serena points to the open ocean behind her. "They deserve to say goodbye to her, too," she says, looking from maiden to maiden. Her gaze falls on the healer who refused to share her stock of ginger with the wolves. "And they deserve our medicine when they are sick."

The healer gives Serena a sharp glance, then trains her eyes back on the floor in front of her.

"What they deserve," a small voice slips out from the back of the ship, "is retribution."

Stepping around webbed feet, Serena moves closer to the maiden that spoke out. Orange scales glimmer under the setting sun as Sophia straightens her back and looks Serena in the eye. "They killed my sister."

"And our king—your father," says the maiden next to Sophia.

Serena addresses the easiest concern first. "Were my father still alive, he would have never agreed to The Migration." Serena fixes the maiden with her best Nerin-like stare. "And we would have died in the caves beside him of starvation or sickness within a year."

The maiden flinches at Serena's sharp words.

Taking a deep breath, Serena turns to Sophia, forcing a softer tone into her voice. "Sasha was the only one of my caste mates who was ever nice to me."

Sophia blinks, and the sharp lines of her cheekbones diminish.

"Sasha was brave, kind, and she didn't give a damn about labels or vengeance or who deserves what. And you probably know that better than anyone."

A slow sigh leaves Sophia's mouth, and her shoulders sag.

"If Sasha were here today, how would she have handled this?" asks Serena.

Eyes drifting out to the wolves playing in the water, Sophia's quivering chin slowly turns into a smile. "She'd be out there, playing with them." Sophia looks back at Serena. "I wish she were here…"

The last of the sun sinks behind the ocean, flashing in farewell across the waves. One especially high crest in the middle of the pack of wolves catches the light. When the swell curls in on itself, it almost looks like a scaled, orange tail. Both of the maidens suck in a breath as they see it.

Serena and Sophia exchange a smile. "She is there—with them," says Serena. "Right where you knew she'd be."

Reaching out, Sophia squeezes Serena's hand. "Thank you. I'll… try harder."

"It would be appreciated," Serena answers. She turns to address the rest of the maidens. "These are our sons. We cast them away for their own survival, though some didn't see it that way. I'm asking you to separate the heinous crimes of a few from the rest of the pack. I'm telling you, what they really deserve is… us." Serena raises her voice so those on the other ships can hear her. "They deserve to see who the Painted Maidens truly are."

"And who are we, Serena?" Evandre says with pleading eyes. "A bunch of... homeless sirens, who get seasick for Poseidon's sake."

"Yes." Serena nods with new energy in her movements. She crosses the deck and points to Evandre. "Exactly. We are homeless." She moves back to point at Sophia. "We are grieving."

From the stern of the boat, pinkish-purple Kiera raises a shaky hand. "We are sick."

"We are low on ginger," mumbles the healer.

Serena ignores the healer because there are more shouts.

"We are fragile," says Sarafina.

"We smell like fish!"

A round of laughter bubbles up.

One of the maidens still looking out at the werewolves speaks. "We gave up our sons."

Laying a hand on her shoulder, another consoles her.

"We were desperate." She looks at Serena. "We still *are* desperate."

"We are too judgmental."

"We are too formal."

"We are chained," says Arista from the next boat over, in a sing-song voice.

Serena gives the maiden a weary look, but amidst more shouting, she moves off the boat to cross the pier, and jumps aboard again next to Arista. Removing the key from the dry bag tied around her waist, Serena undoes the lock. The chains drop to the ground, a heavy clunk putting an end to the shouts.

Serena looks up to find everyone watching her. "You are all right—we are all of those things. But this is a new beginning for the Undine. And we can be so much more than we ever were."

Stepping onto the side of the boat so all of the maidens can see and hear her, Serena speaks up. "So let the wolves see everything. Let them see our faults. But let's also show them our strengths." Wavering slightly, Serena steadies herself on a rope. "And we can't do that if we are constantly turning our backs to them."

No one speaks up, but Serena takes that as a good sign. No one is disagreeing.

"I'm not asking you to wrap them in hugs as soon as they board. But I am asking you…" Serena trails off, looking at Sophia. "To try harder."

The maidens don't get a chance to respond. The first of the wolves filter down the pier and onto the ships.

Serena hops down from the boat to meet Liam.

"Did you enjoy your swim?" she asks.

Shaking his head to rid his hair of extra water, Liam smiles. "Yeah—I think we all did."

"There are better ways to do that, you know." Serena gestures to the torn fabric in his hand.

"Oh, right." Lifting his ripped shirt to dry his hair, Liam grimaces. "Wonder if there will be any seamstress on this race."

"Wait." Serena grabs the torn material. It is bright red, the same color as the ribbons tied to an arrow that will signal for Undine reinforcements. "How do we plan on communicating amongst the vessels during the race?"

"We can't risk using radios in case one of the Ungainly ships is listenin' in on our broadcast." Liam shrugs. "We don't have enough satellite phones and there is no cell signal most of the way."

"I know how we can do it," says Serena. "But I need more material in several different colors."

"You heard her," Liam turns to his pack mates. "Hand over the ripped clothes."

A large pile of scrap material starts to grow at Serena's feet.

Liam takes a step back so as not to get submerged in it. "I hope you can sew."

"Well." Serena thinks. "I am pretty good at stringing together seashell necklaces."

"Seriously?" asks Liam.

"I've got a steady hand, your majesty," Sarafina offers, giving a quick curtsey before bending to select several torn shirts in the same purple hues. "Do you have the tools needed?"

"Here," says Simone, dragging the other two healers along with her. "We brought plenty of needle and thread for sutures—hopefully, we won't be needing them."

Undine working groups for each ship are cobbled together with enough material to make signals in a variety of colors; red for an emergency, blue for maidens in the water, white for rough waters ahead, plus several others Serena and Liam think they may need during the race.

"Smoke! It's the signal!" Conner shouts from the cockpit of the sailboat, pointing to a grey plume rising into the sky. "The first racer has been spotted!"

There is a flurry of feet—both webbed and hairy, as everyone rushes to get themselves and the supplies on a boat.

"What order are we going in again?" Serena asks Liam as they both scramble to gather the last scraps of material.

"Sailboat—it is the fastest and won't draw suspicion if it is among the first of the racers to come in," he says. "Then the center console fishin' boat. It isn't particularly fast, but it is most likely to sink. I figure it'd be better with more of us comin' up behind it to help if that happens."

Serena nods. "Put more maidens on that one, and only a few wolves. No more than they can manage to help in the sea. You'll remember how many of us it took to hold up you and Aiden in that storm?"

"I'm not likely to forget that incident—in this lifetime or the next. Anyway, the cabin cruiser and trawler will come next, with the tugboat last. It can hold more people and pick up any strays the other boats lose along the way."

"Hopefully that won't be the case," says Serena. She nods to the end of the boat. "I'll be on the tug, then. I want to make sure nobody gets left behind. And Conner seems confident enough with the route—he'll remain on the sailboat?"

"Yep," says Liam. He lowers his voice. "I'll stay in the middle on the trawler—and continue to keep an eye on your Sophia."

"I honestly don't think it's necessary anymore," says Serena. She pauses, then nods. "But that works for now."

"All maidens and guards accounted for and aboard the ship," says Kai, joining Liam and Serena. "Except you, your majesty."

"And the werewolves?" asks Serena.

Kai looks from Serena to Liam and back again. "I... didn't count them." He points to Liam. "I figured—"

"Would you mind?" Serena interrupts.

Kai's hand drops to his side. "We need to leave if we are going to catch up with the racers."

Serena crosses her arms. Kai sighs but turns to the first ship.

"And Kai?" Serena holds out her hand.

He hesitates only a moment before passing over the key to the trident trunk. "All are returned and locked."

"Thank you," says Serena, her voice cold.

After Kai returns to the counting task, Liam clears his throat. "We'd better get ourselves on board," says Liam, turning toward the trawler. "Fair winds, Serena."

"Following seas," she finishes the traditional mariner's farewell.

It will only be a few hours of sailing before the racers pull into the next port, retiring for the night, and it is certainly the easiest leg of the entire race. But Serena can't seem to calm the nerves in her midsection. She boards the tugboat with one hand on her stomach, as if she can physically push away her anxiety.

Kai finishes counting the wolves and waves his hand for the all clear. Serena nods and waits until he boards the sailboat before she issues the command.

"All ahead full!" Her voice bellows over the sound of crashing waves.

Leaving the pier in the order they will race, the sailboat pulls away first, carrying Conner, Kai, and an even mix of Undine and werewolves. The rest of the ships follow, one by one. Serena's tugboat falls into line as the last boat. The sight of the vessels lined up, carrying almost all of her people straight into one of the most treacherous races on earth is too much for her to bear.

She turns to look at those on her boat. Several of the Undine are busy piecing together material for their communication flags. One maiden runs out of the bright red needed for the emergency signal—the flag only stands half the size it needs to be. On her knees searching through the pile of scrap material, the maiden stops as a piece of red material is held out, right in front of her face. She rises to find one of the pack mates has taken his shirt off his back. It isn't even ripped.

Slowly, the maiden takes the offered material, nodding her head in thanks. Not a word is exchanged, but it is the most cordiality Serena has seen between the two groups yet.

Further down the line, Sophia's eyes are trained on the area where she spotted a glimpse of orange scales. She is still hoping for another sign of her sister.

Turning back to the line of boats, Serena pulls her shoulders back and lifts her chin. Poseidon has yet to grace The Migration, but at least they now know Sasha has.

Chapter Twenty-Six

The two maidens that were sent to watch for the first racers at the northern most end of the island have now doused the signal fire with wet leaves, and the smoke grows whiter in color. It is time for the first boat to merge onto the racecourse. Unfurling its longest sail, the boat picks up speed. In no time at all, Serena can no longer make out Kai's silhouette at the stern of the ship. It rounds the corner of the island and disappears from view. A noticeable buzz of tension runs up and down the lines of both the werewolves and Undine on Serena's boat.

The color of the smoke once again changes to a brownish grey—the result of more wood, and the center console fishing boat lurches forward, causing the maidens on board to grab the handrails in consternation.

One by one, each vessel vanishes around the northern end of the island, until only the tug is left. When the smoke changes for the final time, the motor revs and the entire ship shudders. Slowly, it inches forward. All of the seasick patients, werewolf and Undine alike, have been grouped and positioned in the center of the deck.

As the boat picks up speed, there are groans from the sick. Serena furrows her eyebrows in sympathy as she watches the pinkish-purple hue on Kiera's face disappear into a sheen of white. Darcy, self-assigned to the boat because of the patients, sees the same. Rising up from the side of a pack member, Darcy takes Kiera by the hand and leads her to the front of the boat, positioning her at the bow facing the sea.

"For the view?" Serena asks Darcy once she returns.

"It is the smoothest spot on the boat," says Darcy. "It should help subside the seasickness, and hers is one of the worst cases."

The pair turns back to the rest of the patients, judging severity simply by the color of their faces. It is difficult when half of them are mostly covered in facial hair, and the other half sport the colors of the rainbow. Undine healers move among the sick, allowing maidens to sip ginger potion from their flasks. Those same flasks are tucked out of sight every time a healer gets close to a sick pack member.

Darcy raises her eyebrow at Serena.

"I'm working on it," says Serena under her breath.

Nodding, Darcy fixes her gaze at her feet, pressing her lips together as if she is struggling to not say something. Finally, she takes a deep breath and looks at Serena. "I have my own medicines that will be depleted by the end of tomorrow. I didn't expect this from so many. But if the seasickness continues past that, my guys will be in danger of becoming severely weakened and dehydrated."

As if on cue, a pack member stands and races for the side of the boat to expel the contents of his stomach. Serena and Darcy have to jump back to keep from being run over in the process.

"We just barely got started today." Serena stares at his heaving shoulders in wonder.

"Yes, well, I'm expecting some of them will recover, but some won't." Darcy walks over to the sick wolf and, once he is done, leads him up to the front of the boat, depositing him right next to Kiera.

After the ocean incident, Kiera gives the werewolf a weary look, but they are both too miserable to do anything about each other.

The last pine trees on the island pass, needles blowing in the wind as if to wave farewell. Occupants on the side of the boat spot shimmering scales in the water. It is the maidens who had signal duty. After putting out the fire, they are racing to catch up to the tug.

"Get the ropes out!" shouts Serena. "Slow it down a bit!"

Her message is relayed to the bridge, and her maidens are on their feet at her command, but they are lost as to how to operate on a boat. Their hands hang by their side, useless and idle.

"Come about!" The werewolves are up, too, and they know what to do. "Throw the lines!"

Ropes are tossed to a pack member standing atop the wheelhouse. He wraps them around the main mast then throws the slack back down. Wound into tight balls, two other pack members take aim and toss the lines. Uncoiling as they sail through the air, the ropes cover a surprising distance. When the maidens grab hold, the line goes taut.

Every pack member who is able grasps the ropes and pulls in coordinated bursts. The maidens fly into the air gripping the knotted ends of the rope.

Pack members continue to pull. Having donated material for the flags, most of them are shirtless. Shoulders and arms bulge each time they heave in the lines. The pack member still at the main mast is shouting commands while watching the maidens come in at speeds faster than they could swim.

"Heave and hold! Steady! One final pull—and heave!"

Pack members at the ropes back up until they hit the other side of the boat, forcing maidens to jump out of the way. Everyone lifts their chins, watching two scaled Undine turning somersaults in the air. Arcing over the water, they begin to descend just as the boat moves underneath them. Pale skin overtakes the colored blur as they transform into legs in midair. Serena can hear several awed gasps from the pack members closest to her.

The maidens land on the deck, one solid thump followed closely by the next. Feet shoulder width apart, they look up, eyes going wide in surprise. They are surrounded by pack members holding the ropes that pulled them in.

The pack member closest to the maidens clears his throat. "Welcome aboard," he says before turning his back to recoil the lines. The rest take his lead, retreating to their side of the tug.

One of the maidens opens her mouth. "We thank you for your—"

A nudge from her partner cuts her off.

Crimson flares at the maiden's cheeks, and she turns her back to the wolves, joining her own group. Blending in with the Undine stitching together flags, she steals indiscreet glances at the pack.

Busying themselves with coiling rope and mopping the deck of excess water, pack members do the same to the maidens.

If only this race were about ten years longer, thinks Serena. *Then we might make some progress.*

"Boats ahead!" the shout comes from the wheelhouse. Just as the bow of the ship turns, heading into Queen Charlotte Sound, another ship ahead and behind come into view—both of them Ungainly racers. Most of the maidens and pack members on the tug sit so their heads are below the rails. Hopefully curious Ungainlies, especially those with binoculars, won't realize how many bodies are aboard the tug. It wouldn't do to attract that kind of attention. Only Kiera and her sick counterpart at the bow, the pack members in the wheelhouse, and Serena stay visible. Darcy passes Serena a hooded sweatshirt, and Serena reluctantly pulls the itchy material over her head.

After making her rounds to provide a few necessities to those who can't move about as freely, Serena surveys the racecourse. Large peninsulas stretch into the ocean like lazy fingers atop blue silk while tiny islands dot the clear water further out to sea. A bank of white clouds roll over the landscape, and as Serena looks up, she feels as though she is back home staring up at the frothy turmoil as a swell lifts then breaks overhead.

Taking a deep breath, Serena pulls herself from The Deep and focuses on her purpose above the water. If she squints, she can just make out the top masts of the wooden trawler holding more of her people. Within minutes it is completely out of sight and she is left with only Ungainly ships to stare at, one ahead and one behind. They are unimpressive trawlers, probably used for commercial fishing on a regular basis.

Behind her one of Darcy's boys complains of boredom. In front, at the bow, the seasick werewolf passes his bottle of fresh water to Kiera. Serena tugs at the itchy sweatshirt, contemplating sitting for a few minutes of rest. Dry flakes flutter to the deck. Her body is already feeling the effects of being absent from the water too long.

When the racers stop for the day at Penrose Island, the plan is for only a few pack members to accompany the boats to check in and join the Ungainly camp for the night. The rest of the pack members will remain hidden on the boats while the Undine will swim on their own up the race course to Hecate Island, which lies further out to sea. While Serena feels obliged to remain close to the group with the Ungainlies, she may have to accompany her maidens for a refreshing plunge in dark waters.

"The flags are complete, your majesty," says Sarafina.

Serena turns at the announcement to maidens holding up several colored flags. Red, blue, white, green, and orange. Serena points to one that appears to be concocted from dozens of different flannel shirts. "What does that one mean?"

The two Undine holding the flag train their eyes to the deck. Serena crosses her arms, waiting.

Clearing her throat, one of the maidens briefly meets Serena's gaze. "We thought it could be a signal for… rogue werewolf."

"Do you have intelligence suggesting this event will occur?" asks Serena.

"Well, they are werewolves…" says Sarafina under her breath. "Besides, it will comfort us to know our sisters on the other boats have a way to warn us."

Serena sighs, but looking over the maidens nods her reluctant agreement.

"A signal!" shouts a pack member from the wheelhouse.

Maidens pop up on their feet running for the bow.

"Stay down!" Serena hisses.

But the excitement of the first signal overtakes their caution for obscurity. Pressing forward into the two seasick passengers, maidens point straight ahead. The trawler carrying wolves and maidens is back in view now that the sailing route has straightened out. Serena joins the group and squints her eyes.

"Blue!" Kiera yells from the front. "I see a blue flag."

"Maidens in the water." The meaning of the signal is muttered throughout the group.

"It means Penrose Island, the first stop must be ahead," says Serena. "We part ways for the night here. Maidens will proceed to Hecate Island. Pack members are to remain with the boats."

Occupants on the boat scurry to action while the maidens rush to clean up from their sewing circles and secure their dry bags around their waists.

Serena looks over the port side of the boat. A wave of excitement runs through her with the anticipation of diving into the cool, blue water.

"For Poseidon's sake," muttering from a nearby healer catches Serena's attention. She is frantically groping through her dry bag. Untying it from her waist, she dumps the entire thing out. Bandages flutter to the deck while vials clink together.

"What is it?" asks Serena, bending down next to the healer.

"My entire stock of hydrocoral," she says, turning each vial so she can see the labels. She looks up at Serena. "It has been stolen." Her gaze flutters to the pack members lining the other side of the boat.

Chapter Twenty-Seven

"Are you sure? When was the last time you saw it?" asks Serena.

"Back on Hope Island. I had all my vials spread out in the sick area. I was in a rush to pack up so I didn't have time to account for them then." The healer lowers her voice. "In powder form, it looks a lot like ground-up ginger." With fire in her eyes, the healer takes a step toward the pack members.

"Wait." Serena holds an arm out, blocking the healer's path. Serena takes one last, longing look at the water. "We can't just outright blame them. There is no proof. I will stay with the wolves and find out."

The healer doesn't budge.

"I will search their belongings if I have to." Serena's arm remains steadfast, and she assumes her best royalty voice. "Go with the maidens. Now."

"As you say." The healer gathers her spilled belongings and ties the dry bag to her waist. Turning to step up onto the railing, she glances one more time at the pack members, then at Serena. Finally, she jumps and dives into the water, far enough to steer clear of the boat's motor.

Serena watches the light-green scales glide away just under the surface of the water. Ignoring the pang of jealousy in her gut, Serena turns to the wolves, practicing what she is going to say in head.

Who stole the hydrocoral?

An outright accusation might trigger a revolt.

If anyone might have taken a vial thinking it was ginger, please return it as I look away.

Mother Rayne would do the same with young calflings.

Clearing her throat, Serena catches the attention of a few of the closest pack members.

"Prefer to run with the wolves than swim with the mermaids?" Colin, Darcy's husband, asks.

"Not really," she says. "Our healer seems to have... misplaced an important vial. It has an orange powdery substance inside. Would you please pass the word that if it is found it should be returned to me immediately?"

"Will do. But just so you know" —Colin points where the maidens sat— "not one of us have ventured to the other side."

Behind her, the last of the maidens splash into the water, and relief runs down the line of pack members. Serena can't help but feel a bit of the relief herself with the tension no longer there. Her shoulders relax, and she unclenches fists she didn't even realize were in tight balls.

"Green flag!" shouts the wolf at the bow. "Land ahead."

Most of the wolves crawl across the deck to make their way down below. All ships have slowed their speed and are a tighter group, which means they are more likely to observe details on other boats.

"So what will it be now?" asks Colin. "Wolves or humans?"

The piers are coming into view, and Serena can already spot the sailboat Kai is on tied to the docks. Male Undine lack the vibrant colors of the maidens and would be more successful blending in with Ungainlies, or so the Undine theory goes. Kai and one other guard will be passing themselves off as crew members of the sailboat, along with three pack members.

"I don't think Ungainlies take too well to blue faces," says Serena.

"Sure they do. Smurfs, Cookie Monster, Mystique, The Blue Man Group…" Colin trails off at Serena's blank stare. "None of which you probably know."

Serena turns, throwing one of the ropes to a pack member waiting on the dock. Several other pack members have already secured their boats and are leaving the docks to set up camp for the night. One of them is Xavier, the wolf who killed Sophia's sister. Serena's eyes fall to a cylindrical object bulging from his pocket. Eyes pinned on him, she moves forward as the tugboat bumps into the dock. He disappears into the trees. When Ungainly voices and laughter filter out from the staging area, Serena stops in her tracks. She will have to leave the Ungainlies to the wolves and the Queen's Guard, for now. It will be a different story once the moon rules the night.

* * *

Rising to its place in the sky, the alloy-silver moon remains suspended and surrounded by thousands of stars, their pinpricks of light mere scatterings. Swaths of moonlight blaze over the water, lighting up the sea like melted platinum. The swell and sigh of the waves is a haunting lullaby.

Below deck on the tugboat, Serena rises to her feet. She tiptoes around sleeping pack members until she feels the warmth of the moonlight bloom across her face from the open porthole above.

Shifting at her feet catches her attention before she can ascend the ladder well.

"You are going?" asks Colin. He sits up and rubs his eyes, careful not to disturb his sleeping boy around him. "I'm not sure that's such a good idea."

Serena shrugs and whispers, "I'll just say I'm The Blue Man Group."

"There needs to be two more of you..." he mumbles as he rolls over, pulling his blanket over his head.

Ignoring him, Serena climbs the steep stairs and takes a deep breath of fresh, salty air. It is a preferable change to the stale smell of wolf that lingers below deck. A few moments later, her feet hit the solid wood of the docks, and she retracts every last one of her scales, pulling the itchy hood of her sweatshirt tighter until her most prominent features are shadowed in dark.

Besides the sleeping wolves hidden below deck on the five ships from Doug's rental business, the docks are deserted. Serena glides past Ungainly ships that sway on gentle waves, and she stays on her toes as she makes the transition from planks to earth, darting up the hill toward the campground. Scattered camp fires emit a subtle glow, guiding her to the most heavily populated section. Even at this late hour there are still voices talking in low tones as racers huddle around fires, regaling their adventures of the day.

Slipping in and out of tents, Serena uses her nose to guide her to the pack. Finally, she spots the same tent she and Kai slept in on Hope Island. There are six more around it signifying her people's camp spot.

Now all I have to do is find that vial.

Pausing by each tent, Serena stops to listen. Several reveal snoring wolves, but the next one she comes to is silent. Moving around to the front, she slowly pulls down the zipper and peers inside. Once her eyes adjust to the darkness, she glances around. The tent is empty. Pulling the zipper down the rest of the way, Serena slips inside and immediately starts routing through bags and clothes.

She freezes when footsteps approach her tent. Squeezing her eyes shut, Serena prays. *Poseidon let him pass, Poseidon let him pass.*

The footsteps pause at the opening to the tent that hangs partly open and Serena is plunged into darkness as an exaggerated shadow is cast by the fire behind him. Lifting his hand to the opened flap, the man mumbles. "What in the h—?"

"Xavier! It's your deal!" interrupts someone from the fire.

The form just outside the tent turns. "I need another jacket."

"No way, last time you had bulky sleeves I swear you were cheatin'. We'll build up the fire."

"Come on, man. I'm cold."

"You go into that tent then you're out of the game!"

"Oh, fine," Xavier grumbles, and the large shadow lurking over Serena falls away as he returns to his cards.

Frantic fingers resume their search once she is safe to make noise again. Finally, they close around a leather belt. Serena feels her way to the front of the pants the belt is looped through, and sticks her hand in one pocket and then the other. Smooth glass hits the palm of her hand, and she pulls out an Undine vial.

"Thank you, Poseidon," she whispers, sticking her head out of the flap. Confirming the coast is clear, Serena shimmies close to the tent around to the back. Stepping backward, Serena keeps an eye on the card players around the fire. There are several Ungainlies participating in the game, too.

A small glowing object bounces against her chest. Serena looks down and holds up the necklace Danny gave her. The Undine's hair is lit.

"What—?" One more step back, and Serena bumps into a warm body. Turning, she covers her mouth before she can emit a sound. Another hooded figure, of the same height and build, releases her own gasp. "Your majesty?!" She pulls back her hood, revealing full lips and an angled face framed with bright red scales along the side.

"Simone." Serena pulls on the healer's arm until they are both well away from the tents and crouching behind bushes. "What are you doing here?"

"I should ask the same of you," booms a low voice behind them.

This time Serena does gasp—and Simone screams.

Chapter Twenty-Eight

"Trust me, I am not the scariest thing out here." The figure crouches, and light from a nearby fire splashes across his face.

"Liam!" Serena and Simone say together as they both frown at him.

"Everything alright back there?" A passing Ungainly has stopped, peering into the woods.

Liam stands up, clearing his throat while the maidens duck further behind the bushes. "Yeah. I, uh, thought I saw a mouse."

"A mouse?" the Ungainly says, voice dry.

"Um…yep," says Liam.

"We have a tough course to traverse tomorrow," the Ungainly reminds Liam of some of the more realistic dangers. "Racers are sleeping, keep it down, will ya?"

"Will do. Sorry about that." Liam watches the Ungainly move on then reaches down to pull Serena up to eye level. "If you would have gone any further into the woods you would have come to the bathrooms they have set up back there."

"Ew," says Simone, standing next to Serena.

"I'm telling you that because this is a high traffic area. It's why we set up tents here—to get as much intel as we could on the other racers." Liam looks behind him. "You can't be here."

Escorting both maidens back toward the tent, it is only then that Serena hears a group of men tromping through the forest toward them.

"Here," Liam whispers. "Get in my tent until I come and get you." He unzips the flap and pushes both maidens inside. "Do not, for any reason whatsoever, come out until I return. It will be a few hours before the camp is quiet enough." Liam retracts his head and zips up the flap without an apology for his rough treatment.

"That was almost not appropriate," says Simone inside the tent.

Serena smiles at her. "He is just looking out for us." She glances around at the contents inside the tent. One duffel bag, one sleeping bag. Liam has the space to himself so they don't need to worry about anyone else walking in. Hopefully. "Come on, we can at least lie down and get some rest."

Kicking aside the sleeping bag, the maidens make themselves comfortable on hard ground. After complaints of the annoying nylon tent floor, Simone settles herself. But sleep is hard to come by for either of them. Liam was right—his tent is directly in the middle of a high traffic area. Booted feet constantly stomping by put Serena on edge.

Attempting to distract both of them, Serena turns to Simone. "Why are you here?" she whispers.

"My hydrocoral was stolen," says Simone.

"Yours too?"

Simone looks at Serena with wide eyes.

"Same with the healer on my boat. I told her I'd search the pack members' things, discreetly, as she was sure it was them."

"I think it was, too. But I haven't had any luck finding evidence. What about you?"

"As a matter of fact..." Serena sits up and fishes the glass vial from her dry bag. "I found this."

"Which is it?" Simone sits up, taking the vial from Serena and popping out the cork. Putting her nose to the edge, she sniffs cautiously. "Ginger. It is gone now," Simone turns the vial upside down, tapping it into her palm. A few remaining flakes drift down and she pops them in her mouth. "Yes, definitely ginger. At Hope Island, we put our ginger in small herb bags so they could be handed out in correct doses. So this vial would have been empty. Why would a wolf want an empty vial?" Simone purses her lips. "But our hydrocoral is still missing. Why would a wolf want hydrocoral?"

"Why are you so sure it was a wolf?" asks Serena. "Oh—shh."

Two men have stopped directly outside the tent. Serena and Simone go still, holding their breath. The precaution is unnecessary. The men are involved in a heated discussion.

"I'm telling you, it is too dangerous. We need to call off the race." The speaker is shorter than the other and his voice deeper.

"Keep your voice down, Smith. Do you know how much trouble we've had keeping this annual race open? And this year we have more racers than ever! If we call off the race now, those entries might never return."

"That storm keeps gaining strength, and we'll cross paths right at the height of it."

The men cease talking as someone else passes on his way to the outhouses. Once they are clear, the larger man sighs. "I'll speak to waterway authorities first thing in the morning, but if they don't forbid us to race, I very much doubt I'll be calling it off."

"At the expense of everyone's life?"

"Quit being so dramatic…" their voices trail off as they walk away.

Serena and Simone exchange a glance.

"A big storm?" asks Simone.

"We can deal with bad weather," says Serena.

"Yes, when we are under the sea. I just don't know how we'll fair above it." Simone lies down, folding her hands behind her head.

Serena does the same and they fall silent listening to snatches of conversation around them. The camp has begun to settle, and with less foot traffic, they can hear those around the campfires talking.

"What do you do with that boat of yours when you aren't racing it?" one man asks his neighbor.

"I contract out to clean up oil spills."

"Oh yeah?"

"Pay is alright—and it keeps me sailing. Been cleaning up from a spill a month back. There are still some slicks floating around from it. Watch for them on the race course."

Across the fire, another conversation is taking place. "What do you do when you aren't racing in the arctic, Jimmy?"

"I'm bush pilot," says another man. He has a strong Russian accent.

"What is a bush pilot?" asks Liam. It is the first time since he left Serena has heard his voice.

"I fly impossible missions. We go inhospitable regions, areas with rough terrain or no landing strips, or in dangerous conditions."

"Why would you do that?" asks Liam.

There is a pause—only the crackling fire can be heard. Finally, Jimmy answers, "The money is good. Besides, what else am I going to do?"

Laughter breaks out from the circle of men.

"Seriously," says Jimmy. "I like adventure. I like crazy people I meet and stories they tell."

"Like what?" asks Liam.

"Oh, stories about adventures they've had. Some are true and some twisted fairy tales. Fun, exotic creatures—"

"Creatures?" Serena can imagine Liam's head popping up. "What kind of creatures?"

"Dragons, trolls, vampires."

Simone leans over to Serena. "We're not fun?"

"Shh." Serena smiles, nudging her.

"But my favorite," says Jimmy. "Is story about animals meeting in a cave."

There is a long pause as if Jimmy is judging his audience for their interest. No one protests, and the fire is still strong, so he begins, "Once upon time, all animals looked the same… on inside. Each year they gather at a sacred cave deep in forest to celebrate their unity. Together, they would take off their skins. Raven shed feathers, bear his fur, and salmon her scales."

Serena and Simone look at each other as the man's words hang in the air over them like stale smoke.

"Stripped of their separate identities," continues Jimmy. "They rejoiced in their unity and danced together."

"Naked dancing?" one man interrupts. "Hell, I'm in!"

Laughter kicks up again, and Jimmy gives an appropriate pause before he resumes the story. "But one day, human comes and laughs at what he sees. Embarrassed, the animals run, and that was the last time they revealed themselves this way."

No one speaks for a long time. Finally, someone spits into the fire. "And that's the end of the story?"

"Yes, sir," says Jimmy.

"Bummer ending."

"I think it holds a good lesson," says Liam. "Underneath our disguises, we can appreciate all we have in common with each other."

Serena looks at Simone, and she can't be sure, but she can almost see a glimmer of wet tears on Simone's cheeks.

"If we could learn to drop our skins," says Liam. "Whether we are human or one of your exotic creatures, and just… dance."

"Here, here!" The group grows loud and rambunctious. Someone pulls out a fiddle and begins to play. Shadows cast onto the tent by the fire reveal dancing men.

Inside the tent, Serena and Simone cannot share in the enthusiasm. Sharp, angled faces and skin tinged with different hues, not to mention their scaled bodies—they would never be accepted in an Ungainly society. Extending her fingertips, Serena finds Simone's hand and they interlock fingers as they lie dead still staring up at the tent ceiling, listening to the music, dancing, and laughter around them.

The party does not last long. Angry campers who are trying to sleep shout their protests. The music stops, and the fire is doused as men depart to their own tents.

Several minutes of complete silence go by before the flap to the tent door is unzipped. "It's clear," whispers Liam. His voice is respectfully somber, as if he is sympathizing with the maidens.

Serena and Simone rise from their places and follow Liam, gliding silently through the camp. They encounter no one else until they get to the docks.

"Should I be expectin' any more scaled surprises tonight?" he asks, crossing his arms.

"Not unless your pack gets hungry for fish, Liam of Clan Werich," Serena shoots back.

"Fine," he growls.

"Fine." She can growl like the best of them. She turns to Simone. "Which boat were you on?"

"The sailboat. But if it is okay I'd prefer to be on the tug with the rest of the seasick patients. I think I can help them."

"As you say." Serena nods her permission.

"Thank you, your majesty," Simone says, leaving to board the tugboat.

Serena turns back to Liam. "Will you stay on the trawler again tomorrow?"

"Yes, keeping an eye on Sophia."

"You should know, someone has taken the hydrocoral stock from two of my healers." Serena crosses her arms. "That is why both Simone and I were at camp tonight. We have reason to believe it was a wolf."

"Hydro-what?" Liam raises an eyebrow. "And why do you suspect the wolves?"

"Well, for one, I spotted a vial in the pocket of the very wolf Sophia is watching. And then I found it in his tent. Turns out it was ginger, which happens to look a lot like hydrocoral."

"I'll have words with him," says Liam.

"Thank you," says Serena. "And thank you for helping us tonight." After one last look at Liam, Serena follows Simone onto the tugboat.

Below deck, Simone pauses at the end of the ladder well. "What is that smell?" she asks.

"Sleeping wolf." Serena, glances around at the bodies covering almost every inch of the floor. "Just… imagine them in the story, shedding their fur. Under their skin they are just like you."

Directly in front of them, one of the pack members rolls over and farts.

Simone presses her lips together and glares at Serena.

"Come on," says Serena. We'll just sleep up on the deck tonight."

Chapter Twenty-Nine

Crew members of the Capital to Capital boat race, whether Ungainly, Undine, or werewolf are up at the sun's first light. Each ship is prepped, the courses are charted, and the expected finish times at the end of the day are reported to race officials.

Serena is in the wheelhouse of the tug, consulting with the pilot. "Why do you need to give expected finish times?" she asks.

"It's how we win the race. Each ship estimates their finish time for the course that day. We aren't supposed to have any timepieces or instruments that measure distance or speed on the boat." As he speaks crew members are pulling heavy canvas over the instrument panel. "The crew that has the best average for estimating their time wins the race."

"We're not really hoping to win, are we?" asks Serena.

The captain shrugs. "We're here. Why not play the game? And if we are handed that trophy in the end, so be it."

"Pure gold, that thing is, or so I've heard," another pack member charting maps speaks up.

"Of which I'm sure you'll find many uses in secluded Ivvavik National Park," mumbles Serena.

Footsteps ping against the ladder well leading up to the wheelhouse. Serena turns to find Liam, already sweaty from doing… whatever werewolves do when they prepare to launch a boat.

"We are about to cast off," he tells Serena. "I'll stay on the trawler, and Kai is moving to the center console. Do you want to be with him for this leg of the trip?"

Looking out the window, down onto the deck, Serena sees Simone and the other healer emerging from the ladder well with their hoods on, whispering but making sharp gestures with their hands. Finally, the healer reaches into her dry bag and hands Simone a pouch. After a quick nod, Simone hurries to the bow where Kiera and the seasick wolf have already placed themselves. Serena recognizes the small pouch as individual ginger portions. Following it closely with hers eyes, she watches it move from Simone's hand to the pack member. Smiling, Kiera hands him a water bottle.

"Well?" Liam asks, still awaiting her answer.

"Our people on the tug are going to be okay." She looks across the pier to the center console. It is the boat most likely to succumb to harsh conditions, so only maidens board it, with the exception of the pilot and his navigator. It would be a selfish move to sit with Kai for a day. Serena catches his eye, giving him a slight wave. *I am okay. And you?*

Kai waves back.

She smiles and turns to Liam. "I think I will take the sailboat today."

After a few more words about the course of navigation for the day, and the plan to board the maidens while sailing past Hecate Island, Serena leaves the tug to board the sailboat. The two large sails are being unrolled and checked for tears and weak spots. Three other pack members stand on deck while eight wait patiently below before they are safe from Ungainly eyes to emerge.

"Her majesty is with us today?" asks a pack member.

Serena turns to find Doug. She gives a slight curtsey. "If you'll have me."

"We'll have you alright, but there are rules. First, we've got no time for formality. Everyone on the boat works or stays below, out of the way. Second, I'm in charge. The deck of a sailboat can be a dangerous place. Yesterday I already had one go overboard."

"A maiden?"

"No." Doug chuckles, twisting the wolf bracelet at his wrist. "Though two of your maidens dove in after him. Not sure we would have got him back before involving Ungainly authorities without them. He hit his head on the railing as he went over and fell into the ocean unconscious."

"Oh no!" says Serena. "Is he okay?"

Doug squeezes past her to help secure the sails. "He's resting below now. One of your healers looked at him but there wasn't much she could do."

Hope blooms in Serena's chest. Maybe she will sail with Kai today after all. Taking a step closer to Doug, Serena lowers her voice. "So relations between the Undine and the werewolves—they are improving here?"

Doug looks at her with wide eyes, then starts laughing. They are great guffaws that eventually turn into a coughing fit.

The rest of the crew members look at Serena and Doug, and her face feels hot with embarrassment.

Once he calms himself, Doug smiles at Serena. "As I said, he was unconscious when he went overboard. Didn't open his eyes until he was being manhandled back onto the boat by the maidens. He lashed out, thinking they were attacking him. They didn't take too kindly to that."

"No, I suppose they wouldn't." Serena frowns.

"Anyway, you'd think the rest o' the pack members would be grateful, but I think they resent the fact they couldn't help their own brother and had to leave him to be rescued by maidens. So after that I had to keep them all divided as best I could."

Serena sighs, glancing at the center console where Kai is. He has just untied the last rope mooring the boat to the dock and jumps aboard. Serena will not be joining him today, she has work to do.

"Heads up!"

Serena jumps at the command, then ducks just in time for a large wooden pole to swing over her head.

"Back to the rules," says Doug. "If you are on deck, stay forward of the cockpit unless I give orders otherwise. Sometimes I'll need everyone to move their weight around to keep the boat from heeling."

"It will be as you say." Serena nods.

Doug looks at her from under bushy eyebrows. "No formality. Hand me that rope."

"Right," Serena says, retrieving one end of a tightly coiled line and passing it to Doug.

"There are certain danger areas, as you have already seen," Doug continues. "You need to watch out for the boom when it swings across the deck. Also be aware of the riggin', the boom vang, and the mainsheet. Try to stay away from the jib and the jib sheets." Doug points as he talks, but it does nothing to help Serena with the sailing terminology.

"The deck can be slippery," says Doug. "Be careful. And if you go to the bow or the stern, hold on tight. The bouncing is exaggerated at the ends."

"And my maidens were able to stay out of the way in all this?" Serena asks.

"We had a few minor mishaps at first." Doug pauses. "But they are quick learners. It was my own pack I had more trouble with. They kept urgin' the maidens out of the way to do everything themselves. But it really takes all hands on deck to run this thing. Finally I sent all my wolves below deck so the maidens had a chance to run operations. Like I said, they are quick learners."

The back of her spine tingles, and Serena is becoming aware of the sideways glances the wolves give her. They aren't malicious, but they aren't exactly friendly. If it's not one group being stubborn bullies, it's the other.

There are shouts of excitement across the pier as the first boats pull away.

"Hold fast!" shouts Doug. "We're the last group to leave."

All five of their boats will be hovering behind the other racers so they can retrieve the Undine waiting on Hecate Island without anyone seeing. As the crowd on the pier disperses, Serena can observe each of their four other boats. On the tug, the wolves are still to one side while the maidens stand at another, but the line of division is no longer defined. It is blurred as some maidens dare to stand closer to the wolves and vice versa. Colin and Darcy's boys dart out in and out of each group, moved along by playful nudges. There are even a few interspecies conversations and food and goods trading hands.

The change in attitude gives her hope, and she turns to seek out the grumpiest pack mate on the sailboat. "Can I help you with that?"

He glares up at her, then spits onto the deck. "I don't need no help from a freakin' mermaid."

Serena was definitely successful in choosing the right wolf. If she can turn him, she can turn anyone.

"Your mother was a mermaid," she says, crossing her arms.

The man jumps to his feet. "What did you say about my—" he cuts himself short as his eyebrows arch with realization.

Not wanting to give him a chance to respond, Serena bends to resume his work. She finishes coiling the rope and looks up at him. "The lines are good, but a figure-eight knot is better on the free end so the rope can't be pulled through the mast."

"Right," mumbles the wolf.

"What did you say?" Serena stands, looking him in the eye.

It takes him by surprise, and he stumbles over his words. "I said you are… right."

"Good!" Serena smiles. "I'm here to help. We all are."

Serena moves across the deck, pulling another pack member down just as the boom swings overhead.

"Like I said—quick learners," she hears Doug say.

* * *

"Maidens in the water!"

The shout causes the crew to scramble into action. The fleet of five ships has remained toward the rear, and now they all approach the northern end of Hecate Island. Already pack members are pulling out ropes and throwing them over anything up top that will hold.

Serena runs to the port side, eyes scanning for colored scales just below the surface of the water. She can spot sporadic bubbles popping up, a sign of her maidens, but they don't show themselves.

Frowning, Serena turns around.

"We ain't got all day," says Doug from the cockpit in the center of the sailboat.

"Look." Serena points to the starboard side.

Directly beside them, an Ungainly trawler is keeping pace. If any Undine were to board now, humans would see. In fact, one of them waves as Doug pops his head out of the cockpit to look.

"We need a distraction," says Serena.

"Your boyfriend is comin' to help." Doug points out the center console boat that is quickly making its way to the other side of the Ungainly trawler. Serena spots two of her more subtly-shaded maidens on deck with Kai, their scales fashioned to look like bathing suits. Skimpy bathing suits.

Almost immediately the men on the Ungainly trawler cross the deck to exchange friendly racing gestures and shouts to Kai and his crew.

"Should we risk it now?" asks Doug.

Serena shakes her head. "It still isn't enough. They could look over at any time." Eyes scanning the resources on board, she cannot come up with a solution—until she spots the white canvas wrapped in three tight bundles. "This is a sailboat," says Serena.

Doug looks at her. "You're just now realizing' that?"

"Doug." Serena looks at him, fingers jittering with excitement. "This is a *sail* boat."

"Ooooh." Doug winks at her. "Now I'm trackin'. Come here and steer for a minute."

"Me?" asks Serena.

"Yes, genius, you." He climbs out of the cockpit leaving the wheel to spin on its own.

The boat lurches toward the island and Serena scurries to grabs hold of the wheel, steadying it.

Already, Doug has begun shouting orders. "Hoist the sails!"

The crew scrambles into action. Hands pull down on thick ropes and crisp, white sails rise into the air. The mainsail flaps violently in the wind, sounding like a series of gunshots. Next go up the two smaller sails on either side.

"Serena!" shouts Doug. "Turn the wheel to nine o'clock."

Blank-faced, Serena looks at the wood-carved wheel under her hands, then back at Doug. "We don't have clocks."

He rolls his eyes. "What about degrees—do you have those?"

"Yes," Serena mumbles under her breath.

"Forty-five o' them, then."

Grasping the wheel so hard her knuckles turn white, Serena rotates it to the left. The ship responds and they veer away from the Ungainly trawler.

"Trim the jib sheets!" Doug's voice bellows above the wind.

Pack members pull on each of the smaller sails until canvas ceases flapping and instead curves gently away from the wind.

"Trim the main!" Doug shouts.

Catching on to the jargon, Serena's eyes dart to the middle sail. It takes almost all hands on deck to push the boom into position.

By now, the pack members are sweating—their brows furrowed with concentration. A hard wind pounds at the boat.

"Stay the course!" Doug tells Serena.

Her hands are still gripping the wheel. She swears she can already feel blisters forming.

One final push on the boom, and the main sail goes taut.

"Ease off!"

The crew releases pressure, allowing the boom to come back inch by inch.

"Hold!"

The main sail calms, matching the subtle curve of its smaller counterparts. The crew continues to work, tying off lines and securing the deck. Their cheeks are red and chapped by the cold wind, but that doesn't keep the smile from their faces. Sailing is gratifying work.

A small square of blue flapping in the sky, dwarfed by giant white sails, catches Serena's eyes. The signal reminds her the maidens are still in the water waiting for the all clear. She motions for Doug to take the wheel again and climbs out of the cockpit. A quick glance at the Ungainly trawler shows they are still occupied with Kai and the maidens on the center console. Quickly, Serena runs to the rails. The maidens below sense activity. They are veering closer to the surface though they are still hesitant to poke their heads above water.

Serena takes a deep breath of the chilly arctic air, then lets it out in a slow whistle. Movement underneath the water grows agitated. The sharp edge of a tail fin slices into the air but disappears again. Pushing out more sound, Serena sings the call to Assembly. Responding to the familiar tune, maidens streamline toward the boat, their colors sleek rainbow streaks under the water.

Looking to her side, she finds pack members on the sailboat lined up along the railing, staring at the spectacle.

"Maiden overboard!" she barks at them. She knows they too will respond to a familiar, or familiar-ish call, and they do. All except one spotter jumps away from the rails, taking up position at various ropes. Loose ends are tossed into the water, and a similar operation to what occurred on the tugboat, albeit to a larger scale, is performed. When a line goes rigid, crew members pull. Shortly after, the ocean delivers a yellow-scaled maiden, the color of warm afternoon light. Arching up until she is just a silhouette against the glowing medallion behind her, she begins her descent. Fins transform into legs and she lands as softly as a sun drop onto the deck of the sailboat.

"Hold!" a spotter at starboard yells to Serena.

Serena stops singing, and no more maidens emerge from the water. One of the Ungainlies is looking toward the sailboat.

A commotion on the other side of the Ungainly vessel attracts attention. The captain on Kai's cruiser is spinning in tight, fast circles, showing off.

Whoops and hollers rise up from the humans and the curious watcher turns back around.

Serena begins singing again, her tune faster and more urgent. Maidens emerge from the water, sometimes two to a rope. Downwind, even more are boarding the tug. The ship is at least far enough away so the action isn't exactly discernable.

At the helm, Doug counts maidens as they land on the deck. "That's everyone for us," he says. "Run up the all clear."

Before his own crew can respond, one of the Undine pull a green flag from the storage bin, clips it to a rope, and runs it up the line. The pack member standing closest glares at her with idle hands.

Serena sighs. *This is going to take some work.*

Chapter Thirty

Waiting until all five ships are flying their green flags, crews turn to their tasks of navigating the racecourse while the majority of the maidens and about half of the pack members move below deck. Recalling the maps in her head, Serena mentally sails through the route ahead of them. Today will be full of passages twisting and turning through a labyrinth of hundreds of islands, and the maneuvering has already begun. Serena remembers to duck as the boom sweeps above her head while they adjust course to skirt the first island. Like trying to swim through a swarm of jellyfish, captains must work to avoid the dangerous sting of running their ships aground.

Leaving Doug to concentrate on his task, Serena finds a safe spot out of the way and turns her attention to the terrain of western British Columbia. Pine trees crowd rocky shores, covering gently rolling hills and, further back, taller mountains. The forest green is a stark contrast to the dark-blue water lapping at the islands.

"The Inside Passage," says someone behind Serena. "Where ice-covered mountains rise straight out of the water and salmon practically leap onto the decks."

Serena narrows her eyes on the intruder. "Is that some kind of euphemism for my maidens?"

"No. I read about this area in a magazine." He sits down next to her, and her breath catches as she recognizes Xavier. Heart pounding, her hand automatically goes to her stomach.

His eyes flicker to the movement, and the small smile on his face tells her he knows he has made her nervous. Leaning back, he puts his hands behind his head and closes his eyes. He has less facial hair than most of the other pack members, and his cheeks and chin have soft curves. There are no sharp angles about this one, at least not physically. "The sun feels good," he murmurs.

Serena's skin begins to tingle, as if him mentioning it makes the sun even hotter. "Not nearly as good as the moon," she responds, tugging on her hood to keep her face in the shade.

An unexpected gust of wind picks up. The crew responds, a combination of Doug's orders and their own instincts. In short order they have adjusted the sails to work with the new conditions.

"They're good," says Serena.

"*They* know what they're doing." His emphasis doesn't go unnoticed.

Serena glances at him sideways. "I hear things didn't go so well yesterday."

"You here to make peace?"

Serena shrugs. "For those who are willing."

He snorts. "We had peace back at the trailer park."

"Knock it off, Xavier," Doug warns from the cockpit.

Serena hadn't realized he was paying attention to the conversation. As she looks around, all of the wolves are throwing weary, sideways glances—but not at her.

"Your trailer park was being shut down," Serena says, dismissing his comment. "All we can do now is look ahead." Serena gazes past the pointed end of the bow cutting through pristine water. The tangled, meandering river bends around a myriad of islands teeming with wildlife. Beyond them, snow-frosted mountains stretch to infinity. "Besides," she says. "You can't tell me you prefer the view of a bunch of rickety trailers to this."

But he isn't looking at the scenery. His eyes are closed. "I prefer the way it used to be. Fish in the sea, wolves in the woods."

"Are you going to try to force us back to that?" asks Serena, her tone void of former kindness.

"Nah. Don't have to." He settles back into his spot. "Things will fall apart on their own."

"You sound very sure of yourself." The cool and peaceful ambiance of the scenery dissipates as Serena's cheeks heat with anger.

The smile is back on his face. He takes a deep breath in, looking like he is finally enjoying The Migration. "As sure as your king is dead."

Serena lashes out with a closed fist before she can stop herself. In the next instant, Xavier is face down on the ground, and Serena is standing over him shouting, "The king was my father, and the orange-scaled maiden on the beach you killed was my friend!"

Xavier picks himself up from the deck, rubbing his jaw. A trickle of blood creeps from his lower lip. Touching it gingerly with his finger, he glares at Serena. "Give me an excuse, mermaid. I've been waitin' for this all week."

Behind her, the rest of the crew has gone silent. Even the wind gives momentary pause, and the sails go limp above them.

Talking herself down, Serena relaxes her shoulders. *This is not the proper way to rule.*

"If it's any consolation," says Xavier. "Your father didn't taste nearly so good as the maiden."

To hell with propriety.

Serena curls her fist again, this time calling forth hardened scales overlapping her knuckles. She rears her elbow back and swings, twisting her body to gain momentum. Her arm jars as she makes contact, raking three long scratches across his face from her scaled knuckles. The wolf flies back into the railing, almost going overboard. Xavier's palm goes to his cheek, and he spits blood. "Even the high and mighty queen has claws of her own," he growls. But his voice is unnaturally deep. He has begun to change, and Serena realizes she played right into what he wanted.

"Stand down before you make things worse for yourself, Xavier," Doug moves to stand next to Serena.

Xavier doubles over until he is on the deck on all fours. His clothes rip as his body transforms underneath, tufts of spiky brown hair pushing through his skin. He looks up at Doug with red eyes. "Things can't get much worse than this," he says. He throws his head back, howling as bones in his face break apart to form a long snout.

Serena steps back, glancing around for something with which to fight. Suddenly she wishes she hadn't locked up her trident.

"How is he changing?" she asks Doug. "It isn't a full moon. Are they still somehow taking Liam's blood?"

Doug pulls her back, putting himself in between the wolf and Serena. "Liam hasn't given blood since you killed Alaric."

"Can you change too?" asks Serena. Doug's wolf might have a better chance against Xavier.

Doug shakes his head, and Serena can see the muscles in his arms tighten with tension.

Glancing around with frantic eyes, Serena needs to find something that can help her. The other pack members have already circled the transforming wolf, but there is no telling how well they can keep him contained.

In fighting werewolves before, Serena always had her trident or her bow and arrows.

Stop moaning about the things you don't have and concentrate on what you do have, she thinks.

Serena looks up at the tall masts but almost immediately rules them out. If she climbs them and the wolf goes after her, he could put the ship out of commission only halfway through The Migration.

Backing up, her eyes are pinned to the werewolf inside the circle of pack members. He is fully transformed and already fighting his brothers, several who have armed themselves with various blunt instruments—one even has an axe. The fact that they are kin means nothing to Xavier, and the feeling seems to be mutual.

Several pack members are already battered and bloody. Doug is on the ground, clutching his leg that is bent at an awkward angle.

Glancing out at the ocean behind her, Serena knows she can always take up safety in her own element. But she has maidens below deck she can't leave behind in the wake of a rampaging werewolf.

Two heads poke out of the hatch leading below deck, but they are quickly forced back under as a flailing body is thrown their way.

Xavier's wolf has made it out of the circle. Pack members left standing give chase, but the wolf is too fast. Sharp talons stretched out in front of him, he swipes at the jib sail rope, and the canvas falls, folding over one half of the deck and trapping the remaining pack members.

Now only Serena and the werewolf are left. He stares at her, chest heaving. But determined eyes tell her he has plenty of fight left.

Serena swallows hard, her own heart pounding. The pair side step, circling each other. Toes hitting something hard, Serena glances down to find the axe, flung aside during the fight. She bends to pick it up, and the werewolf leaps while she is still in a precarious crouch.

Rolling onto her back, Serena grips the axe handle at either end, holding it like a shield in front of her. As the wolf comes down on top of her, Serena thrusts out with the axe and her legs. Both hit the wolf's soft underside, and she parry's him over.

The wolf lands hard on his feet. He slips, skittering across the wet deck before slamming into a mast.

Aware of the precious few moments she has, Serena runs toward the main sail with the axe. Quickly, she slices through the rope that prevents the boom from swinging across the deck. On her feet now, she faces the werewolf. Saliva dripping from in between yellowed teeth, he coils back on his haunches, then leaps. Claws extended and mouth wide open, he locks his red eyes on his target.

Serena glances to the cockpit where Doug is dragging himself. She nods to him. He pulls himself the rest of the way in, reaches up, and spins the wheel to the right.

The boat lurches with movement, and the wind catches the sail from a different angle. A low whistle of a large mass moving quickly behind her alerts Serena to duck. The boom comes swinging across the deck. Flying over Serena's head, the massive cylindrical piece of wood catches the werewolf at the chest. He flies back with it and into the water.

The entire crew, now free of the jib, runs to the rails. The boat tilts with the weight change, and they all hover above the werewolf frantically splashing in the water.

Cheers rise up from the crew. Serena steps back from the railing, breathing hard and shaking hard from the fight. Maidens emerge from below deck at the commotion. They glide cautiously through the wolves toward their queen and the railing. Small smiles light their faces as they look at Serena, deducing what happened.

She licks her lips, trying to gain her composure.

The wolf is barely keeping his head above water, and he can't spare the energy to take his human form.

"Aren't you going to pull him in?" Serena asks.

No one makes a move toward the ropes.

"Nothin' but trouble, that one," says Doug, leaning with one elbow on the rail, glancing in the water. The sailboat continues to move forward and soon will leave him behind. He is already out of reach of any rope they can throw. "Maybe we ought to let another boat pick him up. If he survives that long…"

"Or if he doesn't," another pack member pipes up to the response of more laughter.

Two maidens step forward, looking at their queen. They will offer their help but only if she allows it. Grim faced, Serena nods. Like it or not, even the big and bad wolves are her subjects, and she intends to see them all to safety.

The maidens step up onto the railing, closer to the stern, and dive in. Serena tracks their colors with her eyes, one bright yellow and one bright red. They crisscross paths back forth, enjoying their time in the water before they reach the wolf. Their colors blend, and for a moment, all Serena can see is orange scales. Sasha is with her again, lending strength from the afterlife and giving her own blessing that her murderer's life is spared.

The maidens stop in front of the wolf, but he is too far gone to notice. They disappear and a second later, so does the wolf.

Several moments go by without any sign of all three of them.

"They drownin' him?" Doug asks, his tone indifferent.

"Not today." Serena smiles. She scans the surface of the water, then points. "There."

A blur of colors underwater is racing toward the top. As the Undine emerge, they each have their hands on either side of the wolf. Thrusting out in unison, they throw him toward the boat. His limp body slams into the side railing, and several pack members have to sink their fingers into his wet fur, latching on, and pulling him over the rest of the way.

He sprawls out in a sopping mess, unconscious but breathing.

"Bring him below," says Doug. "Put him in restraints."

It takes more than one pack member to heave him along the deck, and they shoot surprised but impressed glances to the maidens in the water who were able to throw him.

Ropes are finally tossed into the water, and the maidens are helped onboard. As the crew begins to clean up from the fight, Serena surveys the damage to all of her people. Doug has definitely broken his leg. Plus, there are probably several stitches needed just judging by the various gashes on faces, arms, and hands.

"Run up the healer flag," Serena tells a maiden. She looks back at the wheelhouse. "Doug—for Poseidon's sake, let someone else do that and rest until we can get your leg looked at."

Frowning, Doug relinquishes control of the wheel to another. The red healer flag is run up the line, and the boat slows to allow the tug to catch up with them.

"You are well?" Serena asks the yellow maiden that is still dripping with saltwater.

"Yes, your majesty." The maiden nods.

The pair steps aside to make room for those hauling the jib sail back into place. Maidens and werewolves alike are working side by side to accomplish the task.

"In less than a day you completely turned around the atmosphere on the ship," the maiden says with awe. "Look at everyone. They are actually talking to each other. And *liking* it."

"I picked a fight with the right wolf," says Serena, keeping her voice low. "I may not be so lucky next time."

"Hey, sundrop," Doug calls out. "You want to pilot for a while?"

Eyes going wide with delighted anticipation, a smile breaks across the maiden's face. "Aye, aye, sir," she says, bounding to cockpit.

The pack members make way, and Doug is able to put every pair of hands, whether claws or scales hide underneath, to good use on the sailboat. Only one sopping wet werewolf sits below deck.

Thank you, Serena mouths to Doug as she takes up a rope of her own.

He responds with a salute.

Chapter Thirty-One

The rest of the day consists of a string of long, thin fiords that cut through the high peaks of British Columbia's west-coast mountains, paralleling the Pacific Ocean. Due to several narrow passages, Doug decides to order the sails taken down, and the crew uses pure motor power, relying on GPS and other instruments to get through without running aground. Everyone is tense, but at least those with injuries have something else to focus on besides their pain.

Because they have had to slow their speed by half, some of the other ships have caught up to the sailboat. When the center console pulls up alongside them, Kai is standing at the railing, surveying the damage and the injured.

His questioning eyes shoot to Serena.

"All is well, Kai Forest," she assures him, talking loud enough so her voice will cross the short distance over the sea to the next boat.

"As you say, your majesty." He bows. "Until tonight."

Nodding her consent, Serena knows he will not let another night pass without being with her. Judging from the dark circles under his eyes, he has not been sleeping well, and a night together would benefit him most of all.

She opens her mouth to say something else, but the center console speeds up to make way for the tug just arriving. Both boats cut their engines, and crews exchange ropes, binding the ships together. A plank slides across from rail to rail, and all three Undine healers cross over. Darcy is delayed as her boys insist on crossing the 'pirate's plank' with her.

"Not now," she tells them. "Maybe you can ride the sailboat tomorrow, but if you keep asking the answer is going to be no."

Colin intervenes, carting their three sullen boys away.

Darcy finally crosses, and Serena reaches up to help her down. "Doug needs you," she says.

The Undine healers focus on superficial wounds. Serena can't recall the last time a maiden, or a guard, had broken bones in their leg.

Setting her bag next to Doug, Darcy takes stock of her patient. "Is sailing your own boat too dangerous for you?" she asks him.

He grunts as she gingerly prods the knee above the break. "No, but keepin' these wolves in line might be."

"It was a wolf?" She looks up at Serena, eyebrows raised.

"Xavier," Serena says.

Darcy shakes her head. "One of Alaric's favorites." She pauses suddenly. "He must've transformed. But how?"

Both Doug and Serena shrug.

"No matter," says Darcy. "I will examine him later. But first, we need to set this bone."

Serena looks at what she has been trying to avoid all day. Sharp white bone protrudes from the side of Doug's calf.

"It is a clean break," murmurs Darcy. "No major blood vessels damaged. Serena, grab him at the shoulders and hold him steady."

Repositioning herself, Serena gives Doug an apologetic smile, then reaches just under his arm, trying to keep her jittery fingers under control. A pack member sidles in next to her to help, and Serena is grateful for the solid shoulder touching hers.

Darcy settles herself at Doug's feet, sliding the palms of her hands under the heel of his foot. "This is going to hurt," she tells him. "But if you move your leg after I pull it into place, it might pop right back out, and we'll have to do it all over again."

Doug's face turns pale, but he nods, lips pulled back in a grimace.

Her hands tighten around his foot. "Okay here we go. Hold him steady up top."

Both Serena and the pack member squeeze Doug's shoulders.

"On the count of three. One... two—" Darcy yanks suddenly.

Doug throws his head back, howling in pain. Eyes wild, he sits up, glaring at Darcy. "Learn to count, woman!"

Ignoring her patient, Darcy is already fashioning a splint.

Serena looks down at Doug's leg. The bone has disappeared back under the skin leaving only a trickle of blood behind, like her scales. She smiles and pats Doug on the chest. "Now you know what is like to be Undine."

Darcy gives Serena a small smile.

"Thank you," Serena says as she stands up. "I'm going to see if anyone else needs help."

Behind her, Doug is still grumbling. "One, two, *three*. Three comes right after two. It ain't that hard."

Spotting Simone's red scales easily across the deck, Serena knows Ungainly crews might do the same. She glances at the pack members assigned to keep watch. The sailboat hovers in a protected area just before a large sound and so far, no ships but their own fleet are nearby.

"Any luck finding the hydrocoral?" Serena asks Simone.

"No, your majesty," Simone is collecting leftover gauze and dressings to store back in her dry bag. "You?"

Serena looks at the hatch leading below, hoping Xavier is well restrained. "I didn't even have a chance to ask him about the empty ginger vial before things got… hairy."

"The guards aboard the tug are insisting you return with us." Simone motions to the boat idling right next to them.

Not having realized it before, Serena notices she is being watched by three of the large Undine guards, who look ready to bound over at any moment. "It might be for the best," says Serena. "I don't want to incite any more fights should Xavier awake. Tell your healers to finish quickly. We want to be underway before any Ungainly ships spot us."

Serena steps up to the railing to cross the plank. The ships move up and down with small waves, and it is enough to cause her to stop to catch her balance halfway through.

"Look!" comes a shout from the sailboat. "Movement in the water!"

All eyes glance to the caller, then follow his point out to sea. A large surface area bubbles up slightly, then goes back down. It is far too much displacement to be Undine in the water.

For a moment, Serena thinks it might be an oil slick, like she heard the Ungainlies talking about. Then another bubble surfaces directly next to the ship, and a huge humpback whale noses up out of the water. Those near the railing give shouts of delighted surprise—backing up then coming forward to catch another glimpse of the majestic beast.

The nose disappears and a rounded back curves the surface, spraying water from its blow hole in greeting. More are spotted further out. Their broad heads are dark grey with bump-like knobs. Flippers span further than the width of the tugboat, and the giant tail always gives a final flap before the entire whale vanishes underwater.

Serena jumps into the tugboat just as the closest whale begins to sing. Only snatches of the tune can be heard above water, but everyone on board listens closely. In a way, the series of notes and clicks are not unlike the ones the Undine use in The Deep.

"Teaching them females some of your songs?" Doug shouts at her from the sailboat, his bad leg elevated on a stool for rest.

Beside him, Darcy tells her patient to hush but she has a smile on her face.

"Actually." Conner leans over the tug railing next to Serena for a better look. "It is the males that sing. They are complicated songs that can go on for an hour or more, then they will repeat it."

"Why?" asks Serena.

"Probably various reasons. Mating calls, most likely."

"Ew," says Robbie. All three of Darcy's boys have joined to watch the whales.

"What do you think they are chattin' about?" Conner asks the boy.

Robbie looks thoughtfully out to the water. "They're hungry. That one is tellin' all the rest where the fish are."

"No, look." Aiden points. "Those two are about to fight. He's singing to tell the others to back off."

"That's stupid."

"You're stupid."

"Knock it off you two." Darcy crosses over to the tug. "Or I'll make you both sing—right now in front of everyone."

They boys wander off separately to avoid any such embarrassing punishment, leaving Serena and the pack member to watch the pod of whales in peace. The tones of the song have gone deeper.

"Maybe it is a warning," suggest Serena.

"Warning for what?" asks Conner.

Taking a step forward to lean against the rail herself, Serena scans the open water in the sound, from the lazy fins of the humpback whale, over pristine, smooth water, and straight to three large fishing boats.

"Those." Serena points.

Fishing nets hang halfway into the passage all the way from the shore, and behind those, where the sound opens up further, there are dozens more boats. Orange floaters mark submerged nets raking the bottom of the ocean. The salmon have no chance of escape, and it would be a miracle if the whales made it.

The last of the healers make their way back onto the tug, and the plank and ropes connecting the two boats are taken down. Each pilot issues orders as they prepare to navigate the labyrinth of nets.

Maidens and pack members disappear below deck as their fleet move into the line of sight of the Ungainly boats. Just as the tug begins winding through the maze, booming claps thunder across the sound. A group of humpbacks closer to the shore have found themselves boxed in and are unable to move forward.

Squinting in the direction of the commotion, Serena quickly walks to the other side of the tug shielded from prying Ungainly eyes. "Aiden?"

Darcy's oldest has found a quiet corner by himself to play cards. He looks up at Serena.

"Do you mind holding this for me?" She unties her dry bag from her waist and hands it to him. "It carries one of Societies most valued treasures."

"Your crown?" Aiden looks at the bag, confused.

"No—the Undine Ancestral Book."

He glances at her as if he can just the value of the book just by the expression on her face, then back at the bag. "Okay. I'll watch it for you. Where are you going?"

Serena steps onto the trailing and winks at Aiden. "I'm going to go sing."

Chapter Thirty-Two

She jumps off the ship, piking her body then stretching out for the dive. Icy cold envelops her body. The shock of the temperature difference between here and the water at home causes her gills to contract. Sputtering, she hovers just below the surface as she works to force them open. At the same time, scales lengthen melding her legs together. Her second skin has become lazy from the lack of use, and the sharp edges poking their way through is more painful than she remembers.

It has been only a few days since she has last had her fins, but she is out of practice. Sputtering and dog-paddling underneath the hull of the boat, this is her clumsiest transformation in years. Once she is full Undine, and recovered from it, Serena swims to the other side of the ship.

The clear blue waters of the sound are teeming with life. It is spawning season, and schools of pink salmon are buzzing with activity, preparing for their journey up river to their own birthing grounds.

Serena starts forward, schools of fish darting out of her way as she swims. Bobbing orange at the surface catches her eye, and Serena remembers what it signals just in time. She darts out of the way as a frayed net swoops past her, scooping up fish she scared into its path. The bottom of the net is rigged with heavy rubber wheels that crawl over the rocky bottom. Frowning at the noise and destruction the net creates, not to mention the sheer amount of life it is destroying, Serena reaches for the knife strapped at her waist. She changes direction and follows the net up to where the web of lines converge into one thick rope.

Wrapping her tail around to steady herself, she begins sawing through the cord. The knife is dull, and she has to push hard to make any headway with it. Arm tiring, Serena pauses to work out a cramp forming in her shoulder. Above the surface, a loud motor whirs to life and the entire network of rope jerks up with Serena still attached to it. Panicked, she pulls away but her tail is caught as the net tightens. The motors above speed up, and the water turns lighter the closer Serena is pulled to the surface. She turns back to sawing at the rope, this time to save herself as much as the fish.

The cramp in her shoulder starts up again, but she ignores the pain and keeps pushing the knife back and forth into the rope. She swears if she were on an Ungainly beach she'd be doing that sweating thing.

The rope just above her head breaches the surface.

By the grace of Poseidon! Serena screams in her head, heart pounding and vision going blurry with panic.

One last push through, and the rope snaps. The entire net floats to the ground, and the salmon inside scatter, several confused fish bumping into Serena as they flee. Serena turns her attention to the rope and is able to untangle her tail.

As her pulse settles, Serena gives weary glances to any other ropes, leaving the fish trapped inside to their fate. Toward the far end of the sound, Serena spots the agitated whales. She watches them as she straps her knife back around her waist.

Boxed in on three sides, the whales barely have room to turn around. Even if they could, maneuvering their large bodies through the maze of nets would be impossible unless they knew the exact path to take.

Humming a low, slow tune, Serena keeps it quiet enough so only the whales in front of her will catch it, working to copy the tone quality of the whale song she heard earlier without mimicking it exactly. She wants to entice them to follow her—not warn them away.

Emphasizing her case with whistles and clicks, Serena works to reason with them. Moving into a higher frequency, Serena's call grows louder as she adds vibration to her song. Slowly, they begin to turn toward her.

Serena backs up as she swims, making room for the mammoths of the sea. Only one of them lingers, staying away from Serena. As the large body alternately sinks and rises, Serena spots a small calf behind it. The mother needs further convincing that Serena isn't a danger to her calf.

Serena ends her song and doesn't repeat it as supposedly the whales do. Instead, Serena pulls out her knife. She swims over to the closest netting and begins to cut it. Mindful of keeping her tail well clear of the entanglements, she works her way patiently through the rope.

Whales are intelligent creatures, and Serena doesn't doubt the mother is watching her actions. Finally, the rope breaks apart, widening the path out.

Following the same trail the other whales took, Serena moves to the next rope. The lead male begins his song. It is just as complicated a tune as before, but this time Serena recognizes one of her signature whistles within the layers of harmony. She pauses her work briefly and smiles. He has taken part of her song to let the other whales know he has found the way out.

Just as Serena cuts through the rope, she jumps back at a large mass beside her. It is the mother whale, grey body gliding through the water past the fishing nets. Swimming on the other side, the calf peers at Serena over his mother's back. He slows, giving Serena three quick whistles, then hurries to catch up to his retreating mother.

There is a series of shouts above the surface—the fisherman are agitated because of their damaged nets. Serena moves along, looking back with satisfaction at her trail of destruction. Keeping a respectful distance, Serena follows the mother and calf until she reaches the tugboat.

Before she can even surface on the private side of the boat, a rope hits the water. Serena reaches up, grasping the frayed ends. She manages to transform into legs before she is hoisted out of the water. Flying through air then landing hard on the deck, her feet ring with the sudden stop. She nods to the pack mates who pulled her aboard.

"You helped the whales, didn't you?" asks Aiden.

Serena turns to find him holding her dry bag in one hand and his playing cards in the other. "Yes," she says. She wipes excess saltwater from her skin and scales then repositions the knife at her waist.

Aiden hands her the dry bag, eyebrows furrowed. "Just by singing to them?"

"Well—"

"I could never do that." He doesn't wait for her answer. "I can't sing."

"It wasn't just about the singing," says Serena. "It was about showing trust and making friends." She ties the dry bag off in a strong knot at her hip. "And I know you can do that."

"You do?"

"You already have." Serena pats her dry bag and smiles down at the boy. He stands up, and she has to step back to look up at him.

He is getting tall quick.

"Do you know how to play poker?" he asks.

"No," says Serena. She glances around the deck. Everyone above is fairly occupied, there are no emergencies or problems. It seems the wolves and maidens are still getting along. Up at the front, Kiera and the seasick-prone pack mate are talking, their shoulders touching as they look out over the railing. Serena's eyes drift back to Aiden, falling on the needle marks marring his otherwise smooth skin along the inside of his arm. There is no doubt he is taking Liam's blood, but his parents have been unable to get him to tell the truth about who is giving it to him.

Serena sits down, motioning Aiden to do the same. "Maybe you can teach me."

"Okay." He smiles and hops down beside her, exhibiting a boyish excitement he has just about outgrown, or convinced himself he has. He deals seven cards each. "All my brothers ever want to play is Go Fish or Old Maid."

"Is that supposed to be some kind of joke?" Serena looks at Aiden.

His eyes go wide. "No… I—its Old *Maid*, not Old Maiden."

"Teasing." Serena smiles.

"Oh." The boy lets out a nervous laugh. "Okay so the point of the game is to have the highest-value hand. You can do that with two, three, or four of the same card, a flush—which is five cards all of the same suit—or a straight—which is numbers of any suit in order. There is also a full house and a straight flush."

"I found this one left behind on a beach one time." Serena holds the Queen of Spades.

Pausing in his explanation, Aiden looks up. "Maybe it was some sort of sign."

"Maybe," Serena mumbles, looking at the two-faced queen, draped in red and yellow robes with a crown atop her head.

"You aren't supposed to show me your cards." Aiden gently takes the queen from her hand and slides it back in her stack. "Don't worry. I'll forget that you have it." He smiles at her.

The boyish excitement is back and Serena can't help but smile herself.

Aiden lays down a pair of sevens.

"You know you can talk to me, right?" Serena gestures to his outstretched arm.

He follows her glance, then quickly retracts his arm and puts on a jacket that was stuffed under a bench behind him.

"We are friends, right?" Serena asks.

He looks up at her from under bushy eyebrows, then shrugs.

"Anything you want to tell me stays between us. I won't tell your parents if you don't want me to."

Waiting patiently for some kind of response, Serena watches Aiden flick back the edges of the cards in his hand without focusing on them, as if he is working his way through a debate in his own head.

Finally, he lets out a breath. "I will keep that in mind, thank you." Shoulders hunching with a burden he refuses to unload, Aiden suddenly looks older than his years.

"As you say," Serena says, hiding her disappointment behind her own stack of cards fanned out in her hand. She runs her tongue over her teeth, aware of a slick, bitter film forming in her mouth.

After a few hands of poker, Aiden breaks the silence. "Are you okay?" he asks Serena.

Rubbing her temples, coaxing them through a forming headache, Serena puts down her cards. "Mind if we continue the game a little later? I think I need to rest."

Aiden blinks and nods his head. Rising after a final farewell nod to Aiden, Serena slips below deck and into one of the hammocks swinging in a darkened corner. She closes her eyes and takes stock of her body. Besides the headache and the weird bitter taste in her mouth, her skin feels flaky and dry, and her lungs are tight. She can't take a full breath without them contracting too soon. It is not painful but definitely worrisome.

Running through a list of possible causes to her ailments, Serena realizes this is how she began to feel when she was out of the water too long when spending time at the wolf camp. But now it is tenfold, and she just did take a dip in the water.

It wasn't until after that when I started to feel sick.

Serena's eyes fly open in realization. The Undine cannot touch these waters, less they all fall ill before reaching their destination.

Chapter Thirty-Three

Serena cannot force herself up to warn others of the poisoned waters, she is too dizzy and weak. Her rest is interrupted constantly by shouts above as the crew maneuvers through treacherous passages. She vaguely recalls this was supposed to be one of the most difficult legs of the race. When she does drift off, she dreams of being caught up in an Ungainly net, just to be brought to their ship and stabbed with needles. Serena wakes up shivering.

"Serena?"

Focusing on a familiar voice, Serena drags herself from her haze and opens her eyes. Darcy's face hovers above the hammock.

"We're here," Darcy says.

"Where is here?" Serena barely manages to croak out the words.

Frowning in consternation, Darcy puts a hand to Serena's forehead. "Another island. I can't remember which—I've lost track of all their names. It's camp for the night."

Serena glances around the large, empty room at the same time the order to disembark is given above. Panicked, she jolts up. The shift in weight causes the hammock to tilt right and Serena falls out. Darcy manages to catch her, and they both stumble across the slippery floor before gaining their balance.

"Why is everyone getting off?" asks Serena, attempting to hold her own weight. "Ungainlies will spot us!" She heads for the ladder well with Darcy close behind.

"We have the island to ourselves," Darcy says. "All five of our boats are docked here—the rest of the racers are across the channel."

Serena pauses at the bottom of the stairs, one hand resting on the railing. "Okay… that's good."

"You look dehydrated. Does that happen to mermaids?" asks Darcy.

"I've been out of the water too long," says Serena.

Darcy puts her hand on her hip. "That seems an easy fix."

"Not quite." Serena attempts a smile. "This water does not agree with us. We need to spread the word my maidens cannot enter it."

"I can do that," Darcy says. "Come on. Let's get you into the open air."

Helping Serena up the steep stairwell, Darcy begins issuing orders at the first person she sees and doesn't stop doling directions out the whole way off the boat, down the dilapidated pier, and onto land. Finally, Liam stops the hobbling pair of women.

"You alright, sis?"

"No, she is not," Darcy answers before Serena can even lift her head. "Where is Kai?"

Liam points to a tent sitting further in the tree line. It stands alone and is surrounded by thick shrubbery so no one could even consider setting up close by.

"Liam," Serena speaks up. "Can you please take care of everything? I will need to be with Kai tonight."

"Sure thing," he says. "I got this. Most everyone is finally behaving. You just get better."

"Thank you," Serena mouths over her shoulder as Darcy shoos Liam away.

Shortly after, Serena hears Liam sending scouts out to retrieve Kai and the Undine healers. Hobbling her way into the tent with Darcy's assistance, Serena pushes aside the mat that has been laid out for her. She curls up on the floor and closes her eyes.

When she opens them, it is pitch black outside, and she is next to something damp. It stirs, and Serena scoots away, now wide awake.

"You're alive."

"Kai?" Serena pushes herself upright, eyes flying open. "You didn't go swimming did you? The water will make you sick. Very sick."

The darkened form begins to take shape as Serena's eyes adjust to the low light. "That is all you, Moonshine. You were sweating out a fever for a while there."

Serena realizes she is the one that is wet. "My apologies," she mumbles, attempting to wipe some of it off. "This stuff seemed way more attractive on you."

"Here." Kai laughs, handing her a blanket that was tossed aside with all the other Ungainly sleeping paraphernalia.

Clearing her head from the fog of sleep while she takes her time wiping off with the blanket, Serena admits she feels much better after the rest. There is still a small tinge of a headache, and she is weak. Her arms drop from the exertion of using the blanket.

Kai scoots closer, taking it from her. He balls up one corner, dabbing at her temple and forehead. Up close, Serena can see detailed features of Kai's face. His eyes glisten with affection, but there are dark circles underneath. His cheeks are pulled up in a smile, but they are too gaunt. He hasn't been eating well.

Serena can't even send him into the waters for restoration. She leans into his soft touch, unexpected tears springing to her eyes.

Setting down the blanket, Kai gathers her up in his strong arms, holding her while she weeps.

"I'm sorry," stutters Serena. "I just didn't expect this to be so… hard. Maidens will get sick if they don't go in the water, but they will get sick if they do."

Warm lips move to her ear. "We are strong, and we have the wolves by our side. We will make it. *You* are going to make it, because I will hold you together until we get there."

Serena breathes in his salty scent. No matter where they are, Kai will always smell like home. Calming herself, Serena puts her forehead against his. Warmth envelops her, and she looks up. The canopy covering the mesh ceiling vent is gone, leaving an unobstructed view of the night sky. Moonlight filters in, bathing the couple in its warmth.

"See," says Kai. "There are other ways to heal."

Serena looks into his sea-green eyes, rimmed by dark lashes. Golden-brown specks flare bright under the rays of the moon. "I've missed you," says Serena.

"I'm here now." Kai's palm moves to Serena's hip.

She flushes under the heat of his gaze.

"Feel better?" he asks.

"I'm getting there," she whispers, her heart pounding in her chest.

Gently lifting her chin with the crook of his finger, Kai whispers back, "What else can I do?"

Serena meets his eyes, her lips inches from his and her entire body buzzing with anticipation. "Restore me."

Eyes flashing, Kai presses his body into hers, grazing her lips with his own. Wrapping one hand around the back of his neck, Serena sinks into hard earth, pulling Kai with her.

A needing ache forms low in her belly.

The pads of his fingers move up the outside of her thigh, working their way in. One by one, scales retract, the pain of it replaced by the heat of his hand against her bare skin.

Kai suddenly pauses, pulling away. Solid arms on either side of Serena's head hold him up. "I don't have any more protection."

Serena pushes up on her elbows, brushing her lips across his. "Just you," she answers. "I just want you."

Chapter Thirty-Four

Serena awakens in Kai's arms to watch the fog roll in. It creeps over their tent, drowning out the warm rays of the early morning moon. Kai stirs next to her.

"You awake?" she whispers.

Eyelashes flutter as he works to focus on the fog hanging above them. "Well, that is ominous," he says.

Smiling, Serena settles into the warm spot between his body and his arm.

"Do you feel… restored?" Kai kisses her on the forehead.

"Yes." She bites her lower lip, and her face goes hot with memories of the night before. "Still a bit weak, though." Moments pass before Serena speaks again. "I can't let everyone think I'm sick."

"The way Darcy had to practically carry you in yesterday is not going to debunk the rumors that are definitely flying around. Plus the healers came to see you at the height of your fever last night."

Serena moans. "Simone can't keep a secret to save her life, much less mine." Serena shifts to look up at Kai. "What about you? Sleep well?"

"Like a walrus at the bottom of a blubber pile."

Serena narrows her eyes. He is trying to be funny, but it is not going to distract her from her next question. "Any nightmares?"

Kai tenses, remaining silent.

Gently, Serena runs her fingers over his bare chest, hoping the intimate contact reassures Kai.

You can trust me with this.

"I am the Head of the Queen's Guard," he finally says. "It is not right that I can't handle the aftermath of a few battles."

Serena looks up at him. "I am a little familiar with the pressure of being a leader," she sympathizes. Her head snaps up with an idea. "If the same were happening to one of your guards, what would you tell them to do?" Serena asks.

Kai sighs. "Good point."

"Soooo…" she prods.

"So I'll talk to someone," he says.

"Do you want me to get one of the healers—?"

"No," Kai interrupts. "Give me some time to put my thoughts together. And I don't want to send my pairing mate to ask like I can't do it myself."

Serena hides her smile by snuggling deeper into his chest. "We're a mess," she murmurs.

"I know." He kneads his fingers through his hair. The bioluminescence crackles to life with the massage. "And I wouldn't exchange our mess for any other in the world."

"Me either," says Serena. "But right now we have to hide that mess under at least a little bit of regal composure. I think I hear the camp packing up."

Kai reaches for a blanket and throws it over the pair of them. "Shh," he says. "If we're really quiet maybe they'll forget about us."

"That is highly doubtful." Serena giggles, but she plays along anyway, holding down a corner of the blanket.

"Your majesty?" Evandre's voice rings through the mist from outside the tent.

Serena and Kai freeze, their eyes going wide. Serena flings back the blanket, attempting to sit up.

"No!" Kai whisper-yells. "I won't let them have you!" He pulls the blanket back over them, wrapping it tightly around Serena.

"Kai, stop," Serena says, having a hard time keeping her laughter suppressed.

A wrestling match ensues and the pair, limbs intertwined with the blanket, roll into one side of the tent, then the other. Now Serena laughs out loud, but it devolves into a coughing fit with the extra exertion. Kai sits her up, patting her on the back while she takes large gulps of fresh air.

"Your majesty?" Evandre asks again. She sounds further away, as if she took several steps back at the disturbance inside.

Serena clears her throat. "Yes?"

"The racers are preparing to launch. We need to get you on the boat."

"The queen requires further rest," Kai's voice booms out. "Inform the Ungainlics that the race is delayed until tomorrow."

"I… don't think we can do that," a hesitant answer is given.

Rolling the blanket into a tight ball, Serena throws the entire thing at Kai's face. As Kai simulates a fierce battle with a face-sucking monster, she stands, smoothing out her hair. "Of course not," she calls out. "He was just kidding. I will be along shortly."

"As you say, your majesty," says Evandre.

Serena listens until the maiden's footsteps fade in the distance, then turns to face Kai.

He has emerged from the battle successful—his opponent laying crumpled on the floor. "Ready?" he asks.

"Ready," says Serena. "Which boat will you—?"

"Whichever boat you are on. We are together today." He takes her hand in his.

"As you say." Serena smiles. "But I'd like to remain close to the healers, so it will probably be the tug."

Serena unzips the flap and steps outside, watching Kai break down the tent while she plays with the mermaid charm hanging from her neck. She does feel better, but even the simple act of standing upright causes nausea.

This is going to take some doing to pull off, she thinks. Recalling the sailing route, she believes it should be a fairly easy day. Once Kai has the tent and blankets rolled up under one arm, she takes his other for stability, and they walk to the docks.

The fog is still thick, subduing noise and the overall mood. Everyone moves about their tasks silently, like ghosts, keeping their eyes straight ahead. Serena is at least grateful for the relative privacy as she stumbles her way to the boat.

On board the tug, the atmosphere is livelier while preparations for launch are underway. There will be no way to spot other racers due to the fog, so the fleet will have to use their best judgment when to launch. A general feeling of euphoria rises up when it is announced no one has to stay below deck to hide. Fog will obscure the presence of those above deck, and spotters placed around the railings should give plenty of warning before there are any incidents.

Serena finds a seat on a bench. Kai is up and providing help where he can without ever straying too far from her.

"Feel better?" Liam sits on the bench beside Serena. It bows with his weight, and she has to steady herself to keep from falling against him.

"This is going to be a long day if people are going to keep asking me that," she says.

Liam shrugs. "I heard the healers had a long few hours trying to bring your fever down."

"I wouldn't know," says Serena. "But no more fever, at least for now. You've issued the order that no maidens are to go into the water?"

"I don't issue orders," he says, leaning back against the railing. "But I spread the word to avoid the water if they don't want to end up like you."

"Lovely," says Serena. "The wolves should probably stay out of it as well."

"Too cold for our blood, anyway," says Liam. He closes his eyes then opens one to look at Serena. "Seriously, though. You gonna make it?"

The ends of Serena's lips turn down. "I'm weak, but I'll be okay. The sooner we get there the better."

"Did you eat breakfast?" he asks.

"A little. You? I think they are handing out food near the bow."

"I've eaten more than I can handle in one sittin'," he says, closing both eyes again.

She looks at Liam. "You are on the tug today, too? Maybe we should split up."

"I'd rather be here."

"Why?" asks Serena.

"Sophia's here. I said I'd keep an eye on her. Remember?"

A bright spot of orange amidst the fog emerges from the other side of the boat. Serena watches as Sophia searches the myriad of faces before her eyes fall on Liam. Sensing her approach, Liam suddenly straightens, smooths back his hair and clearing his throat.

"Breakfast?" Sophia offers a small basket of rolls, fruit, and sliced fish.

"I'm famished." Liam takes the basket with a wide smile.

Sophia blushes, smiling back. It isn't for several moments—until at least Liam has downed two rolls, that Sophia sees Serena. "Your apologies, my majesty! I mean, er, my apologies, your majesty." She bends in an awkward, rushed curtsey. "May I retrieve sustenance for you as well?"

"No, thanks," says Serena, glancing at Liam. "I've already eaten more than I can handle in one sitting."

Narrowing his eyes, Liam gives Serena a silent warning. *Do not ruin this for me.*

Shouts from the wheelhouse interrupt. The captain orders ropes untied and the anchor lifted.

Sophia curtseys again before facing Liam. "I'll check in with you in a bit," she says before disappearing back into the fog.

Watching his eyes follow Sophia, shoulders sagging a little when she is no longer in sight, Serena smiles at Liam. The sun has gone behind the clouds. "I think you are no longer a child of the moon," says Serena.

"What?" Liam forces down his last bite, brushing crumbs from his face.

"Nothing," says Serena. "Are you going to eat all of that?"

He shrugs. "She'd be disappointed if I didn't… "

The boat jerks, and the entire fleet pulls away from the docks. A fine mist falls from the air, and it does nothing to dissipate the fog. The five ships stick close together.

Pushing himself up, Liam offers his support for Serena to stand at the railing. Kai joins the pair and the three spend the morning scanning the low-hanging clouds for any sign of land or Ungainly boats. In the early afternoon, the wind picks up and the fog thins just in time to reveal a majestic waterfall. It cascades down the face of a mountain that springs straight out of the ocean.

Serena gasps, craning her neck back as she follows the mountain to the top. The fog lifts a bit more, this time in front of a blue-iced glacier that towers over the sailboat. A chunk of ice falls away, cracking into the ocean below causing the boat to rock from the tidal wave.

Further on, Liam points out swarms of sea otters and dolphins playing in the waters beside the ship, beckoning for its occupants to come join them.

Serena smiles and gives a rueful wave.

"Look up," says Kai.

The skies, cleared of clouds and fog, bare no shortage of wildlife. Scores of eagles soar above the boat, a few brave birds swooping close to the ship for a better look.

"They might be taking an interest in our fish," says Kai, gesturing to the barrels of cold food storage a few feet away.

"They can have them," says Serena, drawing Kai's warm arm tighter around her shoulders.

Liam scoffs. "So says the vegetarian." He stands to cover one of the open barrels with a tarp. "But I say she doesn't know what she's missin' out on." He looks at Serena; one eyebrow sits higher than the other.

"Okay." Serena gives in. "Enlighten me."

"Well, now, let's see. Other than the usual poached, smoked, broiled, roasted, baked, or seared salmon, you have your salmon spread and salmon jerky."

"Don't forget about sushi." Kai leans in, joining the conversation. "And I've seen picnickers with salmon burgers – oh, and barbeque salmon too."

Serena elbows him. "Don't take his side."

"You've got to admit it, Serena. Your boyfriend knows his salmon," taunts Liam.

"Perhaps." Serena glares at Kai. "But my *boyfriend* certainly doesn't know when to hold his tongue."

Gusts of wind move across the channel. At the front of the fleet, the sailboat is a flurry of activity as they adjust to the change in weather.

"Ahoy, there!"

All heads whip back in the other direction to the sound of the call. With the distraction of watching operations on the sailboat, no one noticed the Ungainly ship creeping up behind them.

Chapter Thirty-Five

Serena turns her back, pulling the hood over her head. She gives a few sharp clicks of her tongue. Maidens recognize the warning call, and they automatically head for the hatch leading below deck. Those too far away simply duck below the railing or make themselves scarce behind barrels, ropes, or lifeboats—anywhere they can hide.

It is too late for Serena to duck, and she would appear too suspicious if she keeps her back to the Ungainly boat, so she turns to face them alongside Kai and Liam, hoping the hood hides the sharp angles and blue tint of her cheekbones.

Everyone watches as the Ungainlies move closer. The tug captain peers out of the wheelhouse ensuring extra maidens and wolves are hidden, then slows his speed. The Ungainly boat is another sailboat, smaller than the one Doug pilots, and has six humans on board, at least that are visible.

"We thought we were the only ones making the run today," shouts one of the men. "We didn't see anyone else leaving the docks."

Liam clears his throat. "Docks were full last night when we came in. The five boats here stayed on an island across the channel instead." He glances back. "Why did the other racers stay back?"

The boats are only a few spans away from each other now.

"Because of the storm," says the Ungainly. "Supposed to be a big one. Race officials gave us the option to dock for a day until it passes. But my crew has to leave the day after the race to get home. If we wait a day, we may not be able to finish."

Liam turns to Serena and Kai. "They were talkin' about possible storms at the camp. I just didn't think they were supposed to come this far north." He raises his voice again for the humans. "When will it arrive?"

Serena glances at the line of maidens hiding from Ungainly view just under the railing.

"Late afternoon," replies the human. "We thought we could beat it, but I'm not so sure anymore," he says, gesturing to the western skies.

Serena, Liam, and Kai all turn, lifting their chins to look. The sky is now void of eagles. Solemn gray clouds silently roll in, a darker more ominous version of the fog earlier that morning.

"Ain't nothing good coming from those thunderheads," says the human. "We better get ready for some big waves. Let's stick close—and be sure to run up your emergency flag if you are in trouble."

"Will do," says Liam. "Good luck."

"Fair winds to you, too, young man."

Just as the human turns away, a strong gust blows across the deck of the tugboat, flipping Serena's hood back from her face.

Kai spins her around as she gropes with frantic fingers to replace it.

"That was close," she says.

"But we aren't out of the woods by a long shot," says Kai. "Look."

The small fleet of ships is just entering Chatham Sound. Land peels away, and the water is as vast as the Pacific Ocean herself. It would be choppy here even without the storm, but as the wind picks up the surface responds, pitching the tug from side to side.

Shouts come from the human boat, and they angle their bow straight into the headwind. The tugboat follows suit, then the sailboat. Loose items roll across the deck of the tug, and those who are in plain view of the Ungainlies jump into action to secure the boat. Maidens who remain hidden below the railing toss out ropes to Serena and Kai, who tie down food supplies, bags, and anything else that could be flung into the sea or become dangerous missiles during the storm.

Thunder cracks across the sound, reverberating Serena's bones and causing her breath to catch in her throat. It reminds Serena of her father's call. "Poseidon help us," she says out loud.

All eyes turn to the sky. Black clouds pitch and roll, turning the heavens as chaotic as the seas.

"Come on," says Liam. "Keep going."

Serena is tying off a knot securing another barrel of salmon when the skies open, blasting sheets of rain over the boats. Almost instantly drenched, fingers slippery and cold, Serena struggles with her last knot.

"Here let me." Kai bends beside her and takes each end of rope, running them through a quick dance of loops, knots, and tugs until he gives one final yank. "There."

His solid warmth beside Serena is reassuring but his shoulders are tense, and he casts nervous peeks at the skies.

Serena nudges the frayed ends of rope with the crook of her finger. "Hopelessly intertwined," she says, looking back at Kai. "Like us."

Without warning, Kai stands, lifting Serena to her feet. His arms slide around her waist, pinning her to him. Leaning in, the tip of his nose caresses her cheek until their lips find each other. The silky pink rims of his mouth contradict Kai's rigid body. Slow, cautious kisses counter the building storm around them, as if Kai is taunting Mother Nature herself.

Taking a shaky breath, Serena inhales Kai's scent, and she knows she is home again. She sweeps the pad of her thumb across his cheekbone until her entire hand wraps around to the back of his head, tangling in his hair and pulling him closer.

Responding, Kai runs the tip of his tongue across Serena's lower lip. The feather-light touch sends electricity through Serena's body, warming her from the cold rain that no longer seems to touch her. It is his turn to take a breath, and Serena willingly gives everything she has, the loss of air a pleasant ache in her chest.

Cradling her cheek with an open palm, Kai plants one more gentle kiss on the corner of her lips before pulling away. He smiles as he meets her eyes, fingers falling to interlock with hers. "Stay close, okay?" he whispers.

"As you say." She squeezes his hand.

Thunder rolls across the sky, demanding Serena's attention. Casting an exasperated look at the heavens, she turns her back on them, resuming her work in securing the deck side by side with Kai.

Liam calls out, "If you two are done dancing around on first base, I need help with this lifeboat."

The small wooden dinghy is barely bigger than a canoe but weighs a ton. Grunting, the trio push, moving it off to the side to tie it down.

"What is first base?" Kai asks Liam as he hands him more rope.

"Oh, um." Liam ties his first knot. "It's part of a human sport—baseball."

"Never played," says Kai. He takes the rope back from Liam to tie his own knot. "But once we've made it to Ivvaavik, maybe you can teach me." Kai tugs hard on the rope to ensure it is secured, then turns to Liam, slapping him on the back. "We can dance on first base together."

Serena bites her lip to keep from laughing—she knows Kai is teasing Liam. Nonetheless, Liam's whole face grows red.

Standing, Liam runs his palm through his hair, shedding it of excess water built up by the rain. He gestures to the sailboat ahead of them. "I should've caught a ride with them."

"Oh, come on—it can't be that bad here," says Serena. "No more kissing, I promise."

"At least just, give me some warning first." Liam keeps his eyes pinned on the sailboat.

All hands are busy on the deck of the vessel. The sails are brought down and tied securely, rigging is checked and double checked, and the wolves all don lifejackets.

"What about our lifejackets?" a passing pack member asks as he follows Serena and Liam's gaze to the sailboat.

"We needed space for food storage," says Serena. "Remember?"

"Won't do them no good, anyway," says Liam, winding more rope around his arm. "Soon as they go overboard, fear will kick in and most of them will transform. They'd rip right through the vest."

The only good swimmers are the maidens, but unless Serena wants a school of sick Undine who still have more than half their journey to endure. Hopefully, no one ends up in the water.

Lightening fissures out from the clouds above, highlighting nervous faces of maidens still hiding under the railing. Thunder follows almost immediately, breaking across the sky like a gunshot. Serena flinches as its energy rattles straight through her, shaking even the sturdy tug.

"Here it comes," shouts Liam.

No longer concerned with loose items, all occupants of the boat race to secure themselves. The brunt of the storm hits them full force, wind and rain pelting at them sideways while the ship pitches and heaves. Maidens under the railing rise without fear of being seen in order to grasp something solid. The Ungainly boat is nowhere to be found, obscured amongst the massive waves.

"Mommy!" the child's shout rings through the atmosphere better than thunder, causing Serena's heart to race.

All eyes turn to Darcy and her boys, huddled into a corner at the stern of the boat. Suddenly the stakes are brought into sharp focus, and Serena wishes they were riding out the storm on solid ground.

"We should have never left," Serena says out loud.

Beside her, Liam gives her a sharp glance. "Too late for that. We can only look ahead."

But ahead lies only terrifying nightmares. Hundreds of whitewater swells, churning rollers waiting to smash into Serena's fragile fleet in order to prove the truth of her words. They should have never left.

There is nothing she can do about it, except endure the storm. The boat keels down as it rides the backside of the wave, dipping into a deep trough. Serena's stomach drops, and she reaches out to cling to the nearest thing she can. It is the sturdy railing. She wraps her arms around it, riding the wave. She watches the front of the boat where Kiera and her seasick partner still are. They too hold on for their lives, huddled together.

Kai shields Serena, her own protective support, blocking her view of the wrathful squall surrounding them.

A loud crack echoes the thunder above and the occupants of the ship are jolted as the hull smacks against the water. Kai loosens his grasp around Serena. Peeking out from his embrace, Serena's eyes attempt to focus directly in front of the ship. Confused at what lies before them, Serena slowly stands. Instead of the churning, white water mess that it was not moments ago, the surface of the ocean is smooth and solid. Serena takes a step back, bringing the angle of the water into perspective. Lifting her chin, she realizes it does not stretch out before the ship. Instead, it is going straight up to the heavens. It is the next wave towering over them. Serena only has the time to look at Kai, mouth open to shout.

No words come. The wave washes over the ship, punching into Serena's chest and gut. Her head slams against something hard and neither her gills nor her lungs can deal with the assault. Her breath leaves her, replaced only with blackness and pain.

Time brings sweet numbness. Serena's eyes flutter behind heavy lids that feel pinned shut. Flashes of light move in the darkness. Serena calls out, her voice working better than her vision. The word she utters stuns even her. "Mother?"

Music fills her brain, responding to Serena's call. It is a sweet song, dripping of lazy bubbles rising from The Deep until they reach the moonlit surface to fall open, exposing themselves to the world. This song is meant for Serena.

"Serenita, my beautiful princess," the melodious voice chants.

"Is it my time?" Serena asks. Peace overwhelms her, and she knows if she crosses into the afterlife now, those she leaves behind will be okay.

"Not yet." The music and the singing stop. "The queen has yet to fulfill her purpose."

Light rushes into Serena, penetrating through to her bones, then pulling back out just as viscously.

Serena comes to, coughs raking at her throat as seawater trickles from the corners of her mouth and the gills behind her ears. Blinking her eyes open, Serena focuses on Simone's red lips. They are no longer full and pouty. They are pinched together with concentration, occasionally parting to release short, panicked breaths. When they round out or open further to form words, it is clipped orders. Simone's voice is the first that reaches Serena, slicing straight through the ringing in her ears. "This one is okay."

Serena finds some solace in being referred to as 'this one' instead of 'her majesty', like she is one of the group again instead of hovering on some lonely cliff above it.

"There is one more unconscious—over there."

Simone moves away. It must be quickly, because her image is blurred, half of it taking longer to leave Serena's line of sight. Almost immediately, Kai has taken Simone's place. Serena's lips quiver as she attempts a smile. She doesn't mind forcing her eyes to focus on this face.

"Is everyone okay?" Serena manages to croak out as Kai helps her to a sitting position. "No maidens in the water?"

"We think everyone is still aboard, but if the water keeps washing over us like this, it won't matter if the maidens don't enter the water. The water will enter them."

"He hates me right now," says Serena, leaning her head back against the hard bulkhead of the ship.

"Who?"

"Poseidon."

Kai grunts. "I'm not sure Poseidon could talk Mother Ocean down from her anger right now, even if his own daughters' lives depended on it." He stands as Serena does. "Maybe you should keep sitting."

Serena grasps the railing as her head sways worse than the ship. Squeezing her eyes shut, Serena waits until the wave of nausea passes, then she scans the chaos on board. She must not have been out that long. Maidens and pack members alike are still picking themselves up from where they slid across the deck.

A few of the pack members have transformed. Sopping wet wolves slowly get up on all four paws. There is not any panic on the part of the maidens—either because they are too exhausted to care, or because they know the wolves are.

As Serena's gaze follows the aftermath up to the front of the boat, she watches as Kiera picks herself up. The maiden is alone now, her frantic eyes skip around the small area.

"Did you count the werewolves?" Serena asks Kai.

"Not yet," he says.

Down the way, Liam is busy untangling one of his own from fishing nets.

"There is one missing." Serena looks back at the bow. Kiera is climbing on top of the railing, her pinkish-purple scales a sharp contrast to the black water spread out before her.

"Kiera—no!"

The storm raging around Serena dulls into background noise as she watches Kiera's feet leave the railing. They point into graceful arches, moving up as she jumps away from the bow, then down when she pikes into a dive.

Hand outstretched as if she can somehow stop Kiera, Serena's feet won't move quickly enough. Against the deafening cacophony of the raging gale, there is a whisper of a splash as the first maiden enters the water.

Chapter Thirty-Six

A different kind of cracking echoes across the water. In a daze, Serena's eyes drift from where Kiera jumped off the ship. The Ungainlies did not get their sails down in time, and now the force of the wind is causing the boat to tip. Wood on the deck splinters as the storm shows no mercy for the Ungainlies or their vessel.

All movement on the tug ceases as maidens and pack members stop to watch. A mammoth wave builds, creeping up to the Ungainly ship. Everyone can see it coming, yet are powerless to stop it. The wave folds over, plunging the entire boat underwater, its red emergency flag visible even under the surface of the churning ocean.

"Half of those men didn't have on lifejackets." Liam steps up beside Serena, his mouth dropping open. "They'll never make it."

Without thinking, Serena rushes past Liam.

"Wait!" he calls.

Before he can even finish the word, she has jumped on top of the railing. Something clasps around her hand. She tries pulling away and it only squeezes harder. Serena looks to the side. Kai stands on top of the railing, their fingers are already interlocked. He is not going to hold her back—he is going to jump with her.

"It has to be quick," she says. "Don't stay in longer than you have to."

Kai nods. "Stay close."

Turning to the churning water, they jump in together. This time, Serena anticipates the cold and the bitter taste. Her transformation is still not pretty, but it isn't a disaster. It is not the same case with Kai, but he will have to work it out on his own. Serena respectfully turns her back as he struggles. Several more maidens splash into the water next, adding to the chaos of the seas as they flop around, grabbing at their chest and gills—both refusing to work properly.

As soon as the majority of them manage to form tails, Serena gives several sharp clicks of her tongue, beckoning her people to follow her. The Undine form a tight, two-column line. Serena is at the front, swimming shoulder to shoulder with Kai. The rest stay close behind.

Serena and Kai angle down sharply to avoid a large chunk of the sailboat tumbling through the water. After the obstruction passes, Serena gasps at the turmoil before her. Ungainlies float in the water, their clothes and hair rippling as if they are in a slow motion breeze. Some are clawing frantically forward, making no progress at all and going in the wrong direction. The dark skies above give them no clue as to which way is up and which way is down.

The unconscious Ungainlies are more worrisome, though in their state of inertia they will find their way to the top faster than those trying to swim.

One Ungainly has latched onto an unconscious shipmate, and he paddles with frantic arms, trying to get them both to the surface. Neither of them will make it.

Serena dives deep and her columns follow. Once they are below the worst of the aftermath, she arches her body and angles up for the ascent. Despite what she know will happen by the end of the day—fevers, nausea, and headaches, the rush of icy cold water through her gills and into her body is invigorating. She picks up speed, Kai remaining steady and strong beside her.

Approaching the humans from underneath, the column spreads out, each with eyes on separate targets. Chins lifted up, the maidens slice through water as efficiently as shark fins. Reaching both arms out, Serena grabs two Ungainlies by latching onto the clothing at the back of their necks. One is not moving, probably unconscious by now, and the other starts waving all four limbs wildly as if he can ward off the mysterious force. Serena keeps him turned away from her.

Further over, Kai has grabbed another Ungainly. This one is more adamant to see what is pushing him. Thankfully Kai has also found a piece of the ship— flat wood he keeps in between him and the man. When they reach the surface, Kai pushes the wood into the Ungainly who latches on, able to keep afloat.

Serena is almost to the top, too, when she realizes the Ungainly she carries that she thought was unconscious has opened his eyes and is staring directly at her. His lids are heavy, and there is no sharp shine, but he gazes at Serena with what curiosity he can muster.

With a grimace at her own blunder, Serena pushes both arms up with all the strength she has. Two Ungainly heads break the surface, transitioning from the turmoil underwater straight into the squall above. Serena moves away before poking her own head above to check on them. They are helping each other but are barely able to stay afloat with the waves intent on pushing them back under.

"Look!" one of them shouts.

Serena turns her head, trusting her scales to help her blend in with the dark water. Both the tugboat and the sailboat from her fleet surge forward, ropes held at the ready for rescue operations.

"Over here!" The Ungainlies wave their arms in the air, hoarse voices shouting for help as they expend what little energy they have left.

The sailboat reaches them first. Fluttering her tail, Serena moves back, disappearing into the storm but staying close enough to observe. Ropes fly over, their knotted ends dipping into the water. Serena holds her breath, hoping her maidens on the ship don't reveal themselves. Only pack member faces peer over the railing. Dipping below, Serena watches as the maidens that were aboard the sailboat dive into the water.

She sighs, knowing they all will have a long night ahead of them, but they have to keep their distance from humans. There was no other choice.

The pair of Ungainlies in the water kick with tired legs and manage to catch a rope but have no strength to pull themselves up.

"Heads up!" Doug's voice rings out from the ship. He throws another rope—this one has a loop at one end. The more coherent of the two slips the rope under the arms of his shipmate, then waves. Almost immediately the human is hoisted out of the water. In short order he disappears onto the deck of the sailboat and the looped rope is thrown back in the water for the second man.

Serena leaves them to it, diving back under in search of more who need help. She finds an unconscious young man—he can't be much older than her. Long hair floats in front of his face, tickling the beginnings of a skimpy beard.

Grabbing hold of the back of his vest, ensuring he faces away from her in case he wakes up, Serena begins the race to the top. She makes better time when Kai moves in on the other side of the Ungainly, helping her with the load. Just before they reach the surface, Serena gives warning by pushing her tail fins into open air, then slapping them against the water.

"Hoy, look over there!"

The pack members on board have seen, and they are attempting to distract the Ungainlies. Kai and Serena dive back under with their patient, making a wide arc then circle back up gaining speed. They break through and sail into the air, each holding the Ungainly under his arms. He is heavier than they expect, dragged down by extra layers of sopping wet clothing. It isn't long before Serena knows they won't make the height they need to.

Luckily, one of the pack members anticipated that. Waiting on top of a mast, he jumps. With one hand on a thick rope, he swings out and around, colliding with the trio in mid-air. Serena and Kai fall back empty-handed, and the pack member and his new load slam into a sail, sliding down to safety.

The Undine are back in the water before the Ungainlies notice them. Finding one more victim, the next transfer goes more smoothly, and the other maidens have caught on. After a quick sweep of the wreckage area, Serena returns to the tug, using the assistance of one of their ropes to board the ship. Kai comes sweeping in after her.

"Darcy," Serena calls. "The humans are going to need your help on the sailboat. I can't send my healers over there."

When there is no response, Serena looks up, staring at the back of Darcy's head. "Darcy?"

Fingernails scratching wood, Darcy leaves marks in the railing that sends chills running down Serena's body better than the arctic waters can.

When Darcy turns to look at Serena, her face is white. "I've lost Aiden."

"What?" Serena takes a step closer.

"I can't find him—I've looked all over the ship… " But Darcy is no longer looking around the ship—she is looking out to sea. "He must've been washed overboard, but I don't know where."

"No," says Serena, thinking back to his reaction after she helped the whales. "He has gone to help."

"Bring him back to me," Darcy whispers to no one in particular. She is in shock, but Serena has to leave her to her own devices.

"Liam!" Serena shouts, looking for her brother.

He drops the rope he is helping to tow in and is by Serena's side quickly. Keeping her voice low out of respect for Darcy, Serena whispers to her brother, "I need your bracelet. The one Danny gave you."

He slides it off his wrist and into Serena's hand. "Why? What happened?"

"I think Aiden went into the water. I need to find him. He was given his own bracelet, right?"

"Right," says Liam. "I'm coming with you."

"No."

"Yes."

Serena is already headed to the railing of the boat, adjusting the oversized bracelet to fit her thin arm. "I can't look for him if I'm worried about keeping your own dumb head above water," she hisses.

"And what if your fevers come back while you are in The Deep? Then what happens to your *dumb* head?"

"Stop it, both of you." Kai steps in between the siblings. "I will go with her. Here." He spins Serena around, unclasping the necklace Danny gave her and handing it to Liam. Then he takes his own necklace off and puts it on Serena. He looks at Liam. "If we are not back within fifteen minutes, now you can find her. Okay?"

"Okay," Liam huffs.

"Okay?" Kai nudges Serena.

She adjusts the new piece of jewelry around her neck in distaste, feeling like Liam's pet more than anything else. "Fine," she says.

For the second time that afternoon, Kai and Serena are diving into the poisoned waters together. Once she is submerged in the darkness, Serena holds her wrist in front of her, paying attention to the tiny, carved werewolf eyes. They are already glowing bright. Kai gestures to the ship above them. Bracelets wrapped around wrists on the wolves above are causing it to light up. Quickly, Kai and Serena swim away from the ship, toward the Ungainly wreckage.

Rushing through the debris field, Kai searches for any Ungainlies or stray maidens left behind. Serena keeps an eye on her bracelet. Angling down into the dark waters, she finally spots a small glow within the eyes of either werewolf at the end of the band. Urging her tired body forward, she watches as the luminescence burns brighter and brighter until they are as red as Liam's the day he transformed while she was pinned underneath him.

Serena looks up and sees the whole of the Ungainly sailboat sinking. In a round window of one of the rooms below deck there are three sharp scrapes smudged across the inside of the window. The spread of the marks match that of a small werewolf's claws.

Chapter Thirty-Seven

Picking up speed, Serena shoots straight for the window. She places her hand against the claw mark, then bangs against it. Nothing.

As she peers inside, the ship sinks further and further. It is dark, but using her own hair's bioluminescence she illuminates the area. A face pops up right on the other side of the window. Serena jumps back, then recognizes the face. Arista.

Eyes wide, Serena moves back toward the window. Arista shows Serena a ball of fur under her arm—an unconscious ball of fur. Keeping one hand tight over Aiden's mouth and snout, Arista looks at Serena.

Banging on the window, Serena grows hot at the cheeks.

What are you doing?

Kai pulls Serena back, pointing to his lips then to Arista. Inside the room, Arista turns to Aiden, places her lips over his nose and blows. She is using the oxygen her own body pulls from the water to keep him breathing.

Quickly, Serena and Kai move to the deck of the ship, locating the hatch leading below deck. It is completely smashed in by the main mast. Serena and Kai both get to one side, pushing on the heavy wood, but it is tied to the ship in a hopeless tangle of ropes and sails.

Serena and Kai swim to the window. Arista is keeping watch, her eyebrows knitted together with worry. Backing up, Kai thrusts forward, ramming the window with his fist then his shoulder. Serena swims a quick circle around the ship, looking for another way in. Kai is still ramming the window when she returns.

Serena leaves Kai, Arista, and Aiden behind. Her fins give frantic flutters in the race to the surface as she tries to fight back the sense of debilitating desperation. Once she breaks through, in the thick of the storm, she opens her mouth and sings.

High notes and a slow, sonorous tune contrast the booming thunder. It stands out from the storm, impossible not to hear. The tug has followed, and its spotlight comes to rest on Serena. She squints, shielding her eyes from the bright beam but does not stop singing. Heads pop up above the railing, but this song is meant only for one.

A dark shadow leaps from behind the spotlight. When it comes down in front of it, Serena can only see the messy outline of fur. Liam has already transformed—his wolf stands ready to help, if only Serena can keep him from drowning.

The tug's spotlight leaves Serena to follow Liam, highlighting outstretched claws and a bulging torso and arms. He splashes into the water. Serena doesn't wait until he comes up for air. She dives under, going straight for Liam. Using the momentum he already has from the dive in, she comes up behind him, pushing down on his shoulders and thrusting with her tail. Kai joins, pushing Liam down and leading him straight to the window. There is no time to search for a weaker entry point.

Once Arista's face comes into view, she holds up Aiden's limp body to show Liam, then backs away from the window. Tails beating against the water in sync, Serena and Kai pick up speed. They don't slow, even once they are close enough to the ship that they know they won't be able to stop in time. With one final push forward, they release Liam and he bursts into the window, scattering sharp shards of glass in a soundless spray. Serena and Kai angle up, crashing into the side of the ship, and turning somersaults over the rough planks. Cracked wood slices into Serena's shoulder. Steadying herself against the ship, she looks up to see Kai with abrasions across his face.

The sound of splintering wood causes them to look down, and they see Liam tearing through the side of the boat. Reaching in through the broken porthole window, he pulls back, slicing a larger hole for Arista. Dodging more ship debris, Serena and Kai slink down, waiting as patiently as they can. Her bracelet still glows bright red, reminding her of what lies inside the boat.

As soon as Arista is through, Serena rushes forward, wrapping one arm around Arista's waist. Careful not to disturb Arista's delicate hold over Aiden's snout, Serena rushes them to open air. Behind them, Kai helps Liam by supplementing the wolf's very unproductive doggy paddle with powerful strokes of his tail.

The ocean's surface, pounded into a white froth by the storm, is just ahead. Arista releases Aiden's face, and the maidens move to either side of the small wolf, picking up speed. It is a risk, but this will be the fastest way to get him on board.

Bursting back into the storm together, Serena and Arista fly up, their patient between them with his head bouncing. Arching their backs, the Undine traverse the small distance to the boat quickly, almost overshooting it. Netting shoots up into the air in front of them and the maidens automatically curl their bodies around the small wolf, absorbing most of the blow. Course rope cuts into their shoulders and backs until they hit the hard deck.

Groaning, Serena unfurls her fins, allowing them to separate into legs. Arista does the same, scooting back to reveal the ball of wet fur between them.

Serena looks at Arista over Aiden. Both of them are breathing hard, limbs limp with exhaustion.

"Thank Poseidon I didn't still have you in chains," Serena says.

"I'm rather grateful for that myself, your majesty." Arista nods.

The storm is finally clearing out, the sun breaking through gray clouds, but a shadow falls over the maidens.

It is Darcy, her face pale and her posture frozen. Colin stands behind her, practically having to hold up his wife. The clan's only doctor, nurse, and mother—always a flurry of activity especially during a crisis—is unable to even move when her own son is seriously injured.

Red flashes behind Darcy like the Ungainly emergency signal. Simone pushes her way toward Aiden, dropping beside him. Briefly laying her ear against his chest she announces. "His pulse his weak." She puts her hand in front of his snout. "And he's not breathing."

Without hesitation, Simone shoves both hands inside the werewolf's mouth, her delicate pinkish skin scraping against sharp teeth. She feels around, pulling only small bits of debris from his mouth, then pulls his tongue forward, and aligns his head with his spine. Tilting his chin back slightly, she is opening the airway.

Scooting around so her knees are in front of Aiden, Simone wraps her hands around snout and lower jaw, squeezing them shut. Finally pausing, Simone looks up at Serena. "I never understood why Hailey taught us this... until now." She takes a deep breath, squeezes her eyes shut, then brings her mouth to Aiden's snout. Blowing five quick breaths into his nostrils, Simone tears her mouth away. Liam has come up beside her and quickly wipes her mouth with his shirt.

Simone gives him a grateful smile, then turns to Serena. "Is his chest rising when I do it?"

"Oh—my apologies," says Serena. "I wasn't watching." She scoots closer, pinning her gaze to the wolf for any sign of life.

Simone's lips curl up in distaste, but she puts her mouth to his nose again, delivering five more breaths.

"His chest is rising!" says Serena, her voice piercing through the hushed silence.

When Simone pulls away, releasing his snout, Aiden's chest continues to rise and fall on its own. A collective sigh of relief runs through the people surrounding him.

"Aiden, Aiden!" Simone shakes the wolf's shoulder.

He blinks open his eyes, pupils shrinking as he focuses. When his gaze moves to his mother, he flips his tail once, giving a sign that he is okay.

Darcy sinks to her knees, shaking and crying. Serena wraps the woman in a hug as a fatigued crowd gathers around the group.

"Can you transform?" Simone asks Aiden, running a hand down his rib cage and spine. "I don't think anything is broken."

Slowly, bones do break themselves in half, protruding out the side of Aiden's face, then sinking in. His tail shrinks between his legs and fur floats to the ground until there is only a small, naked boy left. Someone hands a blanket through and his mother tucks it around him. "I'm so glad you are okay, honey." She wipes tears from her cheek. 'But if you ever do anything like that again, you will be grounded for the rest of your life."

Lips quivering, Aiden nods while making a brave attempt at keeping the tears from coming.

Colin kneels down next to his son and wife. His hand brushes through a pile of Aiden's wolf hair. "What's this?" he asks.

Darcy takes one spindly piece of the mane, squeezing the length of it with her other thumb and forefinger. An oily sheen of film is left behind on her fingertips.

Simone turns away from her patient to look. "From the oil spill they have been talking about. Oil doesn't dissolve in the water, it just floats in large globs. Looks like the storm put us right through one."

Darcy drops the hair, looking up as Arista. The maiden uses a blanket to wipe the oil off her body. Kiera, the first maiden to dive in, joins the group, coming to stand right behind Arista. Serena breathes a sigh of relief, but Darcy waves her hand wildly in front of her. "Don't retract your scales. Tell all the maidens—don't!"

Arista glances at Kiera, who has bare skin already showing on the majority of her legs, arms, and midsection.

"Why not?' asks Kiera, having already retracted her scales.

Darcy turns to Serena. "The oil must be what made you sick. When you retract your scales, you are introducing it directly into your bloodstream, and possibly your digestive system."

Standing next to Darcy, Liam begins wiping frantically at himself.

Simone rolls her eyes. "The wolves just shed their fur—they won't be poisoned."

"Right," Liam says, handing his towel to Serena instead. "I knew that."

Using one end on herself, Serena helps Darcy towel off her son, too. He is still very weak, barely able to hold up his head and shivering. Gently taking his wrist to extend his arm, Serena runs the towel down his limb, wiping away any remaining smudges of oil.

Fresh pinpricks appear on the inside of his arm. Serena wipes again and beads of blood pop up under the pressure.

Darcy leans in to see what Serena is studying. "Oh, Aiden… not again."

The child does not bother to look, he knows what they have seen. "It's important," he mumbles.

"This is extremely fresh," Serena says. She looks up at Arista, the only maiden Aiden has been alone with in the recent hour.

Chapter Thirty-Eight

"Chains!" Serena orders, pointing to Arista.

"Wait, I—" Arista can't finish. Kai is jerking her around to place the chains on her wrists.

"Her dry bag," says Serena.

Unclipping it from around her waist, Kai opens the flap and reaches inside. It isn't long before he comes up with a full pouch of thick, red liquid.

Hushed silence falls over the maidens and werewolves on the tugboat deck as Liam steps forward to take the blood from Kai.

"Oh, Poseidon," Arista mumbles. "Why do you hate me so much?"

Liam looks at her, eyes blazing. "Where did you get this?"

Arista sighs. "Where do you think?"

Taking a step forward, he holds up the pouch, squeezing hard enough the veins in his arms bulge blue. "Nothing good ever came from this," he growls.

Chains clink as Arista squares off with Liam. "Only when it is in the wrong hands."

Simone dumps the rest of the contents of Arista's dry bag out on the deck. A syringe, tubing, and a plastic bag of wet wipes lay in a heap. Then three vials of hydrocoral roll across the deck. Simone stops one with her foot, picks it up, and removes the cork to smell it. She looks at Arista. "You thief."

"I needed it for a new potion." Arista's eyebrows rise into pleading arches, but she is pushed back when Liam shoves her aside. "Wait! I need that, too!" Arista shouts as Liam walks past with the pouches of blood.

Without looking back, Liam throws them overboard into the retreating storm. Arista lunges toward him. Liam turns, wrapping his large hand around her throat. "Quiet, mermaid—before I silence you myself."

"And if he doesn't, I will." Simone steps up beside Liam. She looms over Arista, even when Liam has Arista on the tips of her toes.

No one protests. As Serena glances at Undine and werewolves side by side watching the standoff, she sees they look ready to join in, and not on behalf of Arista. The traitor Undine is universally hated, and it is bringing the two species closer together.

Serena remembers what it feels like to be the outcast, nothing frustrating her more than the whole of Society looking at her like she was a traitor when she was only trying to help.

"Wait!" shouts Serena. "Let her go, Liam."

He glances over his shoulder at Serena but does not release Arista.

"And both of you step back," Serena continues. "We will hear her out. And it will not be after we've already made our judgments." To prove her point, Serena puts her hand out in front of Kai for the key to Arista's chains.

Thankfully, Kai obliges and the key drops into her palm. Squeezing her way in between Simone and Liam, Serena unlocks Arista. Rubbing her wrists, Arista turns to face the crowd.

"Tell us everything," says Serena.

Arista takes a shaky breath. "I've been giving Liam's blood to Aiden, Xavier, and a number of other werewolves."

"How long?" demands Colin.

"Alaric started it," says Arista. "And once he passed to the afterlife, I continued." Arista meets the angry father's eyes. "Even when I was in chains, I was able to talk Aiden through doing it himself."

Darcy lunges for Arista, and there is a shoving match that almost results in both Arista and Serena going back in the water. A loud, shrill whistle slices through the air. Those closest to Liam jump or lean back, covering their ears. He scans the people around him, satisfied all movement on board has stopped, then he smiles down at Serena, pulling her upright. "You aren't the only one who can sing."

Nodding her thanks, Serena turns to Arista. "For Poseidon's sake, tell us *why* you did it." *Preferably before I regret stepping out on a limb for you.*

"Very well." Arista straightens herself, running a soft palm down her braided hair. "Liam is the only werewolf that has the royal bloodline—and it is the most powerful blood we have."

Most of the crowd has relaxed their posture, and the sky above lightens as the sun attempts to break through the clouds. The hazy glow lessens the harsh angles on Arista's face as she speaks. "By administering Liam's blood into a host body, which is preferably young, strong, or one with a hardy build, the host begins to produce antibodies. From that, I hope to ascertain immunogoblins from the host's system."

"You mean anti-venom?" asks Darcy. Her breath is under control, and her face isn't quite so red. She moves back to sit down by Aiden. "You are trying to cure him of being a werewolf?"

"No." Arista shakes her head. "It won't work like that—your son will be hairy the rest of his life, I'm afraid."

Darcy lets out a sigh of relief, and Serena doesn't blame her. Darcy has come to love all of her son, including his beast.

Arista continues, "The anti-venom, when mixed with other properties used in the original potion—

"Like the hydrocoral," says Simone.

"Please don't interrupt." Arista doesn't skip a beat, she is on a roll, excited about explaining her work. "But yes, like the hydrocoral—it will create antibodies which then can be administered to a pregnant Undine."

All subtle movement from the crowd—shifting from foot to foot, scratching, and drying off with towels—ceases, as if they are frozen at the mention of pregnant Undine.

Arista catches on to the change in mood, and her voice goes soft. "But it takes several small doses administered over eight to ten weeks until antibodies peak in the host system, and it hasn't been without its side effects, obviously." She runs her palm over her braid again, shifting the hair so it lies over her shoulder. "I was going to call it Cordelia's Serum, in honor of our fallen maiden. With this medicine, mothers shouldn't become so sick during the birthing process, and it should reverse the effect of weak male calflings so we won't have to give them the transformation potion." Arista is looking at Aiden now.

Colin helps him to sit up, supporting his back. "She explained all this to you? And you agreed?" he asks his son.

Aidan slowly nods, looking at Serena. "I wanted to help."

Darcy hugs him, her tears starting all over again.

"Do you think it will work?" Liam asks her.

Releasing Aiden, Darcy wipes her cheeks and nods. "It has potential, but it is not without its faults."

Arista frowns, watching Darcy get to her feet.

"The humans use certain animals, like horses, to create antibodies, not each other," says Darcy.

"I was fresh out of horses," mumbles Arista.

"Right. But there are other options. Sharks being one of them."

"We can help there." Simone steps forward. "Hailey taught us how to care for certain animals, even administering injections if needed."

"But most importantly, how did you plan to purify and separate the antibodies from the blood?" asks Darcy. "How will you isolate the active ingredient?"

"Sneaking blood transfusions into the werewolf population was difficult enough. I am approaching this solution one problem at a time," says Arista.

There is an awkward silence while Darcy appears to be mulling over the medical procedures in her head. Finally she sighs, her fingertips going to her temples. "It will be difficult getting necessary supplies, especially sequestered in Ivvaavik as we will be. But with a little outside help, I think this is possible."

"Then it will be as you say," says Serena. "Arista will continue to investigate medicinal potions, but under the guidance and with consultation of Darcy and the Undine healers. And Arista—no more injections on any werewolf."

Arista raises a finger in question.

"Or Undine," says Serena before Arista can even ask.

Arista's shoulders slump.

"Your heart was in the right place." Serena touches Arista's elbow softly. "Just not your head."

"Many thanks, your majesty." Arista curtsies. "I think."

"Heads up!" shouts a voice from the wheelhouse. "Comin' up on the sailboat. Humans on board."

Occupants on the tug's deck reluctantly move into action. Sick and injured are escorted below and those left above help clean up the storm's aftermath.

"Stay with your son," Serena tells Darcy. "Besides, you look like you could use some down time, so to speak." She smiles.

"Thank you," says Darcy, starting to follow Colin, who is carrying Aiden below. She stops and turns. "Our stop at port tonight will have freshwater rivers running into the sea. We should find a way to get all of your maidens on land to wash off."

"As you say," says Serena.

On her knees in front of Serena, Arista is cleaning up the spilled contents of her dry bag. Serena holds out her hand and Arista pauses. Finally, she sighs, passing over the syringes and tubes. "I have none of Liam's blood left, anyway."

"But he does. And I want to make sure you are not tempted to get at it," says Serena. She gives the paraphernalia to Simone.

The healer stores it carefully in her own dry bag. She closes it and looks up, frowning when she sees the look on Serena's face. "Not to worry, your majesty. I think this is going to work."

"I hope so," says Serena. "But right now we need to focus on surviving the night. Imagine the difficulty you had with my fever, and multiply it by at least twenty." Serena snaps her head to Simone. "Were the healers in the water at all?"

She shakes her head. "Liam forbade it."

"At least someone was thinking ahead," mumbles Serena.

A loud clunk behind the two maidens cause them both to jump.

"It's starting," says Simone, kneeling beside an Undine who has collapsed mid-stride.

Serena helps roll the maiden over. Blonde hair falls back from her face. "It's Kiera…"

"She was weak already," says Simone. "And the first Undine in the water. Let's get her below—the Ungainlies don't need to know we have an emergency."

"I'll help." A pack member kneels, sliding one arm under Kiera's head and one under her knees before Simone can protest. Serena recognizes him as Kiera's partner patient, the seasick werewolf.

Serena watches the innocent maiden as she is carried away, her blonde curls blowing in the breeze and limp limbs jostling with every step. Thunder echoes in the distance as the gale makes its way inland. Serena sighs. "The storm is just beginning."

Chapter Thirty-Nine

The next scheduled stop is Juneau, the last stop of the race.

"We have time," Liam says. "The rest of the racers waited a day."

"Let's pull off before the city." Serena can already see the subtle glow of lights further up the coast. "We need to heal, and we don't need to do it under threat of discovery. Besides, we have to wait for the rest of our fleet."

Only the tug and the sailboat got caught up in the heart of the storm. She is hoping the other three vessels stayed in the protected narrows before entering Chatham Sound.

"Okay," agrees Liam. "I'll go tell the captain to signal the sailboat. We'll tell them to go ahead to Juneau so the injured Ungainlies can get help, and they can intercept any of our other boats if we miss them."

Serena goes below deck as they get closer to the sailboat. The enclosed space is stuffy and Serena is still fully armored with scales, not able to retract any until she can bathe in fresh water. Another maiden besides Kiera has fallen sick, both of them already running fevers. The three Undine healers plus Darcy are working hard to combat the first signs of sickness. Serena notices Darcy never strays too far from Aiden or her other boys, and that Arista has very wisely chosen to keep to the far corner of the room.

"When we go ashore, we'll need to set up a sick camp, preferably close to the river." Simone pauses by Serena long enough to wipe her hands.

"As you say," says Serena. "I'll send scouts out for fresh water."

The boat stops soon after, the entire hull shuddering as the anchor drops. Liam pokes his head in from the hatch. "Nowhere to dock. We'll have to go ashore using the row boats."

Transferring the entire crew to land is slow going with only two small boats for the job. It is dusk by the time everyone is ashore except for a skeleton crew of pack members left behind to watch the tug. Serena stands on the beach looking south for any sign of the rest of her fleet.

"Your majesty?"

Serena turns; it is Arista.

The maiden fidgets, nervous fingers jittering at her sides. "It still feels unnatural to call you that."

Smiling, Serena nods. "Sometimes it still takes me a moment to respond to it. I look around for some other queen that is being addressed, until I remember the new queen is me."

Arista seems to relax at the candid conversation. "Well, for the record, I think you are doing a good job."

"Thank you, Arista." Serena raises an eyebrow, wondering what the maiden wants.

"Oh, I was just going to suggest you don't wait too long to wash."

"I see," says Serena, running her eyes over Arista's scales. They still carry the thin sheen of oil themselves. Serena suspects Arista does not want to face Society alone just yet—not unless she can have her pseudo-ally next to her. "Let us go together, then."

The ground is still wet from the storm, but soft moss prevents the evidence of webbed feet imprints from forming. A thick pine scent permeates the air.

"This way," says Arista.

They follow the sound of babbling water. As they walk, Serena spots Kai working to set up tents. He must have already bathed, as his scales are retracted showing bare skin from the waist up. The oil is replaced with a different sheen—sweat.

She looks down as he glances up. There is still work to do, and she doesn't want to keep him from it. Liam steps forward from evenly spaced pack members. "We've scouted the area and we'll keep guards posted around the camp. Simone wanted the sick bay set up on the other side of the river so the noises don't keep everyone else up."

Serena frowns.

"It is a good idea," says Liam. "Half of you will be exhausted tomorrow either from fevers or from treating them. The other half needs to at least be functional."

"As you say," says Serena. She raises her nose the air and sniffs, glancing sharply at Liam. "I smell wolf."

He shrugs. "I gave them the go ahead. They can help keep away any curious humans, or animals."

Serena makes a pointed look at the moon. It is exactly halfway through its cycle—as far away from full as it can get.

"I know, I know. At least we can tell who has been—" Liam stops mid-sentence as a large wolf limps past the group.

"Is that Xavier?" she asks once he is out of sight.

"Yep," says Liam.

"That one was my fault," mumbles Arista. "I upped the dosage on his request. I suppose exacerbated anger issues were a side effect." Arista turns to Serena and curtsies. "My apologies, your majesty." Next Arista looks at Liam and waits, almost as if she expects an apology from him for her treatment earlier.

Liam stares down his nose at Arista and crosses his arms, his lips remaining firmly stuck together.

"Will there be any side effects in discontinuing the treatments so suddenly?" asks Serena, interrupting the stalemate.

"We'll find out," Arista says. "But if there is" — she puts a hand on Liam's shoulder— "we have our solution right here."

"Over my dead—"

"Liam!" interrupts Serena. "Take care with your words." She leans in closer to him, lowering her voice. "We don't want to give her any ideas."

Serena is only half kidding, and Arista giggles behind them.

A distant, anguished moan floats through the woods. The trio look in the direction of the river. It is the sick bay.

"You know," says Liam, voice soft. "Since we left our homes... since we have been travelin' together, workin' together—"

"Sleeping together, saving lives together," offers Arista.

"That too." Liam stiffens at her interruption. He clears his throat, getting back to his original thought. "No one has died."

Serena takes a moment to remember all who perished up until The Migration. Scores of male

Undine—either as calflings or in battle, her mother, the King, Cordelia, Ervin, Sasha, Alaric, and several other werewolves during the battles. "You are right," Serena says, looking in the direction of the moans, then back at Liam. "Let's keep it that way."

"Whatever it takes," he agrees.

A few moments pass, and Arista has to chime in. She apparently can't stand silence. "Well, maybe not everyone has escaped the afterlife. We don't really know, do we?"

Serena's hand automatically goes to the satellite phone in her dry bag, and she exchanges a glance with Liam. "Maybe we should," says Serena.

He considers Serena for a moment before shaking his head. "We ain't callin' no one until we reach Ivvavik."

Serena knows he is right. They can't go back, and she doesn't even want to be tempted. She runs the pad of her thumb over the smooth rectangle that bulges from the bottom of her dry bag one more time, then lets her hand drop to her side. "I need to wash off," she says. "These scales grow cumbersome after a while."

Arista follows Serena toward the river, bidding Liam goodnight for the both of them.

Zigzagging through the trees, Serena steps quietly, evoking the same sense of adventure and thrill she used to get when absconding to the forests just outside The Deep. Behind her, Arista walks with similar dexterity, and Serena has to remember Arista has just as much experience with the woods, if not more.

Stepping out from the tree line and onto a large boulder, Serena drinks in the sight of the stream.

"The water is warm," says Arista. "Or at least warmer than the air."

Steam rises from the babbling river, blanketing the area and hugging the bathing maidens.

A steep drop in air temperature is the direct result of the storm passing through—it's as if Mother Nature is offering a reward for having endured her wrath.

Dropping their dry bags, Serena and Arista step carefully down a cascade of slick rocks, helping each other as they go. Arista enters the water first, not hesitating to lie down until she is fully submerged. She wiggles in delight, inadvertently splashing nearby maidens who frown then move away. Serena laughs at the indifferent maiden.

When Serena enters the water, it is slightly more graceful. She is aware of too many eyes on her, as if they are at Assembly and she is ascending the throne. Despite the awkward itch that runs down her spine, Serena feels a pang of homesickness for the familiar caves.

Maidens shift, giving Serena a respectful distance and opening up the deepest part of the river for her. The queen does not object. Here the water is crisp and runs slightly faster, already brushing at her scales in a cleansing wash.

She takes in a deep breath of steamy air, imagining the healing atmosphere sloughing away what oil might be left inside of her. Maidens in a circle around her tend to themselves, their colors casting effervescent hues on the surrounding steam and water.

Rainbow-colored oil seeps off their bodies, gathering in pools on the surface of the water, and beginning the trek down river back into the very same sound it came from. Serena imagines the pod of whales she helped through the Ungainly nets. They've survived one obstacle just to swim through another.

Shaking her head, Serena continues to rub the oil from her body. Once her upper arm is clean, she carefully retracts the scales. Rustling in the foliage on the other side of the river causes all maidens to look up. Simone and another healer each carry one end of a blanket cradling an unconscious maiden.

Blonde locks droop over the edge of the fabric, and Serena knows which maiden it is. When the healers lower their patient, nearby maidens gasp. Kiera is pasty white and her skin is covered in a sheen of sweat. Her chest rises slowly—too much time passes in between her breaths.

Angling their patient so her lower body up to her waist sits in the water, the healers lay her back on a mossy bank and begin scrubbing exposed skin and scales.

Sarafina, who stands closest to Kiera, begins to hum. Evandre joins in, their voices wavering together until they complement one another. It is the Undine healing song. Serena sang it once to Robbie, Darcy's youngest boy, in a motel bathroom as he suffered separation pains.

One by one, each maiden joins the song adding underlying base beats, sonorous high notes, or steady median tones that blend the song together in perfect harmony.

Inserting lyrics, the Undine call upon the ancients to restore Kiera. They call upon Poseidon to heal the water that is their home, and they call upon their werewolf protectors for a safe journey through perilous territories.

The forest moves around them, and Serena knows the song is working. Pack members, some transformed and some not, appear around the rocky banks. Encouraged, Serena stands up in the river, opens her mouth, and allows tentative notes to breeze past her lips. Although Serena is perfectly content to find harmony within the hymn, as usual Society has other plans for their queen. Maidens soften their voices, blending them into background composition.

Serena pauses briefly, glancing around as river water cascades down her scales. She steps onto an underwater boulder that lifts her above the rest of the maidens. They are now surrounded by pack members, waiting and watching. Even Xavier, still in his wolf form, settles onto his belly to show he will not be a threat.

Chest expanding as she takes a breath in, Serena pushes it out again, her vibrant voice gliding over the river like silk strands. A gentle wind moves in, carrying Serena's voice further. It wraps around Kiera, tousling her hair. It touches each of the maidens and, in turn, each of the werewolves. It breathes strength into Aiden, who stands at the river's edge with his parents and brothers. Serena surreptitiously sneaks in her own small prayer for Kai and all those suffering from memories of past violence between the species.

The pace of the song quickens as Serena ascends a series of tones, each note melding into the next. She is supported by her surrounding maidens who still sing, adding layer and depth. Rich and vibrant, the song climaxes in an interlacing ambiance.

Serena turns, almost stunned to find Kai standing directly in front of her. She releases her final note in time with the maidens.

Stepping forward, Kai wraps one arm around her waist, pulling her close in a brazen move. Serena only has a second to consider that everyone is watching before his lips join with hers. They kiss while fragments of the song still echo over the water.

Too soon, Kai pulls away. Fiery green eyes burn through Serena. "It shall be as you say," he says.

It takes Serena a moment to remember her healing song and all of the maidens' pleas to the ancients.

Kai bends to one knee in a deep bow, and the maidens follow suit with curtsies. Around her, pack members place closed fists over their hearts, and the wolves dip their heads.

Everyone is vowing a safe journey to their queen, and Serena knows they are united at last.

Chapter Forty

Once the very public bathing procession breaks apart with the wolves resuming their patrols and the maidens either retiring for the night or offering assistance to the healers, Serena and Kai retreat to their own tent. This time, it is very close to neighbors. After the storm, no one wants to remain too far apart from each other.

Kai insists Serena lie down while he settles the rest of the camp. She doesn't argue, but sleep doesn't come. Every time she closes her eyes all she can picture is the depths of the ocean where Aiden almost ended up.

The sounds of the encampment settle, replaced by a crackling fire that heats those still awake. She discerns the voices partaking in the type of inconsequential conversation that occurs around a late night blaze. Identifying the voices of Liam and Kai is easy. They sit next to each other, based on their number of low-spoken side conversations, and they are close to Serena's tent. Arista is also there—her high-pitched voice seeming to grate on everyone's nerves as they interrupt her each time she attempts to talk.

She has a rough road ahead of her in making friends, thinks Serena—almost endearingly.

There are a few other voices of pack members Serena doesn't recognize.

Conversation floats from storms to ships to animals of the forest. Just as Serena starts to drift off to sleep, Kai's nickname for her—*Moonshine*—snaps her back to the conscious world.

"You know it's a drink, right?" Liam says. "A human alcoholic drink."

"What does it taste like?" asks Kai.

"It's strong—kind of bitter, at first. It takes some gettin' used to," says Liam. "But it's addictive. Some of the pack members started makin' it during the worst of Alaric's reign. It takes the edge off. It makes things better."

There are a few moments of silence before Kai speaks. "What you just described, is Serena to me."

"Strong and kind of bitter." Liam snorts. "Yeah, I suppose it fits."

"I was leaning more toward the 'makes things better' part," says Kai.

Serena smiles to herself inside the tent.

"I could use a little moonshine," pipes up one of the pack members.

Serena can imagine both Liam and Kai going tense with closed fists.

"Er—the drink kind, not the queen kind," he clarifies.

"Me too." Arista laughs.

Serena turns her head, and she can see Arista's shadow cast by the fire scoot closer to the pack member. He places an arm around her shoulders.

Serena sighs. *She is going to find friends wherever she can.*

A few moments later Serena finally succumbs to restless dreams. She is awakened in what seems like minutes by rough shaking at her shoulder.

"Serena wake up!"

She pushes away a hand that feels awfully familiar. "Kai?"

"Arista has gone missing."

Serena sits up. "What?" Her brain struggles to process his words. "Where?"

"If we knew where, she wouldn't exactly be missing."

Running a hand down her face, Serena glares at Kai. "Don't get smart with me—not now."

"My apologies," says Kai. He holds his hand out to Serena.

She pulls herself to her feet with his assistance. "Who else is missing?"

"Liam is getting a count of the wolves now."

Serena and Kai step out of the tent just as Liam approaches. "All my wolves are here—it is just your maiden missing."

Serena looks at the smoldering ashes. "We need to go find her." She holds out her hand toward Liam.

Glancing at her outstretched palm, he removes her necklace from his pocket. It should help Serena locate Arista more quickly.

"I'm coming with," says Liam, still holding onto the necklace.

"Wait." Serena stops him. "What if it's a diversion—or a trap? Like for your blood. I don't fully trust Arista yet."

After a brief pause, Liam looks at the ground and kicks at pebbles. "Maybe," he mumbles.

"I'll go," says Kai.

Reluctantly, Liam hands over the necklace.

Serena wraps its chain around the werewolf bracelet she still holds so she can keep an eye on both as she walks.

"Take this, too," Liam says. "It's a rape whistle."

Serena squints, looking at the small device dangling from the end of a rope. "What is rape?" she asks. "And what in Poseidon's name is a whistle?"

A blaze of moonlight bounces off the smooth, silver contraption, flashing across Serena's eyes. "I don't want that thing—" Stumbling back, Serena trips over a fallen log.

Liam extends a hand, catching her at the wrist. Once he has her upright and steady, his arms drop to his sides. "That's it. I'm comin' with."

"I want you here, where I know you are safe." She puts force behind her words, as if that alone would make Liam obey her.

It doesn't have the effect she wants, and Liam turns to start walking.

Kai follows Serena, staying well back from the pair of squabbling siblings.

"Liam, just…" She ducks under another branch that snaps at her face—backlash from Liam's momentum. "I will not allow you to accompany me. And that is an order!"

Liam stops in his tracks. When he turns, his eyes fix on Serena. "Fine, I won't accompany you, then."

Serena takes deep breath and tries to recover some composure, smoothing back stray strands of hair from her braid. "Thank you."

"I'll just have to get there first." Liam grabs both the necklace and the bracelet from Serena's hand and takes off through the forest.

Serena's mouth drops open at Liam's retreating back. She snaps her lips together, drops her head in a determined stance, and runs after him. Unable to go full speed in the dark while trying to keep his eye on a few glowing stones, Liam zigzags through the forest, and Serena is able to keep up.

Once she is close enough, she makes a lunge for the jewelry splayed out in his palm. He pulls his hand back just in time, stepping out of the way, and Serena flies past him straight into a prickly bush.

"Argh!" her shouts of frustration are loud, causing almost as much of a ruckus as the thorn bush she tries to fight her way out of.

Kai catches up and reaches in to pull her out.

"You know, you could help me with him," says Serena. "Tie him down or something."

"Watching you two fight it out is far more entertaining."

"Ow!" exclaims Serena as Kai pulls another thorn stuck in between scales on her shoulder. "This isn't funny, Kai. I see human lights just up the way there."

"Is that so?" Kai turns and looks. "Are you trying to let them know we are coming?"

"No!" Serena pauses, realizing her mistake. "No," she says again, whispering this time. "Let's get Liam before we lose him."

It turns out the Undine sense of smell works better for locating werewolves than any glowing stone. Serena finds Liam in short order, convincing Kai to scale a tree with her so they can come at Liam from where he least expects it. Shuffling out onto a branch, it creaks under their combined weight. Serena crouches down, eyes glued to Liam who kneels behind a bush below her.

Kai glances forward, toward the lights. His eyes go wide. "Wait, Serena—no!"

But Serena is only focused on revenge. She leans forward, dropping from the tree directly on top of Liam. They both roll until they hit hard pavement.

Untangling themselves, Serena and Liam exchange nervous glances before they turn their attention to the semi-lit parking lot.

A group of five men who have just left a building are staring in their direction. Loud music booms from behind closed doors, shaking the shuttered windows. Reaching back to pull the hood over her head, Serena realizes she no longer even wears the sweatshirt. "Liam—maybe we should go... " Serena whispers out of the corner of her mouth. She risks a glance behind her. Kai waits as steady as the tree that holds him, not taking his eyes off the five men that stand in front of Serena and Liam.

Movement in the group draws attention. The men shift, and Arista peeks out from around one of them. He keeps his heavy arm draped over Arista as a smile lights her face. "I found some new test subjects. Look how big they are!"

"Arista," Serena growls. "Come here. Right. Now." Remembering Ungainly manners, Serena adds one more word. "Please."

Confusion, then indecision flits across Arista's face.

Serena steps forward. "If you do not obey of your own accord, I will have to sing."

Now confusion flits across every Ungainly face. Finally, Arista steps forward, but the arm around her tightens. "I didn't say it was okay to leave yet, missy."

"Let her go!" Serena shouts, taking a step forward.

Liam puts his arm in front of Serena, stopping her.

"That's okay, sweetheart." One of the bigger men comes toward the pair. "You can join us, too."

As he steps into the light, Serena's eyes go wide. The man is twice as big as Liam, and he continues to walk forward.

"Stop right there." Serena says. "Please?"

"I'm not sure these are the type you can order around, negotiate with, or sing to," whispers Liam.

Serena glances from them to Liam and back again, her pulse racing with panic. "Then what are we supposed to do with them?"

"Fight 'em." Liam's hands curl into fists.

"Absolutely not," says Serena. "We have to find another way."

"Just let me know when you have it figured out... sweetheart." His use of the Ungainly nickname sets her cheeks in flames. He steps back, making it clear she is in charge of the situation.

"Simply infuriating," mumbles Serena.

The Ungainly walking toward them seems to grow in size the closer he gets.

"Stop right there, or I'll have to stop you myself!" Serena tries again.

"With what, sweetheart?" he scoffs.

A quick glance around, and Serena's eyes settle on Liam's whistle still dangling from his hand. Grasping his elbow, Serena pushes up to force his hand in the air. "We have a rape whistle!"

Beside her, Liam buries his face in his other hand.

Chapter Forty-One

Laughing, the Ungainlies whoop and holler, some whistling and some even shouting out the word 'rape'.

Liam steps forward, lifting his chin and crossing his arms.

"You gonna blow that whistle?" someone shouts out. The laughter starts up again.

"It ain't my whistle you have to worry about it," says Liam. He waits until the last of them go silent. "It's what lies in wait in the dark behind me."

"He's just bluffing!" yells the one with his arm around Arista. "Let's take the other one, too and get out of here."

"Don't believe me?" asks Liam. He takes another step to the side and holds an inviting arm out toward Serena. "Fine. Take her."

Serena's mouth drops open as she looks at Liam.

The large Ungainly hesitates, and suddenly he doesn't look so threatening.

Liam takes another step aside just to prove his point.

Interpreting this as a challenge, the Ungainly sneers. "Fine."

Three more steps and he is directly in front of Serena. She lifts her chin to meet his eyes. Light from the streetlamps spills across her face, illuminating her deep blue cheekbones.

His hand freezes inches from her shoulder. This close, Serena can see right into his reddened, bleary eyes. After a night of drinking, he is struggling to process the creature before him. Serena doesn't blame him. She does not belong in his world.

Serena holds her breath, waiting for the Ungainly's decision.

It is a poor one.

With his extended hand, he reaches out, grabbing Serena by the braid. Pulling it into him and slightly down, he smiles having Serena under his control. She is bent back at an awkward angle with her neck exposed.

Pure agitation, both physically and mentally, causes her hair to come to life. Her bioluminescence burns brighter than any streetlamp.

"What in the—"

The man is cut short before he can utter even one of his god's curse words. Kai lunges from the tree, plowing into Serena's captor. By the time she straightens herself, the pair are rolling on the ground. Liam has gone for the rest of the group, which she now understands was why he kept sidestepping away. He needed a clear path.

It leaves Serena in an awkward position with nothing to do. By pushing back three humans at once, Liam leaves Arista free of watchers. Making direct eye contact, Serena points to Arista, then to the area right in front of herself, mouthing the words. "Come here."

Having the grace to look sheepish, Arista walks forward hugging her elbows and keeping her eyes pinned to the ground. She sidesteps quickly when Kai and his human roll by.

"I know you mean well, really I do," Serena chastises Arista. "But from now on before you make any decisions—and I mean *any*—you must seek my approval first."

"I explained my intent to the Ungainlies," argues Arista. "They agreed to give me blood samples so I could test for compatibility before I injected anything into them."

Serena shakes her head, ushering Arista back to the woods. "I don't think those were the kind of samples they were intending to give."

A dueling pair slams into the ground in front of the maidens. They jump back, Arista squealing. Kai is on top, and the human beneath him has hit his head against the pavement. Blood splatters across the blacktop.

Arista reaches out toward a small pool of the thick, red liquid. "Could we just—"

"Absolutely not!" Serena pulls her away.

Despite the loss of blood, the human has plenty of fight left within him. He kicks Kai off, then lunges, catching Kai in his midsection with a hard shoulder. Both Kai and Liam have their hands full, but they won't abandon the maidens. Serena needs to get Arista safely away before they can bow out of the fight.

Still ushering Arista, Serena is almost at the tree line. The forest leans forward, ready to welcome them into its dark embrace.

But someone steps in their way, casting an even darker shadow over the pair of maidens.

It is Arista's original suitor, and he isn't giving her up so easily.

"You're with me." He sneers, reaching out for her other arm.

Serena yanks back, pulling Arista out of his reach. His swipe hits nothing but air, and he stumbles forward. Stepping in front of Arista, Serena uses his momentum and pushes down on his head. Keeping one of her webbed feet solid and strong in front of his boots, she manages to trip him. He falls hard, slamming into the pavement.

Groaning, he attempts to push himself up. He reeks of alcohol and blood, his clothes are disheveled and half falling off from the fight, and he looks as if it might be another few days before he is able to get himself off the ground.

Nonetheless, he is making the attempt, and Serena doesn't want to risk anything. She takes off the belt that barely holds his pants up and uses it to tie his hands around his back. In the process, an Ungainly weapon clatters to the ground from his waistline.

Serena picks up the shiny black handgun, checks it for bullets, and raises it above her head.

The shot splits the air and leaves a ringing echo in her ears. A nearby streetlamp shatters, sending a spray of glass across the pavement. The fights before her stop cold.

"What are you—?"

The question is cut off when Serena pulls the trigger again. Ungainlies pull themselves apart from Liam and Kai.

Another man attempts to speak, putting his hands gently in the air. "Listen, little blue miss, we were just having some fun."

She pulls the trigger two more times. She lifts her chin and, out of the corner of her eye, she can see the chamber of the pistol hanging open. There are no more bullets left.

Confidence wavering, Serena lowers the weapon before anyone else can see. "We shall retire for the night," Serena says. "Go back to your party and leave us in peace."

No one moves for several seconds. There are no sounds save for the music coming from the building behind them.

"There's nothing in those woods for you." One of the Ungainlies nods to the dark forest behind Serena. "Except trouble."

Liam and Kai have started toward Serena now, keeping a wary eye on the humans as they pass.

"We are accustomed to trouble," says Serena. "And we will not bother you again." Serena makes a pointed look at Arista.

"Let me." Kai takes the weapon from Serena and disassembles the parts, dropping piece by piece as they walk toward the forest.

"When did you learn to do all that?" Arista asks the group as she follows them into the tree line.

"When you were sitting in prison eating sponge worms," says Serena. She lays a hand on Arista's shoulder. "Come on. They aren't going to leave it at that. We need to hurry."

The group starts toward their camp at a light jog, but it isn't long before they can hear someone crashing through the trees behind them. It sounds as if the Ungainly herd has doubled in size. Serena leads the way, dragging Arista behind her. They duck under branches, plough through shrubbery, and hop over bushes. Scratches form across Serena's legs and arms but she doesn't want to bring her armor forward for fear it would slow her.

Sprinting through a brief clearing, Serena risks a glance back. She can see the first Ungainly on Liam's heels. In front of her, glowing eyes peer out from the next clump of trees. Smiling to herself, Serena repositions her hand on Arista's arm to get a better grip. She charges straight for a thick, fallen trunk.

"Serena…" Arista manages to squeak out in between heavy breaths.

"Duck!" yells Serena.

They both slide under the tree followed closely by Kai and Liam. Feet slipping on loose soil, Serena looks up to see the hairy underbelly of a werewolf leaping over the fallen tree. A chorus of growls tell her several more follow. Serena leads her group behind a bush and they stop to catch their breath, peering through a screen of leaves.

The werewolves stand their ground in the clearing, forming a line so the Ungainlies can go no further.

"Hold!" The first human raises his arms until his friends skitter to a stop. After at least ten of them crowd the clearing, one more man lopes up from behind. Serena recognizes him as the one she tied up. He whips the belt in the air above his head like a lasso. After peeking around his friends, his arm drops and the belt goes limp in his hands.

"Stand together!" the one in front tries to direct his friends. "They won't attack something that looks bigger than them."

"That's bears, not wolves," a comrade whispers through gritted teeth.

"It applies to all animals, dummy."

In response, one of the wolves pulls back his lips in a snarl and lets loose a round of vicious growling and snapping. The men lose their nerve, turn tail, and run.

Rising from their hiding spot, Liam, Kai, and the two maidens brush themselves off, nodding their thanks to the wolves.

"Better pack up camp." Liam gestures to the sky. It begins to lighten as dawn approaches. "We have one more day of sailing ahead of us."

Chapter Forty-Two

Once they return to camp, it is a mad rush to pack up and board the boats before Ungainly authorities decide to investigate a wolf pack too close to an Ungainly city. Back on board the tugboat, Serena double checks the sailing route with the navigator. It will be an easy day—only a couple of hours until they reached the finish line: Juneau, Alaska.

They cast off and take it slow, Serena keeping watch until she spots the other racers coming up behind them, the three other ships from her fleet included. Serena breathes a sigh of relief. The ships are whole and have run up the green flag. All is well.

With Ungainlies approaching quickly, all of the Undine and most of the wolves disappear below deck. Serena goes with them. She pauses at the bottom of the ladder well, searching the dimly lit room until her eyes lock onto Simone's bright red scales.

Weaving her way through bodies packed into the hull of the ship, Serena finds the sick area.

"It is at least considerably less," she murmurs to Simone.

"Yes," says Simone, straightening to wipe her forehead with the back of her hand. "But for those that are still here… " She trails off, as if a lump forming in her throat makes it impossible for her to speak further.

Serena understands—their chances aren't good.

Taking a deep breath, Serena turns to look at the sick maidens. There are three of them, one is pinkish-purple Kiera, her damp blonde tresses curled and sticking to a reddened face—the result of a fever sustained far too long.

Simone slumps down beside Kiera.

"Can you help them?" asks Serena.

"I have," says Simone. "I've done everything I did for you and more. But they are showing no signs of improvement. They just keep getting worse." Simone dabs at Kiera's forehead with a cool, wet rag. "They need to be in their natural form in healing waters. It is the only other thing that I can think of that will help."

"How quickly?" asks Serena.

Simone looks at Serena with a steady gaze. "Within 24 hours."

Mouth dropping open, Serena holds out empty hands as if she has nothing to offer. "We have at least three more weeks of sailing ahead of us!"

Lips tight, Simone doesn't acknowledge Serena. She only picks up the rag, and dabs at Kiera's forehead again.

"Excuse me." A pack member practically shoves Serena aside. "I have more cold water, and here is the axe you asked for, Simone."

"Axe?" Serena exclaims.

The queen is ignored.

"Use it on these." Simone hands the pack member a small, wooden bowl and a vial of herbs.

Without question, he sits down and grinds at the herbs with the handle of the axe. A flowery, soothing scent fills the air.

"He hasn't left her side," Simone says to Serena. "So I had to put him to good use."

"End of the line!" shouts on the deck ring below. The finish line to the race is in sight, but it gives Serena no sense of glory or accomplishment. Their race against the clock starts now, and this time, everyone might not survive.

Fishing through her bag, Serena pulls out her hooded sweatshirt and slips it on. She makes her way above deck, pulling the material low over her head. Cheers ring out from a distance. Following the sound, Serena watches as the Juneau port comes into view. The piers are crowded with people waving. Sitting amongst the crowd is a white judges' tent—a tall trophy sits inside, its gold beaming out.

"What is that flashing?" Serena asks, coming to stand next to Liam and Kai at the railing.

"They are taking pictures," says Liam. "Smile."

"Oh," Serena turns her back, pulling her hood down even further. "What now?"

"We will need to check in for the final leg," says Kai. "Then there are awards and acknowledgements—"

"Why do we need to stay for all that?" Serena asks, frowning.

"We need to stay at least long enough so as not to appear suspicious," says Liam, leaning out on the rail. "It'd also be good to find out what came from last night, and if the authorities are looking for anyone. Why? In a hurry?"

"Yes, as a matter of fact." Serena crosses her arms. "There are three sick maidens, and they don't have much time left. We need to get them to healthy waters, and we need to do it by tomorrow."

There is no response from Kai and Liam. They stand still, processing the information until Ungainlies on the ports are in front of them. Imitating sailors on the other ships, Kai and Liam raise their hands to wave. The motion is purely mechanical.

Serena knows they are racking their brains for solutions.

Even going over land wouldn't be quick enough. Kiera and the other two maidens are out of time.

We need a miracle, Poseidon. Serena glances over her shoulder at some of the other boats coming in.

We need speed. Serena looks at limp sails. Yesterday's storm took all of the wind with it.

We need wings. A pair of bald eagles fly overhead.

We need..."Bush pilots," she says out loud. Her eyes are back on the boats. One, in particular, that holds an Ungainly she recognizes.

"What?" Kai and Liam ask simultaneously as they turn around, looking to where Serena points.

"Bush pilots," she repeats.

Understanding dawns on their faces.

"We'll need to do a whole lot of convincing," says Liam.

"We can find some way to pay him," says Kai.

Liam nods. "I know we can. I was talking about the rest of us."

"No convincing needed," says Serena.

They both look at her, skepticism scrunching up their faces.

"I am the queen," says Serena.

Now Liam raises an eyebrow.

"Well, I am," she mumbles.

"I'll go get some form of payment," says Liam.

"And I'll go talk to the pilots," says Kai.

"And I'll go... be a queen," offers Serena.

As the tugboat pulls into port, Serena disappears back below deck. Despite the loud cheers, music, and clapping from the pier, the mood below is somber.

Kiera has taken a turn for the worse, and everyone sits quietly.

Previously prepared to issue a decree worthy of a full Assembly, Serena changes her mind. She moves through the crowded room quickly, whispering to those closest to her so as not to distract the healers from doing their jobs. "We will be traveling by plane to our destination. Bring only that which you can carry with you. Everything else will have to stay here."

There is no hesitation and no refusal by anyone to the new form of travel. The urgency at which the healers work speaks to the need.

Serena continues moving through the room. As she skirts around a group of mixed maidens and werewolves holding hands with heads bent together, she realizes there are no more lines of division. Instead of the maidens huddled together on one side, with the werewolves lined up on the other, they are all interspersed. They are encouraging each other, they are helping each other, and beyond that, they care for each other.

Her sense of pride is dashed as a flurry of activity near the sick bay draws Serena's attention. Victory comes at a steep price.

Chapter Forty-Three

As soon as Serena receives word that Kai and Liam have returned, she races above deck and out on the pier to meet them. She is taking a chance, but the crowds have dispersed for the most part and Simone has already had to resuscitate Kiera once. Every second counts.

"Did you make arrangements?" Serena asks.

"We have a ride if we can find payment," says Kai.

Liam nods. "I thought we could sell the boats, but no one wants them. I'm not even sure I could give them away with such short notice."

"Sir! Excuse me, sir?"

An Ungainly is racing down the pier toward Liam and Serena.

"Uh-oh," Serena pulls her hood further down her forehead. Behind her, two more Ungainlies are unloading a large pallet of supplies. She is trapped. "Just get rid of him quickly," she whispers to her brother.

Kai edges closer to Serena and takes her hand. Her quickening heartbeat evens out, and she takes a deep breath, putting most of herself behind Kai and Liam, stealing small glances of the approaching Ungainly in between them.

He jogs the rest of the way to the group. He is a heavy man and already breathing hard with the excrtion.

"Congratulations," Liam says as they wait for him to catch his breath.

The man glances at the trophy he carries in one arm. It is a huge cup mounted on driftwood. A small plaque nailed to the wood reads, 'First Place, Capital to Capital Predicted Log Yachting Race'.

"Thank you—though after the events of the race, I could care less about winning any trophy. You see, my son was on one of those ships that broke apart during the storm. I let him travel with his uncle, my brother. Damn fool thought he could get out ahead of the weather. They left before I could stop them." His voice catches in his throat. He shakes his head as if warding away thoughts of what could've been.

Vaguely, Serena recalls a teenage boy she pulled from the depths of the sound during the storm.

"I know your ship pulled him out of the water, and I wanted to thank you." He shifts the trophy to the other arm and holds out his hand.

Narrowing his eyes, Liam scrutinizes the human. The human lifts his eyebrows, glistening blue eyes looking harmless enough. Kai elbows Liam.

"Oh, right." Liam shakes the human's hand. "Weren't nothin'."

"Nothing?" The man scoffs. "It was my son's life—he means everything to me. This" —he holds up the trophy— "is nothing. Thank you for saving my son."

"You are most welcome," Kai offers, his sense of manners exceeding what Liam can give.

The man nods once to Kai. "Anyway, I heard as how you were looking to sell your ships."

"You interested?" asks Liam.

Serena has a brief moment of elation, until the man speaks again.

"No," he says. "But I gather you're in need of some money." He looks at the trophy again, a tiny flicker of regret flashing across his face, then he shoves the award into Liam's arms.

Liam takes a step back, looking down at the trophy in his hands. "Heavy," he comments.

"Pure gold," says the human. "I imagine you can get a pretty penny for it."

"You…" Liam's eyes go wide. "You're giving this to us?"

"Like I said, don't mean nothing compared to what you did for me. I only wish I could give you more."

The group goes quiet, staring at one another in awkward silence. Finally, the human gives a nervous laugh. "My son said something about angels in the water. Swears he saw something out there…" he trails off, shaking his head. "Proves more than anything how close to death he really came." His voice cracks again.

Liam lays a heavy hand on the human's shoulder, snapping the man out of it. "Best not to dwell on it," he says, half turning the man back down the pier.

Before Liam can steer him away, Serena steps in front of them in a bold move. The Undine have already been exposed, and she has to know how these Ungainlies will react. She is counting on the fact that he is obviously not as heartless a creature as those in the parking lot in Juneau.

Against all instincts screaming at her not to, Serena reaches up and pulls back her hood. Out of the corner of her eye, she sees Liam's mouth drop open and his hand starts to rise, as if he is going to put the hood right back on her.

She gives him a hard look and his hand freezes mid-air. Satisfied he won't interfere, she returns her gaze to the man before her.

His eyes examine her face, everything from her angled, sharp chin to her blue-tinted cheekbones. Expression neutral, he finally meets her eyes and does not waver from there as he speaks. "You know what?"

Serena waits, holding her breath and lifting her chin slightly, clinging to her own confidence.

"I do believe my son was right... 'bout them angels in the water."

Chapter Forty-Four

The old cargo plane is a patchwork of metal squares held together by rusty nails. One faded stripe runs along its side. Serena squints, trying to make out the foreign lettering.

"Russian," says Liam, crossing his arms to stare at the plane alongside her.

"Oh," says Serena. She knows little to nothing about Russians or their machinery. "What does that mean? Will it be safe?"

"It means we'll get there—but it ain't goin' to be pretty." Liam glances behind them. Several werewolves are transporting sick maidens in sheets. The healers walk alongside them, holding the limp wrists of their patients to keep apprised of their pulses. "Come on," says Liam. "The sooner we get to Ivvavvik, the better."

Liam is the first to climb the steep stairwell to the plane, and Serena stays tight on his heels. The whole thing sways as they pull themselves up each step. Serena swears even the flight can't be as dangerous as the stairwell.

Once they enter the plane, Liam hands the trophy to the pilot.

"As agreed," he says.

The pilot inspects the trophy, rubbing the back of his hand under his nose. "You ain't trying to trick us with no fake, are ya?"

Crossing his arms, Liam stares at the pilot from under bushy eyebrows. "Just get us there—
whole. And don't say nothin' about who or what you see that is about to board this plane."

"That there's my job, ace." He passes the trophy over to his co-pilot, then salutes Liam. They both disappear into the cockpit to prepare for takeoff. Amidst all the button-pushing and switch-flicking, they are making jokes and passing a flask back and forth, taking swigs of a liquid that Serena can smell from where she stands.

She crinkles her nose. "What are they drinking?"

Lifting one side of his lips up in a devious smile, Liam looks down at her. "Smells like moonshine."

Having just boarded, Kai pauses to follow their gazes into the cockpit.

"I dislike it," says Serena.

"Now I have to think of another pet name." Kai rolls his eyes and sits down on a bench running on the inside of the cargo walls shaking his head. "It was such a good one, too."

Liam and Serena move aside to allow maidens and wolves to board and find a seat. Conner and Xavier carry the trunk of tridents to tie down on the floor of the plane. Zeke is helping Doug hop to his seat on one foot. Darcy and Colin keep a tight grip on their boys as all three have different ideas about where they want to sit for the ride.

"Buckle up back there!" the co-pilot shouts over his shoulder as they engines sputter to life.

Subtle shifting down the rows of benches cause a commotion until Kai yells back, "There *are* no buckles!"

Both pilots feign a look of surprise, then let out a bout of maniacal laughter. Exchanging an exasperated glance, Serena and Liam hurry the rest of the maidens and wolves on board, giving false assurances despite the prankster pilots.

The wheels begin to roll even before everyone is seated, and when the aircraft is at its top ground speed, Serena still has her head out thc door checking to see if they've left anyone behind. Several alarming bumps later, Kai pulls Serena in and helps Liam figure out how to seal the door.

Settling into the bench, Serena peers out the window. The ride becomes smooth as the aircraft rises into the air, and Serena sees the tops of the five ships they left behind. Liam made arrangements for an agent to watch over them and sell them if he can, splitting the difference in half, leaving Danny's address for his share of the money.

The plane tilts its nose up, causing everyone to hold on to the person next to them. The sick maidens, the healers, and Colin and Darcy and their boys are all on the floor in the middle of the plane. Wolves and maidens close by reach out to help secure them in place. Arms link together down the line creating a tight-knit web of intertwined limbs, scales and furry hides against one another.

Serena releases her grip on the maiden next her once the plane evens out. She swallows to relieve the pressure in her ears, then turns to Kai. It is too loud to speak to one another, but his furrowed eyebrows tell her he is worried. He rubs the pad of his thumb over her bare arm. The skin there is flaking and dry.

Attempting to calm his thoughts, she lays her hand over his and buries her head in his chest. The public intimacy would be unheard of just days ago, but maidens and wolves who have no romantic tendencies toward each other are doing the same. Sometimes the simple, solid warmth of another is enough to keep monsters at bay, even for the monsters themselves.

* * *

Waking with a jolt, Serena rubs her eyes.

"We are descending." Kai leans in close so she can hear. "We are almost there."

The flight was supposed to be short—only a few hours—but she must have managed to doze off. Fully alert now, Serena presses both palms and her nose against the window. All she can see is grayish-white. She fights back a moment of nausea as she realizes the clouds are underneath her. Adjusting in her seat, she moves her face up the window so she can see at a better angle looking down. Suddenly the clouds break and a glassy-blue ocean spreads out before them. Everyone on Serena's side of the plane gasps in awe. Ripples of pristine water roll across the expanse of the Beaufort Sea, tendrils of white froth accenting the blue.

Serena feels a ripple just under her skin. Squeezing her hands into fists, she fights back the urge to release her scales, form her tail, and jump out of the plane just to dive in.

"The forest," says Liam.

"What about it?" Serena asks, shifting her gaze to the land mass neighboring the sea.

"There isn't one." He frowns.

Darcy steps up to the window by Liam. "There are thicker trees further inland," she lays a hand on his shoulder. "But... the idea here is that we won't need to hide in the forest anymore."

Serena smiles at Darcy's use of the word 'we'.

"Here we are," announces one of the pilots from the cockpit.

"Set us down there." Liam points out the window. "As close as you can to that peninsula."

"Right." The pilots glance at each other. "We're gonna need our payment first."

Confusion tugs Liam's eyebrows together. "I gave you the trophy."

"Eh?" The pilot brings his hand to his ear as if he suddenly can't hear.

Liam stands and stomps toward the cockpit. "I already paid you!" he yells over the roar of the engine.

"Oh, right." The pilot nods. He half turns in his seat to face Liam. "That covered takeoff and the flight. We're going to need payment for the landing before we set her down." Both men look at each other and chuckle. "And the bigger the payment, the softer the landing."

Serena knows what is coming, but before she can even stand from the bench, Liam lunges for the pilot. Huge, hairy hands wrap around a fat, red neck.

The entire plane gives a violent tilt to the left. Maidens and wolves from one side slam into those across from them. Serena fights her way free of heavy bodies. Despite the pilot's refusal to land, the plane makes a series of stomach-flipping drops. With each one, Serena chokes back fear and nausea, imagining they will slam into the ground any minute.

Spotting the chest that holds their tridents tied down at the back of the plane, Serena moves more quickly. A glance over her shoulder reveals Liam in a full blown wrestling match with the pilot. Her brother has yanked the man out of his seat and is now slamming him repeatedly into the dash. Instruments light up with every thunk.

The co-pilot attempts to fly the plane himself, working around the pair of wrestlers. Beads of sweat slide down his face, but every time there is another thunk, he lets out a bout of maniacal laughter.

"Poseidon damn me if I've led them all the way here just to die at the hands of these crazy... Russians," Serena mumbles, refusing to even grace them with the name of Ungainly. Flipping open the lid to the trunk, Serena reaches in, her hand wrapping around cold, familiar metal.

Pulling her arm out, she runs the pad of her thumb over her mark etched into the stem of the trident. Moon Shadow—a double circle representing the full moon and the shadow it casts upon the ocean.

One last favor, Dagon.

Serena turns and yells, "Everyone down!"

Fortunately, the maidens know their Queen's command voice. The wolves are a bit slower, but they are quickly pulled down by maidens. The last head is shoved aside just as Serena releases her trident.

The elongated center prong narrows in on its mark, with the two outer prongs spinning around it. At the front of the plane, Liam cocks his ear. Even above the roar of the engines, Liam knows the sound of a trident slicing through the air.

He holds his man by the scruff of the neck, pushing him into the direct path of the trident.

Serena's eyes widen in horror, and Liam's own words run through her head. *Since we left our home, no one has died.* The trident is almost to the cockpit and Liam still hesitates.

Don't do it.

At the last second Liam pulls. As the trident rotates past, one of the prongs scrape the man's cheek, drawing blood. Prongs slam into the instrument console spitting out a spray of sparks.

Every head turns to look at Serena.

"There is your payment," she says, chest heaving and eyes full of red. "Now set us down before we rip this Russian beast apart."

Slowly, and with a wary eye on Liam, the pilot sits down in his seat. This time there is no laughter and no drink passed back and forth. They bend their heads in concentration, working around the obstacle the trident presents, making do without the systems that have been damaged.

The aircraft makes a wide turn, then straightens out coming around for a long strip of clear beach.

Chapter Forty-Five

Late morning fog rolls across the beach. Two snow-white caribou pause in their grazing, ears perking at the sound of engines overhead. But the alien noise cuts off abruptly, and the caribou go back to nosing through sand, searching for sparse grass blades. The gentle arctic sea laps at their hooves as they amble along.

The bull sees movement in the fog, and he turns, putting his fuzzy antlers on full display. A wavering dark shadow forms, and the bull decides it is not worthy investigating. He gives a short grunt, urging his female out of the way, and they both lope along to the next beach.

Cautiously, the shadow moves forward onto the shoreline.

A lone pack member steps into the sun. Stumbling with exhaustion, he catches himself before he loses the precious load he carries in his arms—an unconscious maiden, pinkish-purple scales glittering in the sunlight. Her blonde hair hangs loose and messy, swaying in rhythm to his walk, swaying in rhythm to the waves reaching out, calling to wolf and Undine alike.

His eyes lock onto the water. A few more agonizing steps and finally frothy white hits his boots. Sinking to his knees, the next wave rushes in. He lowers his arms, relinquishing the maiden to healing water. It scours over her, scrubbing scales and skin in a cleansing rinse. Her body's natural response takes over. More scales emerge and legs meld together to form a tail. Ribbed gills behind her ears burst open to catch the surge of salt water.

The wolf releases her completely, allowing the wave to take her with it as it retreats. He holds his breath, waiting and watching, refusing to feel the relief that threatens to flood his system.

More shadows emerge from the fog. Their silence is respectful as they wait with him.

Further out in calmer waters, there is a disturbance. All eyes are pinned on the spot. There is more movement, however subtle. The surface breaks, the sound of it whispering across the beach.

The next wave builds, and the wolf smiles. He can hear the song of the maiden before she even surfaces. As the wave crashes on the shore, he pushes himself to his feet, catching a glimpse of a finned tail, arching up and out of the water.

All is well. They are home.

Epilogue

"Hello?" The voice crackles with static, and it sounds distant, like it comes to Serena through a long tube.

But Serena would recognize that voice in any form. Her eyes are already glistening with tears. "Mariam?"

"I do not believe my ears..." the voice trails off and there is a clunk, like the satellite phone on the other end has been dropped.

"Mariam? Mariam?" Serena practically yells into her handset through a series of fumbling, clicks and exclamations on the other end.

"Serena, dear, did you make it? Are you in trouble?" asks Mariam.

"No, no," Serena answers. "We made it. We are all well and here at Ivvavik. What about you? Is everyone okay?"

There is a brief silence before Mariam speaks again. "Two of the elders have passed into the afterlife."

Serena shakes her head. "We have a way to bring you here, by plane. Before anyone else—"

"Serena... we've made our decision. No one has changed their mind. Now, no more talk of that. What is it like there?"

Maidens have gathered in a large circle around Serena, and they've started shouting.

"Tell Hailey I resuscitated a wolf." Simone leans forward, talking into the handset herself.

"Shh." Serena waves Simone away.

"Ronan and Rayne send their love," says Mariam. "And Murphy wants to know if you still have your trident."

Serena's laugh turns into a sob. "Tell him no—I don't. But it served its purpose. It got us here."

Mariam laughs in response. "I'll let him know."

"Listen, we don't have much time," says Serena. "I don't want to risk being tracked, but we'll figure out a routine where we can make calls regularly. Others want to talk, too, so I'll pass the phone on now."

"Okay, Serena. We are so proud of you, and we send our blessings. Be careful."

"Always am." Serena is barely able to complete their old exchange without choking on it. She passes the phone on to the group of maidens who immediately begin arguing over it.

Stepping away, Serena wipes her cheeks with the heel of her hand. She ascends a bank of large boulders into one of many caves carved into the shoreline.

The sharp smell of boiling hydrocoral drifts out. Arista looks up from her grinding stone when Serena enters. Darcy stokes a smoldering fire.

"The potion is coming along?" asks Serena.

"We hope so," says Darcy. She stands, wiping her hands across an apron she wears. "As long as we can find a way to cultivate the anti-venom in sharks."

"It'll be tricky," says Serena. "But it was either the sharks or humans." She narrows her eyes at Arista. "And the latter is harder to come by in these parts."

"Well, I'm off," says Darcy. "I have to get dinner started. Colin has the boys out hunting nearly every day, and they are always starving by the time they get back."

Months ago, after their arrival at Ivvavik, one of the first projects was to build a temporary home for Colin's family. The rest of the pack are making themselves comfortable in the caves on the beach, and the Painted Maidens have all found homes in The Deep.

The entire group decided to wait until they were settled and the sick maidens were recovered before they called home.

"We'll see you tomorrow?" asks Arista.

"As you say." Darcy gives a curtsey, causing Arista to giggle.

Darcy turns and waves to Serena, then exits the cave, making her way carefully over the rocks.

When Serena turns back to Arista, the woman is bent over the grinding stone again.

"Has her majesty come for a reading?" Arista raises a curious eyebrow.

"Are you able to see now that you have your hydrocoral?" Serena asks.

"Some paths are clearer than others." Arista shrugs. "Is there something in particular you wish to know?"

Sitting down on a hard rock across from Arista, Serena waits until the Undine psychic is finished turning the batch of hydrocoral in front of her to powder. Arista carefully pushes the small pile into a tube, corks it, then looks up at Serena.

"When I was sick during The Migration, in the midst of my fevers, I had a dream."

"A dream?" Arista interrupts. "Or a vision?"

"I don't know…" Serena shifts on her rock. "But I believe I was on the verge of death, until I was told I had yet to fulfill my purpose." Now Serena shrugs. "And then I came back."

Arista nods, quiet as she stares into the fire. Noise from maidens flocking around the phone on the beach filters in. Finally, Arista turns to look at Serena. "I have foreseen something that could certainly be interpreted as your purpose."

"Well?" Serena puts her hand to her heart—it is beating so hard it feels as if it might burst from her chest.

Slowly, Arista leans over. "Not there," she says as she takes Serena's wrist, moving the queen's hand until it rests over her stomach. "There."

Serena's eyes go wide as she looks down. "A child…"

"No," says Arista. "A single blessing is reserved for Liam and Sophia." She gestures out onto the beach where Sophia's bright orange scales stand apart from the rest of the maidens. She walks along the tide line, hand in hand with Liam. "Theirs will be named for Sasha, our lost maiden."

Serena smiles, a bloom of warmth spreading in her chest that wards away the cold of the cave.

"Her majesty," continues Arista, "will take after her mother."

"Twins," says Serena, her voice hollow. "A boy and a girl?"

Arista nods. "They grow already."

Serena looks down again, her fingers spreading wide over her stomach. Suddenly, she looks up, spotting the hydrocoral. "The anti-venom—"

"Will be ready," interrupts Arista. "Why do you think I've been working so hard?"

Serena nods, biting her lip for the first time in a long time. In a burst of emotion, she throws her arms around Arista, burying her head in the psychics braid. "I'm so glad you're not still in chains."

Arista laughs the high-pitch, annoying laugh that Serena now finds endearing. "Me as well, your majesty."

"So they will both be born healthy? What will we name them? Will there be more after the twins?"

Putting both hands in the air, Arista puts a polite stop to Serena's questions. "I'm sorry, your majesty. But the first thing Isadora taught me was to never reveal too much." Arista leans closer to Serena and winks. "Takes the magic out of it."

"Out of what?" asks Serena.

Arista makes a wide circle with her hands. "Life."

Nodding, Serena swallows her next hundred questions with an audible gulp. She puts her hand to her stomach again, focusing on the here and now. "Oh," says Serena. She digs into the dry bag at her hip and pulls out a large book. "Since none of the caves in The Deep here escape high tide, I thought we could leave this with you."

"The Ancestral Book," says Arista, eyes wide. She runs her hand gently over the cover. "I didn't realize Mariam gave it to you."

"She believed it was ours for the taking." Serena smiles, placing her hand over Arista's. "So we can add to it."

Arista nods, then hugs the book to her chest. "I will watch over it, your majesty."

"I would be much obliged, Arista." Serena rises and turns to leaves. "Oh, and Arista?"

"Hmm?" the Undine psychic murmurs, unable to tear her eyes from the book she holds.

"We'll be holding elections for a new council tomorrow. As Isadora's former understudy, I plan on nominating you."

Arista finally glances up. "Are you sure? Society... doesn't really like me."

"I think they'll come around," says Serena. "Besides, having you on the council will give Assembly a bit more... " Serena makes a wide circle with her hands. "Life."

Before Arista can protest further, Serena says her goodbyes making a promise she will return tomorrow with more questions about her twins. She exits the cave, spotting Kai on one end of the beach. He stares up into the sky, following the white contrail of an airplane from east to west.

"Can they see us?" Serena asks.

Kai brings his gaze back to earth and smiles. "No, too high up." He wraps his arms around Serena. "Though I've been talking to Liam. There are other things out there that can see us. Satellites, I think he said. We should consider only coming onto the beaches at night."

"Is that an official order from The Head of the Guard?" asks Serena.

He straightens, clearing his throat and rotating his trident in a full circle once with his free hand. "My first decree."

Serena laughs. "As you say."

He spins the trident again then brings it to his side, looking at Serena. "Do you miss your trident?"

She buries her head in his chest, looking out at the sea as he squeezes her tighter. "No," she says. "I have no use for Dagon here. It felt... appropriate as final payment for our passage to the birthing grounds."

"I wish you'd stop calling Ivvavik 'the birthing grounds'. It sounds so feminine."

Serena smiles to herself. *There is a reason for everything*, she thinks. But for now, she keeps Arista's news to herself. There will be time for an announcement to Kai. There will be time now for a lot of things.

"Will you ever tire of kissing me?" Serena asks.

Knitting his eyebrows together, Kai lifts her chin with the crook of his finger, searching her eyes. "Serena," he begins then pauses, perhaps searching for the right words. He twirls the small mermaid charm that dangles from her neck around his finger.

Above them, the clouds have finally broken and snow falls, dusting the pair of them with white flurries.

Eyes lighting up, Kai looks at her again. "Serena, every kiss with you is as unique as a snowflake."

He leans in, touching his lips to hers. It is a sweet, lingering kiss, and before it's done she can feel his lips curving in a smile.

"I think I just found a new pet name for you," he murmurs.

Her eyes widen. "No."

"Come here, snowflake," he growls. "Give us a smooch."

"The name makes no sense!" she laughs, pushing him away.

He bends, scooping her up in his arms, teasing and snarling at her as he walks into the ocean.

Serena's laughter skips across the water one more time before they disappear beneath the surface, heading to the dark embrace of The Deep.

About the Author

Terra is author of the eco-fantasy novels in the Akasha Series, 'Water', 'Air', 'Fire' and 'Earth', as well as the Painted Maidens Trilogy. Born and raised in Colorado, Terra has since lived in California, Texas, Utah, North Carolina, and Virginia. Terra served a 5½ year enlistment in the Marine Corp, has earned her bachelor's and master's degree and presently runs the language services division of a small business. Terra currently lives in a suburb of Washington, DC with her husband of fifteen years and three children.

Connect with Terra:

E-mail: terra.harmony11@gmail.com
Facebook: http://facebook.com/terraharmony
Blog: http://harmonylit.wordpress.com
Twitter: https://twitter.com/#!/harmonygirlit

Discover other titles by Terra:

The Akasha Series

Elemental powers in the palm of her hand, and it won't be enough to save her. When Kaitlyn Alder is involuntarily introduced to a life of magic, she becomes part of an organization hell-bent on saving the Earth. Follow the saga as one of the most terrifying men the human race has to offer stands between Kaitlyn and Earth's survival.

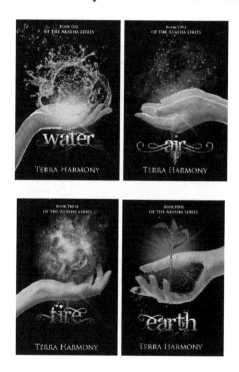

Read more great novels from
Patchwork Press
www.patchwork-press.com

Featured Title:
The Lost Locket of Lahari

The six novellas of the *Lost Locket of Lahari* anthology pause a moment in time when the locket finds the ripples of its ancestry. From the Victorian-era to the Roaring Twenties, the 1940s to modern day and beyond, this anthology is a collection of stories as dynamic as the authors themselves.

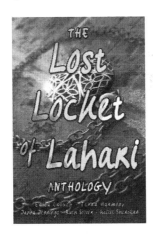

In a dusty, dilapidated stall tucked away in an alcove of a bustling Bazaar in India, a man with a rickety spine and a spindly beard bends over his work bench, forging a locket with accidental magic. There's power in a wish, and there's nothing he wants more than for his children to return home. The locket was intricately crafted, adorned with one dragonfly for each of his children—and the power to find them.

With the guidance of fate, the locket skips through time and journeys across oceans, traveling from person to person in a constant search for the souls whispered into its vessel. Centuries after the magical old man in the Bazaar became near-forgotten myth and whispered legend, the locket has fallen into the hands of those with echoes of the six dragonflies: the seeker, the empath, the dreamer, the confidant, the adventurer, and the dancer.

In the hands of its new owners, the power of the locket adapts, bending and remaking itself to answer need. While the locket never found the children of Lahari, it found the next best thing… Their spirits.

Made in the USA
Lexington, KY
28 March 2016